# CRONGTON KNIGHTS

# ALEX WHEATLE

ATOM

First published in Great Britain in 2016 by Atom

3 5 7 9 10 8 6 4

A CIP catalogue record for this book
is available from the British Library.

ISBN 978-0-349-00232-3 (paperback)
ISBN 978-0-349-00233-0 (eBook)

Typeset in Palatino by M Rules
Printed and bound in Great Britain by
Clays Ltd, St Ives plc

Papers used by Atom are from well-managed forests
and other responsible sources.

MIX
Paper from
responsible sources
FSC® C104740

Atom
An imprint of
Little, Brown Book Group
Carmelite House
50 Victoria Embankment
London EC4Y 0DZ

An Hachette UK Company
www.hachette.co.uk

www.atombooks.co.uk

CRONGTON
KNIGHTS

*Also by Alex Wheatle*

Liccle Bit

Dedicated to Heather Thomas,
a beautiful spirit, too good to be forgotten.

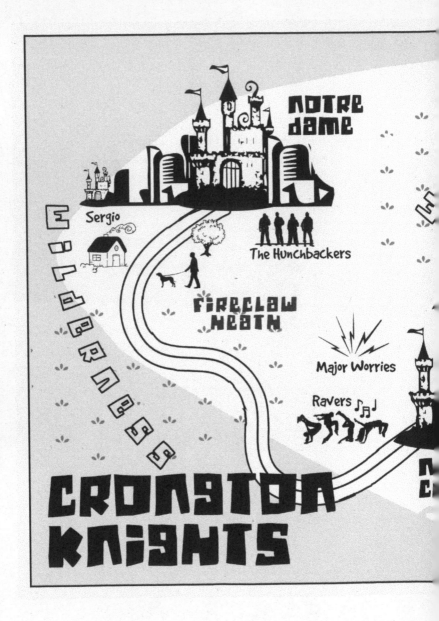

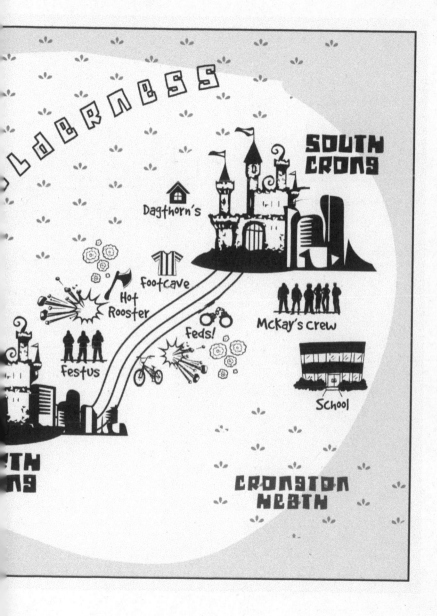

My mum told me I was named after her Scottish granddad, Danny McKay. Apparently, once a year, he served food to the best golfers in the world in some top-ranking hotel by the sea. I don't love golf but Mum was proper proud of her grandpops. She wanted to keep his surname so I was branded McKay Medgar Tambo. It's not the coolest of names but it smacks the insults out of the Gateau Kid, Slop Bag and Dumpling-Butt which I had to put up with in primary school.

My maths teacher, Ms Riddlesworth, reckons I'm fourteen and fifteen–sixteenths years old. I dunno how she worked that one out. I live in Dickens House, South Crongton estate, with my seventeen-year-old brother, Nesta, and my dad. Mum died a few years ago. Pops works the twilight zone in a biscuit factory. He drives a forklift truck in the warehouse. Going by his curses, he hates his boss.

My bredrens are Lemar 'Liccle Bit' Jackson and Jonah 'Rapid' Hani. I've known them long before anyone called me a nickname.

Six months ago, Liccle Bit had some serious drama with the top G of our estate, Manjaro. He couldn't quite keep out of Manjaro's way cos the crime duke is the daddy to the baby of Bit's sis, Elaine – a bonkers situation. Bit made things a trailer-load worse for himself when Manjaro manipulated him to hide a gun. It was a time when beef between North and South Crong exploded with the merkings of at least three bruvs.

Bit was ordered to return Manjaro's gun. My bredren finally came to his senses and put up resistance. Him and his gran got a beat-down for his trouble but, since that day, Manjaro went all fugitive. The feds hunted him high and searched for him low. They couldn't find him. Graffiti in South Crong shouted 'Manjaro woz 'ere' and 'Manjaro woz there'. The feds and the social services offered Bit's fam a flat in Ashburton – they turned it down. Bit explained it was on the eleventh floor and in that tiny castle you couldn't swing a baby's dummy.

We all lived on a red alert. Feds patrolled around the tall slabs and the quiet alleyways. Teachers checked our lockers once a week. Security guards followed your steps in phone shops. Only two kids were allowed inside the Footcave store at one time. The local council wanted to open a new youth club in Crongton Broadway but the residents all signed a five-hundred plus petition. Even the popping of bubblegum made us jump. Most of our parents banned any missions out of the ends after dark. After a few nerve-jangling months the graffiti began to disappear. We stopped looking over our shoulders. Things were getting on the level once more. Bruvs and sisters started to chill again, soccer games booted off in the park, summer jams pumped out of ghetto blasters. A-class chicks rolled by in their sexy denim cut-downs, big boots and check shirts – wannabe players had to smile away their put-downs. Gs spent their time smoking rockets in parked cars, balling in open-air basketball courts and counting their notes from dragon hip sales. But just a few weeks ago, a North Crong soldier got carved in the Crongton Movieworld car park. General Madoo was his name. Sixteen years old. His fam leaked tears on the 6 p.m. news. My dad and Bit's mum joined the 'Knives Take Young Lives' march to Crongton Town Hall. The mayor gave the world's most boring speech. Manjaro's name was whispered again. In North Crong, Major Worries, the King G in those ends, stirred up his crew. We became even more careful of our movements. Man! Living in Crongton has never been easy. I had no idea things were gonna get a world more dangerous . . .

# 1

# Uninvited Guest

'*Don't* answer the door!' barked Dad from the kitchen, the washing-up suds popping on his grimy white vest.

'Mr Tambo!' a voice boomed from outside. It was deep. I imagined the owner of that tone strutting in the park with a rhino on a leash. 'We know you're in there! Let's be adult about this, Mr Tambo. Let us in so we can sit down and talk about your repayments. This is *not* going to go away.'

I breathed in a dose of pure fear. *Why are we in so much deep debt? Dad's working. Why won't he give me the full score on what's going on?* Dad dried his hands on the dishcloth and then draped it over his shoulder. He looked at my older brother, Nesta, who was standing in the hallway only a couple of metres from our drawbridge. Dad beckoned him to retreat. Nesta shook his head. I put my fork down on my plate. Suddenly, I didn't love my pasta and mince even though I had grated some cheese on top to nice it up. The letter box crashed again. My heart rumbled. 'Mr Tambo!'

Dad walked out of the kitchen and switched off the light in the front room. He gestured to Nesta again but Nesta took a step towards the door. I closed my eyes and willed for the men outside to go missing. I also prayed that Nesta wouldn't let loose his temper.

'Why are you scared of them pussies?' spat Nesta, glaring at Dad like he wanted to go head-to-head with the debt brothers outside. Dad raised his palms, trying to calm Nesta down. I could hardly bear to watch.

I strained my ears and could just about make out muffled conversations. Nesta took another stride forward. We all looked at each other. I sank half of my blackcurrant. When I placed the glass down I nearly knocked it over cos my hands were shaking. *Kiss my knights! Will evenings like this ever stop?*

'They're moving on,' said Nesta. 'Yeah, I can hear them bouncing down the stairs.'

My heart put its brakes on. Dad closed his eyes and let out a mighty sigh.

'Why do you let them chat to you like you're a pussy?' charged Nesta. He rolled towards Dad, taking his hands out of his pockets. I stood up from my chair and stepped between them. I didn't want them to be warring again. 'Stand up to them!' raged Nesta. 'Or go outside our gates and tell them to remove their grimy, money-sucking asses from our slab!'

'Nesta,' I called. 'They're gone now. Calm down, bro.'

Dad picked up the dishcloth, turned and entered the

kitchen. I sat back down and pushed my half-eaten dinner away.

'It's not as easy as that,' said Dad, resuming the drying of dishes. 'I owe them a whole heap of money. I can't afford to get myself into any confrontations that might make tings worse. I have responsibilities.'

'Why you owe so much money?' I asked.

Nesta and Dad glared at each other. They didn't give me an answer.

*'Why don't you two ever tell me a damn thing!'* I raised my voice.

Dad stared at the floor.

Nesta flicked me a warning look. He was simmering now. 'They shouldn't be shouting at you through the letter box like you're some kind of mouse! Like you're a boy or something. I swear, if they slap on our gates again, I'll deal with them myself.'

'No you *won't*,' replied Dad. 'You're only seventeen . . . it's *my* problem.'

'Then deal with your problem instead of pussying out!'

I wished I could make them stop. They did this time after freaking time. I used to retreat to my dungeon and slam the door behind me but that made no difference. I was getting tired of them fighting and getting pissed with their stupid pact not to tell me what the freak was going on.

'I'll deal with it in my own way,' said Dad. 'I'm doing a lot more over time and—'

'That ain't gonna do zero nish!' argued Nesta. 'You need to tell 'em you're not paying the interest they slapped on your bill! Tell them to ram their interest where the number two hides!'

Dad took in another deep breath. He glanced at the ceiling as if he was asking God for some wise words. 'I'm doing my best,' he said.

'Your best?' Nesta repeated. 'So hiding in the darkness like a freaking rodent is what you call your best? *Man up!* When are you gonna take your stance again?'

'Nesta—'

'I'm *out of this damn place!*'

Hot-stepping to his dungeon, Nesta collected his faded denim jacket. He then pulled back the curtain in the front room, opened the balcony door and picked up his bike. He wheeled it towards the drawbridge. Dad's eyes followed him but he didn't say a squawk. Nesta turned to me before he disappeared. 'McKay, don't stay up too late – you got school in the morning.'

'I won't,' I said.

'If I come back at mad o'clock and I see you playing games, I'm gonna kuff you in your head-corner ... Me gone.'

'*Nesta!*' Dad suddenly called. 'The police are stopping and searching teenagers on the estate since that kid got killed. Don't—'

'You think I'm fretting about the feds?' interrupted Nesta. 'I'm more worried that my pops ain't got no heart.'

Dad had his faults but he didn't deserve those lyrics.

Nesta slammed the door shut. Dad smacked his right palm against his forehead. He might as well have stamped on my nerves. Nesta gone. Again. And to who knows where, on his lonesome at night – it'd never been safe round here, but since the latest merking it'd been mental.

I picked up my plate and made for the kitchen.

'Can you get your brother's dirty plate from his room please?' asked Dad.

'Don't worry, Dad, I'll wash the rest of the tings up. You rest before you roll to work.'

'*No*, you cooked.'

'I'll do it,' I insisted. 'And please, Dad. Just tell me what's going on?'

'I don't want you fretting about it,' Dad replied. 'Just concentrate on your schoolwork.'

'But I'm nearly fifteen!'

'McKay! I *don't need* this now.'

Anger surged through me. I had to step off.

Nesta's dungeon was beside the bathroom. A bare-chested Tupac Shakur, the old-school hip-hop legend, overlooked his single bed. My brother had copied a tattoo on to his chest that Tupac had written on his back.

*Only God Can Judge Me*

His dirty plate was on the bedside cabinet beside his boom box – some phone-in show was broadcasting on a low volume. I switched it off. His wardrobe doors were open. Every time I saw Mum's clothes hanging up in there, something icy cold-footed through my veins. Dad wanted to give Mum's clothes to charity when she passed, but Nesta switched big-time when he heard that. That was one mother of an argument. By the time the bad lyrics between them were over, a window in Dad's room was blitzed and his clock radio was kissing the concrete ground far below. But Nesta got his way so here there they were, Mum's nice blouses and skirts alongside his own garms.

There was a framed picture of Mum on his dressing table, angled in such a way that it was the first thing Nesta saw when he woke up. He asked me once if I wanted one, but no – it was hard enough trying to deal with Mum not being here let alone having her by my bed watching my every flex.

When I returned to the kitchen, Dad was staring into the sink as if he might find the meaning of life floating in the soap suds. 'I'll do the rest, Dad,' I offered once more. 'You get ready for work.'

Dad moved aside to give me room. He then turned around and forced a smile, the kinda messed-up smile that parents use to hide what's really going on behind the eyes. Whatever it was, I knew it was bad. The logs were about to spill over the toilet seat.

'I'm *still* gonna get you someting for your birthday,' Dad insisted. 'I promise that to the fullest!'

I started washing Nesta's plate, satnavving my frustration with a scouring pad. 'You don't have to—'

'I *do* have to!' Dad raised his voice. 'I'll find a liccle someting from somewhere and get you a present.'

'Dad, please—'

His expression switched. His eyes narrowed and his eyebrows turned into a V shape. 'What you saying? That I can't provide a birthday present for my youngest son for his fifteenth? You think I'm that useless? Huh? Do you?'

'No . . . I didn't mean that, Dad.'

'I hope not.'

Dad gave me a hard look and then glanced up at the ceiling again. 'I hope Nesta'll be all right out there,' he said after a while. 'There's too much badness on the estate nowadays. The feds *still* haven't found Manjaro, you know. The brother's wanted for not one but two murders and nobody'll say a ting. Someone must know what's become of him ...'

A few weeks before Manjaro disappeared undercover, I'd seen him banging fists with Nesta in the park. When I asked Nesta about it he told me to seal my lips. I concentrated on the soapy water.

'What time did your brother come home last night?'

'I ... I don't know.'

'I don't like him going out all hours, but if I put my foot down it'll only make tings worse. He doesn't listen to me anymore, McKay. You know how he is.'

Dad wasn't wrong. I knew how Nesta was.

I placed the plate on the drying rack. Dad looked at me again. This time there was a messed-up sadness in his eyes, like he just didn't know what to do any more. 'I'm gonna have a shower and take an hour's nap before I go to work,' he said. 'Don't stay up too late.'

'All right, Dad.'

'You got credit on your phone?'

'Yeah.'

'Remember, any liccle ting, just call me, OK. Or text. Don't kill out all your credit chatting to your school friends.'

'Yes, Dad, I know the deal.'

*

An hour later, Dad was gone. I didn't go to bed. I parked at the kitchen table for a while and thought about Mum. If she were around she would've banged Dad and Nesta's heads together until they kissed and made up – but she wasn't and I was gonna have to face up to another night home alone cos Dad had to work and Nesta was hot-pedalling around the estate in a rage.

I didn't like to admit it to anyone but being left alone in our castle at night freaked the living kidneys out of me, especially with all the slayings going on in our ends. I was thinking of dinging Liccle Bit and Jonah just to hear a voice but I wanted to save my credit. Instead I played FIFA 14 on my PS4.

Tiredness must've licked me at some point cos something woke me at half three in the morning. My game was on pause but the TV was humming. It was shadowy. I heard footsteps.

'McKay! What's a matter with you?'

Nesta! He was home and standing watching me in the darkness.

'Don't you do any frigging thing I tell you to?' He sounded proper angry. He must've had a hard-lick night. His tone was fierce – it definitely woke me up.

'Where's your bike?' I asked, sitting up.

'Why aren't you in bed? What did I tell you before I rolled out? You're asking for a kuff in your freaking eardrums. Get your big ass to bed before I—'

'Where's your bike?' I cut in again.

I jumped up and switched on the front room light. Nesta flinched and squinted. His bottom lip had swollen to the size of a hovercraft's bumper, blood was trickling down from his forehead and his left eye looked all mangled.

'What happened to you?' I asked.

'You have good hearing, right?' Nesta asked.

'Er, of course,' I replied.

'Then you must've heard what I said. Get your butt into your bed. *Now!*'

I didn't bother packing my PlayStation away. I just scrambled to my dungeon and shut the door behind me. I lay on my bed fully clothed, quiet and still. I heard Nesta clattering about in the bathroom. I turned to face my poster of Usain Bolt. I'd pinned it right above my headboard. 'Another crazy day in the Tambo castle, Usain,' I said to him. 'Not sure of how much more I can take.'

I don't know what time sleep finally caught up with me but it must've done because next thing I knew I was being woken up by someone rocking my shoulder. I tried to open my eyes but sleep was putting up a damn good fight. A heavy hand rolled me again. I forced my eyes open a fraction, enough so I could just make out Nesta. He had slapped a plaster on his forehead, his left eye was the size of a ping-pong ball and his bottom lip still looked like it could save refugees in a mad sea.

'McKay! Wake up, bruv!'

I sat up a little, wiped my eyes and checked my mobile on my bedside cabinet. Quarter to six.

'What's a matter with you, Nesta?'

'Delete your noise and listen up,' he ordered.

He looked proper serious so I shut up.

'I have to go missing,' he said.

'Why?'

13

'I got caught up in a feud tonight and I don't want Pops to see me like this. I wrapped untold ice cubes in my flannel but the damn swelling won't go down. He's gonna go all *Question Time* on me how my face got mashed up.'

'Where you gonna go?'

'You don't have to know. But I have to keep a low profile. I got involved with one of Major Worries' crew.'

'Major Worries!' I sat bolt straight. The hairs on my arms stood to attention. My heart started to pound. I glanced at Nesta's right hand and I could see his knuckles were bloodied and grazed. 'Spill the score!'

'You don't need to know the whole deal,' said Nesta. 'Just keep your backside in our ends and *don't* tell Dad zero squat. I *mean* it. You hearing me?'

'No one tells me sweet zero around here!'

'McKay! I don't need to stress about you as well! As I said, *don't* spill a drop to Dad. I need your help on this one.'

I stared at him hard but finally nodded. 'So what do I tell him?'

'Tell him ...' Nesta paused. 'Tell him I'm staying with a chick.'

'What chick?' I wanted to know.

'It doesn't matter what chick!'

'All right! Keep your plaster on.'

'I'm missing again,' Nesta said, turning around. 'And I don't know when you'll see my ass next.'

'Will you text or ding me so I know what's going down with you?'

Nesta offered me an angry look. 'What am I? A rolling

freaking news channel? You'll hear from me when the time is good.'

The time was never good with Nesta.

He closed the door gently behind him, as if Dad were listening to his movements. I lay back. Home alone. Again.

# 2

# A Problem for Venetia

I ejected myself out of bed at seven, flung away my BO in a
long shower and, after I niced up my armpits, I dropped the
bent frying pan on to the cooker. I fried myself some bacon,
scrambled eggs, onions and a spin of pepper and ate it fast –
and I left some in the oven for Dad to sink when he got home.
Before I left my castle I tried to flick my afro out as far as it
would stretch – if Liccle Bit wanted to see who'd got the sickest fro he was gonna get a dose of disappointment.

As I stepped out, I fretted about seeing the debt brothers.
Bless my armour! What would I say if I bumped into them
bouncing down the stairs? Luckily enough they weren't
around. Man! Going to school was a relief – some kinda
normality.

I jogged across the green to Liccle Bit and Jonah's slab
wondering how I was gonna get away with not having done

my history homework. I wasn't gonna tell Mr Lockton no excuse about being stressed out by the debt brothers or Nesta getting grief on his night-ride. I thought about asking Bit and Jonah to copy theirs, but I bet neither of them had done it either. I'd just tell him I forgot. If I got a detention, then hey-ho.

I climbed up the steps to Liccle Bit's floor and smacked his letter box. Bit opened his door and I noticed two things straightaway: one, he wasn't smiling (*strange*); and two, his fro wasn't looking as neat as mine (*good!*).

'What's wrong with you, bruv?' he said. 'How many times have you called for me at my yard in the last four months?'

'I don't count,' I replied.

'Over a hundred times,' Liccle Bit raged. 'And you still can't press the freaking doorbell? Use the damn ting! When you slap our gates like that it makes us all think you're the feds, or worse, that it's Manjaro coming back to Voldemort us! My fam is giving me nuff grief about it.'

'Stop going on all Hollywood, bruv,' I said. 'Isn't it about time you stopped sweating about Manjaro anyway? No one's even seen his bald head in six months. Now get your short self in motion and let's step to school.'

Man! Ever since Bit had been trying to sample a touch of loving from Venetia, he got touchy about any small ting. Frustration was chewing his sad ass.

Bit said bye to his fam and we jumped down three flights before calling for Jonah. Jonah came out in a rush but Bit and I overheard some cussing going down in his castle. His parents were raging at each other. Something about money.

Bit and I swapped glances. Jonah didn't say diddly about it so we rolled on.

'Have you linked up with Venetia yet to ask her about that new chick?' Jonah asked Bit.

'What new chick?' I wanted to know.

'Some fit new girl,' smiled Jonah. 'I think she's Indian or someting.'

'Her mum's Turkish,' said Bit. 'I think she's only been in this country for three or four years.'

We stepped downhill along a pathway between two slabs. We all heard a distant siren. There was new graffiti on the side of Shaka House. In big orange letters it read:

STOPPING AND SEARCHING US ALL IS WRONG, JUST COS WE'RE YOUNG AND LIVE IN SOUTH CRONG.

I thought of Nesta who had been stopped by the feds untold times. *Where is he?*

'Haven't you seen her yet, McKay?' Jonah asked, getting all excited. 'She's prettier than any chick in a Bollywood film. She has a sweet front display and her legs are begging for my strokes. Trust me! I'm gonna be on it in a rush if Bit sets me up neatly!'

'The only thing you're gonna be on,' I said, 'is a detention for stalking this ripe chick. So you'd better not go on like a hound when you see her.'

'Her name is Saira,' said Bit. 'Saira Aslan. Her fam used to live in Ashburton and before that they were in some kinda refugee place. Venetia says she's had one hard tough-lick life. And, Jonah, you're my bredren and I got your back, but I'm not gonna introduce you to her, bruv. You always go on too hungry around fit girls.'

'You're not wrong,' I agreed. 'Jonah, you have to stop spilling drool when you're around them, bruv. Or put some batty paper in your mouth when you're near them to dry tings up.'

'I don't spill drool when I'm around ripe girls!' Jonah protested.

'*Yes*, you damn well do!' I insisted. 'What about that time Syreeta Davis sat beside you at the cinema? Your tongue was going on all lizard-like. Niagara Falls was spilling from your mouth. It's embarrassing, bruv. You wanna keep that tongue on lockdown before the feds arrest your ass for perving.'

As we hit the road that led us out of the estate, I noticed Jonah had been smacked with a bit of evil on his face. I thought it best to ease up on him – he could sulk longer than a red carpet full of divas.

'After all the crap I've done for you,' he said to Bit. 'I borrow you games and you've been sampling my mum's cupcakes forever. I even sold you my last phone on a Black Friday discount, bruv. And you can't set me up with this Saira? You're going on dark! Maybe it's because you can't get to second base with Venetia. I bet you haven't even stroked her yet!'

'Venetia's got a man,' replied Bit. 'I'm just friends with her.'

'But you want more than that,' I said. 'You wanna burst into the in-zone, slam a touchdown and take a mad lap of honour.'

'At least I *have* a close chick friend!' Bit suddenly got angry.

'What girl do you chirp to? Not a damn freaking one! Even the B-class girls blank you.'

'I don't wanna be friends with any B-class chick,' I said. 'I'm not into that first-base friend-zone crap. The only time I'm gonna be chirping and linking with any girl is when I'm touching fourth base with her and getting my strokes on. And she's gonna be A-class. Believe it!'

Jonah and Bit both started to laugh. 'With your fat ass?' Jonah remarked.

'They'll be too scared to link with you. You might wanna eat them for dinner!' added Bit.

I quickened my pace and left them behind. I always got pissed when Jonah and Bit spat lyrics about my weight and anyway I had better tings to worry about than linking with a chick. Nesta was still on my mind for one; no way was *he* with a chick today ...

They caught up with me just as I entered the school gates.

'You better not flop, Jonah,' Bit was stressing. 'I'll chat to Venetia at break and put in a good CV about you. But you have to promise to keep your damn phone in your pocket. No pics!'

'That's why chicks think you're hungry, bruv,' I put in.

'I'm not gonna go on hungry, or take pics,' said Jonah. 'Just put in a neat word and I'll run tings from there. Me and Saira are gonna be twined like barbed wire, trust me.'

'OK,' agreed Bit. 'But don't blame me if you get a big dose of disappointment.'

'I won't get a dose of anything but sweetness,' returned Jonah.

'And one more ting,' said Bit. 'When you chirp Saira *please* don't leak anything about the Manjaro issue. She'd tell Venetia quick-time.'

Bit had made us both swear that we wouldn't spill anything to anyone about what happened with him and Manjaro. He didn't want Venetia to find out – it would mash-up their relationship for good.

'What do you take me for?' challenged Jonah. 'As if I would spill that! I wouldn't do that to you. Ain't I your bredren? Stop fretting! Why you even dragging this up again? I just wanna run around the bases with Saira and—'

'Promise!' Bit insisted.

Jonah nodded. 'All right! I promise. But it was months ago now, bruv, and you still fretting about it. Manjaro's long gone. Someone probably blazed or burst him.'

'Nah. Don't believe the hype. He's out there somewhere on a low profile tip. I can feel it,' said Bit.

'Are you a freaking Jedi now?' I joked.

No one laughed.

We finally bounced into school with Jonah smiling like he had smoked something funky. 'Did anybody do the history homework?' I asked.

'Yeah,' Bit replied. 'I did. My sis had me on lockdown until I finished it.'

'Let me see what you've done.'

Bit rolled his eyes but relief was surging through me – Mr Lockton had given me a final warning.

Borrowing Bit's books, I did my history catch-up in science

class. I didn't give a spit about physics, chemistry or slicing up frogs but I kinda liked the idea of kings riding on horses and having to fight for the land, castles and chicks they won.

Bit had drama for the first two lessons of the day – he only optioned it cos Venetia did – so Jonah and I went to meet him at the drama studio at break time.

When we arrived, Bit and Venetia were in a corner having some deep one-to-one. Venetia was looking well upset. She kept on rubbing her eyes. Another person who wasn't singing the Happy Song was Ms Crawford, the drama teacher. She was parked on a chair in the middle of the room, nibbling an apple and staring into space. She always had this vibe of doom about her.

'It's a lovely day outside,' she said all of a sudden, looking at us and a few others. 'Why don't you go out and enjoy the sunshine?'

We all ignored her. I looked over at Venetia, now clearly leaking tears on Bit's shoulder.

'Man! The effect you have on chicks!' I teased Jonah. 'Bit's told her you wanna link up with Saira and she doesn't wanna give that news to a new friend. Look, bruv, she's inconsolable!'

Jonah slapped me on the back of the head and started hot-stepping over towards them. 'Where're you going?' I hissed. 'Stop going on so peckish! Can't you see something deep is going on?'

'But I wanna find out if Bit linked me up,' said Jonah.

'Get back here!' I warned Jonah. 'This is what I'm talking about. You ever heard of a word called *patience*? Learn to spell it and google it.'

Jonah kissed his teeth and folded his arms. He would be sulking about this for the rest of the day.

We had to wait five minutes while they finished their convo, and when Venetia rolled away – man could that girl roll – Bit came over to join us.

'So who pissed in Venetia's perfume spray?' I asked.

'It's no joking matter, McKay,' replied Bit. 'She's on a downer. She's well upset.'

'Did you put in a nice lyric about me?' asked Jonah. 'Where's Saira?'

'What's a matter with you, Jonah?' I cussed him. 'Can't you see how trauma is licking her?'

'But she just smiled and waved right at me,' said Jonah.

'Yeah, but she's faking it,' said Bit. 'She was crying lakes before the lesson.'

'So who shat on her make-up mirror?' I asked again.

'Her boyfriend,' answered Bit. 'Or I should say her *ex*-boyfriend.'

'Ex-boyfriend?' I repeated. 'That's all good, isn't it? Shouldn't you be saying thanks and praises to Cupid and hanging up the flags in your bedroom? Isn't that the best news you've had since your mum let you stay out till ten o'clock on a Friday night?'

'I haven't got a curfew time!' argued Bit.

'Yes you have!' Jonah jumped in.

'All right, all right!' I said. 'So, Sergio's been sacked and put in a bin bag. Bit, this is your time, bruv. Your ass has been waiting for this chick for what? Six months and three-eighths? Maybe even more than that? There ain't no bruvs ahead of you on the racetrack so crank up your charm, fling away that old cabbage smell in your armpits and conquer!'

'It's . . . it's not as easy as that,' said Bit. I couldn't quite work out why he looked so stressed.

'Why isn't it easy?' I asked.

'If that was me I'd just rush in there,' laughed Jonah.

Bit sucked in a long breath. When he did that, I knew he had serious crap to spill.

'When they were warring with each other,' he explained, 'Sergio jacked her iPhone. Venetia wants me to go with her to get it back. I was wondering if you bruvs would come with me?'

# 3

## Stepping to Distant Ends

Jonah and I swapped worried glances. 'How old is this Sergio?' I wanted to know.

'Eighteen,' Bit replied.

'Eighteen!' Jonah repeated. 'Venetia was linking with an eighteen-year-old! I saw him once, picking her up after school. He's kinda crusty, isn't he? His arms are thicker than my legs! I ain't risking my looks on this mission. It's not like Venetia's showing *me* any loving. Bit, you haven't even sampled a kiss, bruv, so why are we even debating this? She's gonna have to deal with her phone-nap on her lonesome.'

'Wait a minute!' I said. 'Why don't Venetia get her dad to deal with this ex of hers . . . What's his name again?'

'Sergio,' Bit helped me.

'I've seen Venetia's dad. And he's not the kinda man you

would fart next to in a packed lift. That man carries boilers under one arm! Believe it!'

An image of V's dad flashed through my mind. Mr King always had his sleeves rolled up to show off his superhero fists.

'Yeah, he's more massive than your dad, McKay.' Bit nodded. 'But she can't tell him.'

'Why not?' asked Jonah.

'Cos he doesn't know sweet diddly about Venetia linking with an eighteen-year-old man,' Bit reasoned. 'If he did, he would let loose the Kraken.'

'What's the Kraken?' Jonah wanted to know.

'Didn't you see *Clash of the Titans*?' I asked. 'The Kraken's a giant sea monster. It tends to get mad and eats people for snacks.'

'Sounds a bit like you,' joked Bit.

'Oh, I get it.' Jonah nodded. 'Venetia's dad would switch to psycho mode if he found out an eighteen-year-old bruv was giving it to his daughter.'

'Nice to know your hard drive's working,' I said.

We all looked at each other. This was serious. Bit needed our help but Nesta had told me to keep my butt in the estate. If he saw me rolling on some mission just to return a chick's phone he would bang me up worse than the Kraken could. I really wanted to help Bit but I had my own issues. I wanted to have Venetia's back too – when she did chat to me she was always encouraging me to get my bake on and to take my cooking seriously. *'Learn something positive and get out of these ends,'* she always said. I always had nuff respect for her.

'This might sound cold, Bit,' I said. 'But can't she just get herself a new iPhone? Or even a second-hand one?'

'Yeah, why can't she do that?' Jonah agreed. 'Kiran Cassidy's always selling 'em. Don't know where he gets them from.'

I knew where but I wasn't going to tell Jonah – he couldn't be relied upon to keep his beak sealed. The phones were being supplied by Pinchers. He was hustling tings in South Crongton now Manjaro was missing. Pinchers' liccle bro got slayed by someone from Major Worries' crew a few months ago, and Crongton had gone all Syria ever since.

It was messed up to me that bruvs were deleting each other just because they had a SOUTH or a NORTH at the start of their address. The feds were para about anyone looking like a hood-rat. And bruvs like Nesta, who didn't roll with a crew, were getting pissed at being body-searched by the feds at every corner. A crazy, never-ending cycle.

Bit inhaled again. He switched his gaze from Jonah to me. 'There's something else,' he said. 'But if I drop this info you bruvs better keep it on lock.'

'Spill, bruv,' I urged.

'I'm not joking,' said Bit. 'Don't even tell your pillow, let alone your fam. Are you hearing me, Jonah, cos your tongue is looser than a baby with the runs.'

'All right.' Jonah nodded. 'I'm hearing you. Nothing will vomit from my mouth. What is it?'

Just then Ms Crawford stood up, looked at all of us and said in a voice just above a whisper. 'Can you *please* leave the drama room? You're not supposed to be in here at break time, you know that, boys.'

We regrouped in the hallway.

'Let me guess – Venetia's pregnant?' said Jonah.

'She's *not* pregnant,' Bit replied quickly.

'Then what?' I asked again, getting impatient. 'Drop the bomb or we'll bang the afro off your head.'

Bit checked along the hallway in case anyone was in earshot. 'There's some images on her phone.'

'Images?' Jonah repeated.

Bit looked at the floor. The fog started to clear in my head but Jonah wasn't up to speed. 'What freaking images?' he said, raising his voice.

'She's naked,' said Bit. 'Sergio took them on his phone when she was … when they were … anyway, he texted the pics to her.'

'Man! That's … that's … sick,' I said. 'All wrong!'

Jonah's eyes widened.

Naked pics on a phone of any girl in our school always went nuclear. Last year, this mixed-race chick, Sharon Goddard, had to leave cos she was so traumatised about embarrassing pics of her online. I could never understand why they'd allow themselves to be snapped like that in the first place. Venetia didn't deserve this.

Jonah would definitely want to check out what these nude graphics of Venetia looked like. I had to admit that I did, too – after all, Venetia was hotter than Miley Cyrus twerking against a bonfire. Bit though … Bit looked as if his world had been blitzed to pieces. He loved Venetia to the core.

We had to come up with a plan, fast.

'Hold on a sec,' I said. 'If Sergio texted those pics to Venetia that means we'll have to jack his phone as well as get hers back.'

Jonah had a dose of panic on his face. 'I'm *definitely* missing from this mission,' he said. 'We can't jack the man's phone. He'll terminate us.'

'Bruv, how would you feel if you were Venetia? You know all of her family are in Team God, right? She's not even supposed to have a boyfriend, let alone an eighteen-year-old perv! Say Sergio decides to forward these pics or upload them to the internet. If her fam finds out it's gonna go off big time.'

'People in Team God don't fling out their kids to the kerb,' Jonah said. 'I think you're being overdramatic.'

'How's she coping?' I asked.

It was a dumb question. Obviously Venetia was stressed to the max. Bit gave me a messed-up look and shook his head.

'Where does this Sergio live?' asked Jonah.

'Notre Dame estate,' answered Bit. 'He's got his own bedsit.'

'Notre Dame!' I repeated. 'That's the other side of North Crong. South Crong bruvs don't step there. SWAT teams with night-vision goggles don't tread there. It's Major Worries' kingdom.'

'And this South Crong bruv is *still* not rolling there,' insisted Jonah. 'Too dangerous. We'll all be jacked, sliced and minced.'

'Then I'll have to go with V – just the two of us,' said Bit. He shrugged, turned and rolled away.

Jonah and I watched him disappear down the hallway.

'Is he nuts?' Jonah said to me as the bell for class rang.

'Crazy-ass Manjaro is out there, the estate's swarming with feds and Bit wants to go on a mission to Notre Dame?'

'Yeah, he's nuts,' I replied. 'Nuts in love with Venetia.'

History was all about the Germans and the First World War, but I couldn't concentrate. There was too much going on in my hard drive. *Who jacked Nesta's bike and mauled him? Where is he hiding out? Will the debt brothers return this evening? And should I go on the mission to help Bit find Venetia's phone and jack Sergio's at the same time?* The only thing I'd learned by the lunch bell was that the German soldiers wore some weird, messed-up hats, and that I was in one bitch of a mess.

My mind was still churning away as I made my way towards the cafeteria. I bumped into Boy from the Hills in the corridor. His real name was Colin but we christened him Boy from the Hills because he practically had twigs, grass, leaves and probably little bugs in his long matted brown hair.

'Heard about your bro,' Boy from the Hills said.

'What about him?' I replied.

'That he mashed up Festus Livingstone – one of Major Worries' crew.'

'Who told you that?'

'It's all around, bruv. You better step safe. I wouldn't like my toes to be in your socks.'

The thought of Boy from the Hills' toes in my socks made me gag.

'You heard wrong,' I said. 'Nesta got his bike jacked. He was probably fighting for it.'

Boy from the Hills scratched his hair and a bit of mud or

something dropped out. He put his arm in front of me to get my attention. His fingernails weren't clean. I wanted to step around him but he blocked me. 'This Festus is in hospital, bruv, having all kinda scans.'

'You're lying!'

'No, bruv,' Boy from the Hills maintained. He gave me a concerned look. 'Just trying to look out for you.'

'You *don't* have to look out for me!' I raised my voice.

'It's only what you did for me, when you stopped Peter Ellison and his crew from jacking my tablet off me.'

'You shouldn't bring tings like that to school, man. If you didn't have them with you, brothers wouldn't want to jack them from you,' I said. 'Doesn't take the *Big Bang Theory* to work that one out! Now, stop cramping me!'

Boy from the Hills slouched away. I stood still for a minute, fretting that Major Worries might want to maul my hide too. Nesta and I looked enough alike – no way could I sack him as my brother (believe me, I'd tried before . . .)

In the hall, Jonah spotted me from his table and beckoned for me. Liccle Bit was sitting at a table on his lonesome. (Sulking, probably.) I collected my shepherd's pie, cabbage and mashed-potato lunch and joined Jonah. As soon as I sat down he was tweeting into my ears.

'I heard about Nesta,' he said. 'What are you gonna do? You're gonna have to keep a low profile.'

'They *jacked* his bike!' I snapped. 'What's he supposed to do? Just let them take it? My dad bought him that bike for his birthday a couple of years ago.'

Jonah soon forgot about me. Venetia had just joined the

lunch queue, and I guessed that the beautiful chick with her was Saira. Jonah's eyes were on them both like a heat-seeking missile. Saira's long hair was blacker than a raven. Her front display had it going on and her backside curved sweetly in her black trousers. I could definitely understand why Jonah was so peckish around her.

Saira and Venetia collected their trays of food and joined Bit at his table. Venetia pushed her fork into her shepherd's pie but wasn't really eating it. Her head was down and it seemed obvious she had been leaking tears.

'McKay, bruv!' said Jonah excitedly. 'You see what I'm saying now? Can you imagine jacking your parents' credit card, booking a week's holiday to Barbados and taking Saira with you? If they said I'd have to do a year's bird I'd still do it anyway!'

'Stop fantasising, bruv,' I said. 'And you know what? I've been thinking. Maybe we should have Bit's back on his mission.'

That got his attention. He looked at me as if I was the dumbest kid on Planet Dumb. 'You feeling all right, McKay? Have you got a fever?' he asked. 'Didn't you hear what Bit said?'

'Yes, I heard,' I replied.

'You know, at six o'clock they have this programme called the news,' he said.

'I know.'

'Just the other day they showed this North Crong bruv's face. He was—'

'I *know* the score.'

'This Sergio brother lives in Notre Dame,' said Jonah. 'Before we even get to Notre Dame we'll have to go through North Crong estate.'

'But we'll be on a bus,' I reasoned.

'And what kind of bruvs might step on a bus in those ends? I dunno about you but I'm *not* one of the Expendables. I don't carry a rocket launcher with me in my PE kit. My parents want me to give them grandchildren one day!'

Jonah had a good point. I sunk half of my shepherd's pie before answering. The mince was rubbish – why couldn't the lunch ladies spin more seasoning in it? – and even the cabbage was off-key.

'If taking the bus is such a mad danger then we'll have to trod,' I said.

'Trod!' Jonah repeated. His eyes rippled with pure disagreement. At least for a moment he wasn't ogling Saira Aslan. 'From here it's about ten K to the Notre Dame estate. Maybe fifteen. If we walk, we'll be catching cramp not jacking phones! Nah, bruv. We should be keeping Bit under a low profile still. Manjaro could've merked him when he broke down his gates.'

I tried my mash. It wasn't smooth. I washed down the dry taste with water. Jonah still looked at me like he wanted to superglue a straitjacket around me.

'OK, you're not wrong,' I reasoned. 'It's dangerous. But how would you feel if Bit with Venetia went on their lonesome and got all chewed up? And another ting. What would this Saira chick think of you?'

Jonah thought about it. He glanced at Bit, Venetia and

Saira. Jonah didn't say anything till I'd finished my shepherd's pie and started nibbling an apple – apples weren't really my thing but Dad said I had to try to sample fruit at school instead of puddings and choc bars. I took three bites and then left it on my plate.

'Maybe we can ask Kiran Cassidy to come with us?' Jonah suggested. 'Or Peter Ellison.'

I shook my head. 'That's a no-no,' I said. 'Especially Peter Ellison – he's a living bully. Venetia doesn't want anyone else to know about these naked pics and Kiran Cassidy's mouth spills more news than CNN.'

'Then there'd just be three of us, right? And Venetia?'

'Four against one,' I said. 'Are you now feeling this?'

Jonah scratched his ear and gave it more thought. My phone buzzed. I checked if there were any teachers about. There weren't. I took my mobile out of my pocket and checked the name on the screen. It was Dad. Hogs on fire! I couldn't remember the last time he dinged me at school. I thought he'd be sleeping after a long shift. It had to be about Nesta. It always was.

# 4

## Nesta's Secret Girl

'Have you seen Nesta?' Dad asked. There was nuff tension in his voice. 'Doesn't seem like he's slept in his bed and there's no sign of him anywhere.'

'I . . . I haven't seen him, Dad.'

'Didn't you see him this morning?'

'No, Dad. I tried to ding him but he's not picking up.'

'I've tried to call him too,' Dad said. 'I'm worried. We have our arguments but he always comes home.'

I hated lying to Dad but what could I do? I could sense his stress and in that moment I vowed to look for Nesta after school. Man! If only teachers and parents could understand the amount of trauma we young heads were all living under in Crongton.

'He'll come home when he's ready,' I said. 'Maybe he's chilling with one of his bredrens?'

As far as I knew, Nesta didn't have too many real bredrens.

He knew all the Gs in these ends, including Manjaro, because he was always on road. But he was a bit of a loner. There was some guy called Sergeant Rizla who he used to chillax with on a regular, but that friendship licked the kerb when Dad found Sergeant zonked out on his bed one night – watching him storm-troop Sergeant's ass to the drawbridge and boot him out was one of the funniest things I have ever seen. He was the last guy who came to our castle to link with Nesta. I definitely couldn't remember my bro ever having a girlfriend.

'I hope so,' said Dad. 'I don't think there's been any trouble from last night. Have you heard of anything, McKay?'

I swallowed a spoonful of spit.

'No, Dad. I haven't heard of anything.'

Guilt on a stick! Another messed-up lie. It felt terrible.

'I know tings haven't been good between your brother and me lately,' Dad said. 'But if you hear from him, let me know as soon as poss, right?'

'Right, Dad.'

'OK. McKay, I'm going to have a bit of a sleep and I'll try to call him again when I get up. I've left some money on your dressing table for your dinner.'

'Thanks, Dad.'

'No worries. Remember, let me know as soon as you hear from Nesta.'

I killed the call. Jonah was giving me a disapproving glare.

'You shouldn't lie to your pops,' he said.

'I promised Nesta that I wouldn't say anything about where he is or what happened to him.'

Before I put my phone back in my pocket I texted Nesta.

WHERE R YOU?

I had English in the afternoon but the shepherd's pie hadn't helped me find my focus. If anything, after that chat to Dad, it was worse. *Why hasn't Nesta texted me back? Where is he?* The logs would float to my dungeon if Dad found out about Nesta putting Festus Livingstone in hospital. *I may as well get pulped by Venetia's ex-boyfriend!*

I made up my mind there and then to help Bit on his mission. And Bit always had my back when I was going through a drama. When my dad was in hospital a couple of years ago, his family took my sad ass in for a few days – I didn't love his mum's cooking but his gran's dinners and cakes blessed up my taste buds to the max. And Bit had had a tough-knock year with Manjaro terrorising his fam. Anyway, what were my other options? Staying in my castle with the debt brothers at the door and trying to deal with Dad's and Nesta's issues didn't make me pull on my smiley T-shirt.

I met Bit and Jonah outside the school gates at the end of the day. Fed cars cruised by – we had all got used to them sitting outside our school with their windows wound down, checking if any beef was about to kick off. An officer asked, 'Are you OK, guys?' and we ignored him.

Bit wanted an answer – were we with him or not? I nodded yes. Bit smiled then turned to Jonah. 'What about you?'

'I . . . I don't know,' he replied.

'What kinda chicken-crowing is that?' Bit raged. 'You either have my back or you don't.'

Jonah stared at the ground. I was sure guilt was booting

him between his legs. Saira and Venetia bounced out from the main school exit. Man! Those two made a sweet sight. For a second or two my worries disappeared. Sometimes you had to appreciate the nice tings in life. They spotted us, waved and rolled towards us. Jonah straightened his back, dusted off his blazer and fiddled with his tie.

Venetia looked a little brighter than she had earlier on in the day. Her eyes weren't so puffy and she was trying to get a smile on. As for Saira Aslan – this was the first time I'd had a close-up. Her eyes were big and darker than midnight, and there was a beauty spot on her left cheek – it could've been a black biro stain but I didn't care. It made her look damn well gorgeous. Jonah was gonna have to step up big time if he ever wanted to get to second base with her.

It was time to make a plan. Venetia was first to speak. 'Saira's gonna come. So that's three of us.'

'Four,' I added. 'Venetia, sis, don't fret about nothing. We have a rebel alliance. This Sergio is gonna get death-starred.'

'And I'm coming too!' Jonah said, getting brave all of a sudden. 'Yeah, man. This Sergio's taking liberties! Can't allow that! Let's boot him up!'

Bit and I both glanced at Jonah with nuff suspicion.

'That's five!' Venetia smiled. 'Thanks, guys. It means a lot. Hopefully, we can get to his ass before he uploads any ... well, you know.'

Our mission made me think of the brave knights in King Arthur's days heading off to rescue fit girls with long hair from warlords who kept them locked away in tall towers. It would be epic!

Suddenly, Venetia kissed Bit on his cheek. Bit's eyes did this strange, messed-up dance as if he had been smoking rockets all day. I have never seen a pleasure download make a brother smile so much. Meanwhile Jonah looked on, jealousy pumping through his veins.

'So when are we gonna get the steel band on the float?' asked Bit.

'Tomorrow night,' answered Venetia. 'Sergio's always at home on a Friday evening waiting for his mum to call.'

'That's good with me,' I said.

Jonah nodded. 'Good with me too.' Envy was still booting his ass.

'What time shall we link?'

'Say around six,' answered Venetia. 'That'll give us time to change and sink some food after school. Come to my slab? I'll tell my fam that you're helping me out with my new dance steps or something.'

'Yeah,' I replied. 'I'm on that programme. Everyone good with that?'

Bit was smiling, no doubt kinda relieved that at least he wouldn't get his short ass savaged on his lonesome. Jonah was grinning too but there was a hint of something else on his face – a dose of dread right behind his eyes. I didn't want to admit it but fear was brewing in my stomach too. At least knights had body armour, swords and maces, and horses that could gallop forever. Our crew? We were trekking up to Notre Dame on the number 159 bus, with just our fists and our afros for protection.

All of a sudden, this hood-rat screeched up to us on a bike.

He snapped his head back to release the hoodie that was covering his head, smiled at Saira and Venetia, then looked at me. Collie Vulture! One of Nesta's bredrens. He was about seventeen, maybe eighteen – it was hard to tell with all the puss mountains that sprouted on his face. All I knew about him was that he got booted out of our school, had an acne issue and his real name was Simon. I had never spat two lyrics to him so why was he clocking me?

'McKay,' he hailed. 'Been told to come and get you.'

'By who?' I wanted to know.

'By my sister,' he said.

'But I don't know your sis.'

'Your bro Nesta does.'

'How does my bro know your sis?'

'Follow me and find out, innit,' Collie Vulture replied.

I stood for a little while, thinking about it. I glanced at Jonah and he was shaking his head. Bit just shrugged. I had vowed to find Nesta and if it meant following Collie on a mad one, then that's what I'd do. I said my goodbyes to my crew.

Collie, performing wheelies, spins and skids, led me to the southern ends of our estate. We left the tall slabs behind. I thought we were going to take the road to Crongton Heath but we headed east to these narrow streets with terraced housing. Graffiti in big black bubble-shaped letters on the side of one house read:

SOLDIERS FROM THESE ENDS NEVER SPILL TO THE FEDS, IF THEY DID WE'D TERMIN-8 THEM AND ROLL THEIR HEADS.

The doors were peeling and the brickwork was grimy. There was only enough room for a couple of bins to be placed outside the front windows before you hit the pavement. Kids rolled by on squeaky scooters and coming from an open window came the sound of some woman wailing along to the radio, totally out of tune, doing her *X-Factor* thing. There was nothing perilous going on but it was one of those places where you glanced over your shoulder every ten steps just to stay sharp.

Collie Vulture laughed then performed another wheelie on the pavement, where he nearly demolished a passer-by before bombing away down the road. When I caught up with him, he led me another three turns before stopping outside a green door with grimy windows on either side. The rank pong of cat piss invaded my nostrils.

'We live in the upstairs flat,' he said.

He pushed his key into the drawbridge, then turned around and gave me a mad grin. I have to admit, my heart started to bang. I thought about turning back – it wasn't every day some hood-rat I hardly know tells me to follow his ass to ends I don't usually step through. I hesitated as he opened the door and pushed his bike through.

'What's a matter with you?' he said. 'Your brother's upstairs.'

Before us was a short hallway with two doors at the end. Collie parked his bike and opened the door to the right. Stairs led up to his flat. I followed him, and I tried to stay cool on the outside while my nerves ping-ponged around inside me.

'Yvonne! *Yvonne!*' Collie called. 'I've got him.'

We reached a landing and turned left. Clothes were drying on a banister. I passed a small kitchen and I was led through to the end of the passageway, where there was a door. Collie used his keys to rat-a-tat it. I held my breath.

'Come in,' a girl's voice called.

I pushed the door open and stepped inside the girl's bedroom. Nesta was propped up on her bed. Red pillows supported his back. He was wearing his black jeans but his top half was going solo. Nuff bruises covered his back and shoulders. His left eye was a bluey-black and almost entirely closed up. A bottle of antiseptic sat on the side table (the smell doing mad battle with the already powerful aroma of cat piss) and a chick with blonde, frizzy hair was dabbing his face with cotton wool. She was wearing a *Matrix* T-shirt and untold bangles danced on her wrists. A tattoo of a green Buddha sexed up her neck. She looked about nineteen, maybe twenty. Nesta's good eye blazed when he looked at me.

'What's your fat behind doing here?' he shouted. He switched his hard stare to the girl. 'Did you set this up?'

'Yes, I did!' said the girl. 'If you won't go with me, then you can go with your liccle bro.'

'Go where?' I wanted to know.

'To the fed station, to report his bike missing,' revealed the girl.

I had to take a few seconds to download all this info. For a start, it was obvious my loner big bruv had a girlfriend. A girlfriend! That was a galaxy far, far away on its own, but it was also clear she – his *girlfriend* – wanted him to go to the feds! Shave Merlin's eyebrows!

Nesta was unpredictable but if there were three tings you could say about him they were: number one, he hated the feds; number two, he loved his bike to the max; and number three, he never had girlfriends!

'I'm Yvonne,' said the chick, pausing from giving her tender loving care. She gave me a half smile.

'I'm missing, sis,' said Collie to Yvonne. He held out his hand. 'Where's my five pound for getting McKay?'

'I'll give you it later, maybe tomorrow,' replied Yvonne. 'My budget's well sad at the moment.'

Obviously frustrated, Collie shook his head before turning and making his way back along the hallway.

'Don't go out troubling anyone and *don't* ride on the pavements!' Yvonne barked. He bounced down the stairs and we heard the drawbridge slam.

'The feds can't be trusted,' argued Nesta. 'I'll get my bike back *myself*!'

'So you think you're indestructible?' Yvonne raised her voice. 'Crongton's very own Ironman?' She kissed her teeth. 'Look at you. You obviously *spill blood* and *bruise nuff shades of purple*! If they see your ass they'll paralyse it! So for once, stop trying to be the hero, swallow your damn pride and report the jacking of your bike to the feds. It's the only way you'll get it back.'

Nesta closed his eyes. Sweet shiners! I had never seen him so humbled. He must've loved Yvonne to the core. If Dad had tried to convince him to leak to the feds he would've got a world of resistance.

'What ... what happened exactly?' I asked.

Yvonne wiped my bro's face with one of those moist face wipes they use for babies' bums before slapping a new plaster on his forehead. Nesta winced. '*Tell* him!' she insisted.

Nesta opened his eyes, or at least his good one. He glared at me so fierce I had to look away. It was then I noticed a black and white cat sleeping at the foot of the bed.

'I was riding up to North Crong the other night,' Nesta began. He stared into space. 'I reached Jubilee Way, near the open-air basketball court.'

'Why did you have to go up there?' Yvonne said, shaking her head. 'You're just looking for beef. Them North Crong bruvs are gonna war with anyone from South. It was only three weeks ago that General Madoo was speared and they're still looking for Manjaro.'

'Last time I looked it's a free country, isn't it?' Nesta replied. 'I can ride to any ends I damn well please.'

'Dumb choice,' spat back Yvonne. 'Sometimes you just *don't* think. Don't expect me to bless-up your headstone with flowers.'

'Don't want any!'

It was kinda weird that in my entire life I had never bounced up to North Crong. I had to agree with Nesta. It was a free country. What kinda messed-up world were we living in if you couldn't even step through neighbouring ends without hood-rats hunting you down?

The cat woke up, yawned and jumped to the floor. It stepped across the bedroom like it was the king of the world.

'They got a new skateboard area,' Nesta resumed. 'I pedalled up there to check it out. I wasn't looking for any beef.

I mean, what can I do on my lonesome? Anyway, I noticed these rodents clocking me so I thought I'd better remove my ass from the scene.'

Nesta climbed off the bed, found his white vest resting on a chair, pulled it on and continued. 'I was burning across a green and hit something – I think it was a freaking skateboard. I fell off the damn bike and three rodents were on me in a rush. Can't remember how many times those pussies kuffed me. While I was down, somebody picked up my bike and started to ride away. *Friggin liberty!* I got mad, pushed the rats off me, ran after the thief. Caught up with him too and kung-fu'd him off my wheels. He kuffed his head hard on the concrete. Nuff blood was leaking. I tried to ride away but his bredrens caught my ass again. They gave me the living kicking. Worst of all, they *still* jacked my mother-freaking bike.'

'You should've told your dad,' said Yvonne.

'*No!*' cried Nesta. 'He doesn't need to know. I fight my own wars. What can he do anyway? He can't even deal with the bailiff brothers!'

The cat leaped on to Yvonne's lap, licked its face and started to get its snooze on again.

'I'm with Yvonne,' I said, fretting that Nesta would blow me down with a cuss attack. 'You should've spilled to Dad . . . he bought you that bike.'

'What do *you* know?' he spat back.

'Look, you want the bike back, right?' Yvonne continued. 'And if you go up North Crong on your lonesome to try to get it back then don't bother to tap on my gates and ask me to patch you up again. I won't do it! You can take your stubborn ass to the friggin hospital and wait for the doctors to sew you up!'

'That's cold,' replied Nesta.

'I don't give a flying cuckoo how cold you think it is. I *mean* it,' Yvonne said, raising her voice. 'If you really want to get your bike back, step to the station and file a report.'

Yvonne turned to me. 'Make sure your mule-like bro gets there, McKay.'

I had never made sure of Nesta doing anything in my entire life.

'Besides, Nesta,' Yvonne added, 'I need some *me* time to do my sociology research. And I've got to clean up the kitchen! I haven't done a damn thing all day cos of *your* issues and Mum will be back from work in a couple of hours so get your hard butt in gear and step off.'

I tried my best to kill my smirk. Nesta pulled on his T-shirt and his denim jacket. I watched him tie the laces of his trainers – he never wore socks. When he was ready he kissed Yvonne on the cheek, looked at me and said, 'Let's bounce.'

# 5

## Crongton Fed Station

Nesta didn't say anything until we reached the southern ends of our estate. 'Do you really think the feds can be trusted?'

I shrugged. 'I dunno. You hear lyrics of woe about them. Bit's sis hates them.'

'It might be a waste of time anyway; those North Crong rodents have probably sold my bike already. Don't know what I'll tell Dad if I can't get my wheels back.'

'Be honest, innit,' I said. 'He'll get it. Crap happens. The other day someone jacked Colonel Slab's laptop – look how tall and crusty he is. Dad knows what the ends are like.'

'*No!* He won't get it. He'll still think I can't defend myself.'

'There's another ting,' I said.

He stopped stepping for a moment and caught me with his one-eyed stare. 'What?' he asked impatiently.

'That guy – that guy you booted off your bike? I think he

had to go hospital for a scan or someting. It's all around the school.'

Nesta paused and gazed into space again, as if he was replaying the drama in his head. 'His head did kiss the ground with nuff force,' he admitted. 'But who tell this rodent to t'ief my freaking bike!'

'His name is Festus.'

'Festus?' My brother repeated. Dread slobbered his face. 'Festus Livingstone?'

I nodded. He wiped his forehead and sucked in a deep breath. The fear in my stomach grew like a beanstalk in a fairy tale. 'Come step it up, bro,' he said. 'We have a bike-nap to report.'

Nesta didn't spill another word until we were rolling by the old factories – I didn't know why the council hadn't mashed them down and built someting else. The only people who used the buildings were the bomb-heads and runaways.

'How was school today?' Nesta asked.

'Same old.'

'You do any baking today?'

'No, that's on Tuesdays.'

'You wanna take that shit serious,' he said. 'You never know, you could be a chef one day, working in some posh hotel like Great-grandpops. Yeah – where the guests give you fifty-pound tips like a dentist gives out lollipops. So get on it.'

'I *am* on it,' I replied. 'But if I do go into the cooking game one day, I don't just wanna be a chef – I wanna own the whole damn shebang.'

Nesta nodded and grinned. I guessed a memory hit his

sweet spot. 'Mum's books came in handy, innit,' he said. 'It was a good ting I stopped Dad giving them away to that charity shop up by the Broadway.'

'Yes, they have been well useful.'

'I should've kept her aprons too, and stopped Dad flinging them out – you could've worn them in your cookery lessons.'

'It doesn't matter,' I said.

'Yes, it does!' Nesta raised his voice. 'Everything she had *matters.'*

Conversations with Nesta always ended up with Mum.

I wanted to ask him about Yvonne. How long had he been linking with her? Why he had kept this ting on a low profile? I'd only met her for five minutes but already I could see she was good for him. Nesta could definitely intimidate people with his crazy stare and off-key ways – but not her. She might be able to calm him down a bit. Maybe she could even help him work out his issues with Mum passing? She was already on the Dad drama.

'I still think you should tell Dad about your bike being jacked,' I said.

Nesta closed his one good eye and shook his head. My phone buzzed. I took it out of my pocket. It was Dad, right on cue.

'Don't tell him you're with me!' Nesta warned.

'But—'

'I *mean* it! Don't tell him zero nish, otherwise Festus Livingstone won't be the only bruv who I give a flying kick to.'

'Hi, Dad.'

'Hi, McKay. Where are you?'

'Oh ... just stepping down to the heath to watch some balling.'

'Who's playing up at the heath?' Dad asked.

'Some Year 11s.'

'Have you heard from Nesta?'

'No, Dad. Still no reply.'

Nesta nodded and raised a thumbs up. I felt bad though. Dad was probably at our castle, stressing out to the max. The inside of my stomach was churning like a gone-wrong blender.

'He'll come back when he's ready, Dad. Don't fret too much,' I said.

'I hope so,' said Dad. 'OK, McKay. Remember I've left five pound for your dinner.'

'Thanks, Dad.'

I deleted the call. 'I'm not lying for you again!' I said. 'You two need to sit down, slap your heads together and sort out your issues. I'm not loving playing the referee in-between your warring.'

Nesta put a hand on my shoulder. 'That'll happen when he starts *listening* to me. You *know* how he is. *His* way or *no* way. He's gonna have to deal with that issue before I even sit down with him.'

I could see Nesta getting vex so I left it alone.

We reached Crongton High Street. School kids were hanging outside the Footcave store, admiring the name-brand trainers. Others were sinking fried chicken legs in the Hot Rooster takeaway. Four feds, two on each side of the road, were on patrol. A bomb-head, wrapped in a duvet on the pavement, was begging for money at the bus stop outside Norley's department store. Charity shakers smiled their fake smiles. The two coffee shops were packed with twenty-somethings working on their laptops and young mums nibbling cakes. More bros and sisters of my age were inside the phone shop, checking out the latest smartphones. Nesta didn't hang around or get sidetracked. He hot-stepped straight to the fed station at the end of the street. I had to get my jog on to keep up with him.

The sight of the fed station made me think about tings. I paused. Nesta turned around.

'What's the matter – why you stopped?'

'Can I ask you someting?' I said, wiping the sweat from my brow.

'What?'

'What happened to Manjaro?'

'How many times have you asked me this?' Nesta barked impatiently.

'Is he dead?' I ventured. 'You'd know ... wouldn't you?'

Nesta took his time in answering. He looked away. 'Hush your words, bro. Remember where we are. No, he definitely ain't *dead*.' He hissed the word under his breath. 'Now bin your questions. And let's get this ting done.'

We bounced through the swing doors and crashed on the two chewed plastic seats in the reception area. There were posters on the walls telling you what numbers to ding if you witnessed a crime. Boot a helmet! If I called the feds about all the badness I had seen I'd never be off the phone.

We could see an old woman through a glass door, bitching

about something at the main counter. A female officer was taking notes. I glanced at Nesta – he was staring vacantly ahead in that psycho way of his. I hoped he wouldn't start kicking off. If he did, I'd definitely have to ding Dad.

This one time just after Mum passed, Dad was called to the school. There had been an incident in Nesta's PE class. Nesta had refused to go on a cross-country run – and when the teacher had threatened to call home and 'get his mother to come down and deal with him', Nesta just lost it. He'd blitzed a display cabinet with a cricket bat. The PE teacher was new – he hadn't known any better.

They'd brought my ass out of my class to chat some sense into his hard drive. I'd found him sitting curled up in the teacher's chair, hugging the bat like it was a baby. No one tried to take the bat off him. Eventually Dad arrived, explained the situation to the school, and persuaded Nesta to kill his rage and drop the bat. Nesta said he would've been cool if they'd just gone running and left him alone to play basketball.

Everyone was sorry. But he still got a week's suspension.

The old woman was coming back out through the glass door. Nesta glared at her and she muttered something underneath her breath before going on her way. Nesta got to his feet. My heart started to drum. I followed him over to the front desk. The female fed was scribbling something down on an A4 notepad. It looked like she had been chomping her nails. She had ginger hair. Her white blouse was cleaner than brand new snowfall.

Nesta made his presence felt. "Scuse me!'

The officer looked up and smiled. She was kinda pretty

for a fed. 'How can I help you, sir?' She noticed the wounds on Nesta's face. Her expression switched. 'What happened to you?'

'Got a beat-down from some North Crong pussies up by Jubilee Way and they jacked my bike,' Nesta answered. 'I can take the beating, I ain't snitching on that, but I want my mother-freaking bike back. It's got a silver frame and I put some gold tape around the handlebars. It's got four reflectors on the back and—'

'Hold on a minute,' said the female fed, raising a palm. 'First of all I need to write down your personal details – you know, name and stuff.' She looked at his face again. 'That looks nasty,' she remarked. 'Have you received medical attention?'

'I don't need any medical attention,' snapped my brother. 'I just wanna get my bike back! My dad bought me it! Why don't you send the military wing of this station to North Crong with some gooey-dripping dogs and deal with the issue?'

My heart banged quicker. *Don't lose it here, Nesta,* I said to myself. *Not here!* I put a hand on Nesta's shoulder. I could feel his body tensing up.

'I need to get a form,' said the fed. 'I'm going to get myself a cup of coffee too. Would you like one?'

Nesta looked proper confused. He glanced at me and then at the officer again. 'Er, I dunno. Yeah, what the ... yeah, I'll have a coffee. What about my liccle bro? Can't he get one too?'

'Yes, of course,' she replied. 'Milk? Sugar?'

'Yeah,' Nesta answered. 'Spill a bit of milk in mine and drop two sugars in it. Thanks.'

They both looked at me.

'Er, I'll have the same,' I said.

The fed clip-clopped away. Nesta studied her ass. I think he liked what he saw. I know I did. He turned around. 'Can you believe that?' he said. 'A fed making me a cup of coffee?'

I shook my head. 'Maybe they don't all work for the dark side,' I said and kinda half smiled, hoping it might chill him out a bit – I could see he was on edge. I certainly was.

'Still haven't tasted this coffee yet, bruv,' he said. 'You never know, they might've laced it with skunks' piss or worse.'

I laughed. 'To tell you the brutal truth, bruv, it's not really a hot drink that my stomach is crying for. I *need* some hot wings or someting!'

Nesta kissed his teeth. 'You and your belly. Always thinking about *food!*'

'I haven't sunk a ting since lunch!'

As we waited for our coffee, I remembered Mum taking me to the supermarket and asking me what I'd like in my sandwiches for school. I said corn beef, cucumber and Branston pickle. *'But you're not getting any fizzy drinks so don't even ask!'*

The fed returned with a tray of steaming polystyrene cups and some forms. The coffee was tame but I was starting to relax because to my surprise Nesta and the fed seemed to be getting on. 'You should've seen my girl's reaction when she saw my mashed-up face,' he said. 'I had to stop her from taking up arms and marching to North Crong to deal with those rodents. She's a proper warrior, not scared of anyting. And she's studying online for a degree in sociology. She's gonna be a social worker one day. Yeah! My girl's well brainy.'

There was nuff pride in his voice. My bro loved this Yvonne to the core.

'I'm sure your family and loved ones were all concerned,' the fed said. 'Now, you need to fill in your name and your full address, a contact number and—'

'My dad doesn't need to know, does he?'

'How old are you?'

'Nearly eighteen.'

'I think at least one of your parents should be informed. If not your dad then perhaps your mum?'

Nesta gripped his cup tighter. Coffee spilled on to the counter. I placed my hand on Nesta's shoulder. For a moment, I held my breath.

'Can't tell my mum,' he said. 'Someone killed her.'

'Oh, God. I'm so sorry to hear that,' the fed replied. Sympathy stroked her face. There was a silence. She searched my brother's eyes. 'I didn't know,' she said eventually, 'and I do apologise if I upset you.'

An image of Ms Archer, our head of year, coming into my food technology class to tell me the news about Mum downloaded into my mind. She was rubbing her knuckles and stuttering. I remember that more than what she'd actually said.

'That's all right,' Nesta said after an awkward pause. 'Sorry about the mess.'

'No problem.' She managed to smile again. 'I'll deal with that.' The officer went to fetch a cloth. I let out a monster sigh. Nesta hung his head.

When she came back, he filled in the form and explained to her how he had to suffer a beat-down and watch his bike being jacked. For a second I wished Dad was here to see this.

'So you're gonna make sure they send a SWAT team to hunt down my bike?' Nesta joked.

'I can't promise you a SWAT team but as soon as someone is available they'll look into it. I'm sure you know that we're a bit overstretched at the moment – so much going on.'

'I hear that,' Nesta replied.

'You have a crime number now,' said the fed. 'I hope your bike is insured. And I still think you should at least see your doctor.'

Nesta shook his head. 'Thanks for everyting,' he said. He spun around, looked at me and added, 'Let's bounce.'

Seconds later we were rolling down the front steps of the station. Nesta was saying something about how Yvonne could get off his back now, but I was thinking about dinner – my stomach had its rumble on.

# 6

# Stop and Search

We walked back along the High Street. There were now six feds on patrol – three on either side. The Hot Rooster take-away was teasing my nostrils. Nesta was still jibber-jabbering away about Yvonne this and Yvonne that. It was funny. He hadn't said a fat zero to me about her before today. It sounds cold but I blocked him out.

A couple or so days ago, Dad had bought a tray of chicken fillets that he had left in the fridge. I wanted to get back, slice and dice up a piece of prime rooster, spin some seasoning on it, chop up onions, peppers, garlic and stir-fry that mother with veg and a serious dose of Jamaican jerk. Yeah, I think there was a liccle bit of olive oil left to fry it in. I'd let it steam for a few minutes under some foil and get it smelling all sexy and ripe for sinking. And a pot of rice too, boiled up sweetly on the stove to go with it. Mmm. My mouth was watering big time.

'So, what do you think?' Nesta asked me as we headed towards South Crong ends.

'Think of what?' I said.

'Haven't you been listening to me, McKay? Yvonne, innit.'

'Yvonne,' I repeated. 'What about her?'

'What's a matter with you? I asked you what you think of her.'

'Oh, she seems cool,' I answered. 'But crush your balls! She has you under lock though! *Go to the fed station . . . Speak to your dad!*'

'No, she ain't,' Nesta argued. 'I just respect her.'

I killed another smirk.

We rolled towards the shop in the middle of our estate cos Nesta was thirsty – I hoped he would buy me a drink too. I was wondering if Nesta was gonna step back to our castle with me, when I saw flashing blue lights about a hundred metres away – not too far from the shop.

'Step it up, bruv,' Nesta told me. 'Someting's going down.'

We hot-toed to the scene. A crowd had gathered on the pavement outside the store. A fed car was parked up and Mr Dagthorn, the forever stressed-out, bald-headed owner of the place, was pointing this way and that, mauling the ears of two male feds. About thirty metres away, two other feds were dragging a hood-rat off towards their car, which they'd parked a little further along the road. Collie Vulture! His hands were cuffed behind his back. Curses spat from his mouth. His bike was abandoned on the pavement. I glanced at Nesta. He was shaking his head and spitting something dark under his breath. I spotted Boy from the Hills leaning against the shop door and bounced up to him. 'What's the score?' I asked.

'Collie jacked a bottle of tonic wine from the shop but when he jumped on his bike the feds appeared out of nowhere.'

I shook my head.

'Collie was raging. He'd promised Mr Dagthorn he'd pay him tomorrow,' Boy from the Hills added.

I rewound to earlier in the afternoon when Collie asked Yvonne for a fiver for collecting me from school. It was messed up how small dramas could turn into major blockbusters.

'I've banned him from coming in here but he's always stealing from my shop,' ranted Mr Dagthorn to the officers. 'Sweets, chocolate bars, chewing gum, porno mags – I'm sick and tired of young people robbing from me. Throw away the bloody key, I say!'

Collie heard what Mr Dagthorn said and wasted no time in biting back. 'Screw you, old man. I said I'd pay for the drink tomorrow and I would have!'

The feds tried to shove Collie into the back seat of their car. Collie put up nuff resistance. *'Get* in the car!' one of the feds ordered.

In trying to get away, Collie banged his head on the door handle. A red mark appeared across his eyebrow. Onlookers raged their disapproval. More people were starting to pay attention now; windows opened in the slabs above us. A council worker, wearing a yellow Day-Glo top, stopped sweeping the street and tuned in to the drama.

'Don't you *ever* enter my shop again,' yelled Mr Dagthorn. 'You'll probably even steal from the prison canteen!'

Someone threw a fat stone, hitting one of the fed cars on its bonnet. We all turned to see a hood-rat Usain-Bolting away from the scene towards Wareika Way. The soles of his trainers were bright orange. I tried not to laugh, but it was well funny. The feds weren't exactly singing 'Always Look on the Bright Side of Life'. Poor Collie yelped and shrieked as they slam-dunked him hard through the car door. Nesta's expression switched.

Someone threw another stone, and blitzed the front window of Mr Dagthorn's shop. A nine- or ten-year-old boy laughed as he burned off through the estate, a fed hot on his heels.

Boy from the Hills and I stepped away quickly, not wanting to get caught up in any trouble.

'Everyone *calm* down,' shouted an officer.

'You see what I have to put up with!' roared Mr Dagthorn, his hands now on his head. 'You see how much respect they have for me? Do I deserve this? If I wasn't here where would they go to get their milk for the morning? I'm just trying to make a living and *this* is how they treat me!'

Nesta approached the officers who had Collie. 'If I pay for the drink he jacked, will you let him go?'

'He's committed a crime,' a fed replied. 'We can't have everybody walking into shops and taking what they like.'

'It doesn't even cost three pound,' said Nesta. 'And Dagthorn charges fifty pence more than the supermarket – freaking t'ief! I'll pay for it and, trust me, after I spill to his sis he won't ever jack from the shop again.'

I wasn't sure if Nesta had three pound on him. My own

funds were low – I only had twenty-seven pence blessing my pocket.

The fed shook his head and slammed the car door. The other officer climbed into the driver's seat and switched the ignition. Nesta slapped the window. Mr Dagthorn had stopped his ranting and was now watching my brother like everybody else.

'Nesta!' I called. He didn't hear me. The Kraken was about to be set loose. *Oh crap!*

'Can't you feds be on a freaking level?' Nesta raged, hammering the top of the fed car. 'Why arrest him for someting that don't even cost three pound? Let him *go*! Nobody was hurt. He hasn't even touched the bottle. It can go back on the friggin' shelf.'

My heartbeat accelerated. The officer inside the car pushed the passenger door open. It smacked Nesta in the leg, nearly knocking him over. 'Why don't you move along!' ordered the fed to my brother. 'And go home!'

I could feel Nesta's rage burst. Without hesitation he ran into the fed and headbutted him dead in the chest. The officer lost his balance and fell hard on to the ground.

Someone cheered from the pavement. A girl giggled hysterically. Even the road sweeper had a smile on his face. Others stared in disbelief.

'Nesta!' I shouted again.

The feds gathered round. *Two* of them grabbed my bro in a hard bear hug, almost strangling him, trying to put cuffs on him. Nesta wriggled this way and that, kicked and flailed. He managed to scratch a face or two, but he was overpowered.

Everyone around me cussed the feds. A voice inside me screamed, *Don't stand up there like a pussy! Help him! Help him!*

I started off to Nesta's aid, but Boy from the Hills barged me to the ground and said, 'McKay, keep your big self still.'

My right knee kissed the concrete.

'The feds are arresting my bro!'

'And how's your dad gonna feel when news beats him that not one but *two* of his boys are sinking oats in a fed cell?'

By the time I climbed to my feet, Nesta was being hand-cuffed. All struggle left him. His chest was heaving but he was weirdly calm. I think he was staring at me. His mouth was moving. I guessed at what he was saying. He wouldn't want me to tell Dad.

They shoved him into another car. Doors were slammed. Engines were revved. I watched as he sped away. He didn't look back. The road sweeper resumed sweeping.

# 7

## Yvonne's Mum

Tiredness licked my ass. I sat down on the pavement. Mr Dagthorn ranted on and on. 'Who's gonna pay for the damage? Insurance companies take months! I'm closing for the day! Why aren't there more police patrolling this estate? Why did I come to this godforsaken place? I just want to make a decent living!'

'There's too many of the feds around here as it is,' argued a voice.

'Why didn't you let Collie pay for the drink tomorrow?' said another.

'Because he's a *thief*!'

'If I had a shop I wouldn't let Collie inside,' somebody else cut in. 'That hood-rat would t'ief the pillow from his granny's coffin!'

'But Dagthorn's a prick,' came the reply. 'My mum wanted to put ten notes on her electric key and promised to pay him the next day. She's never robbed from him and he just shook his freaking head, telling her a big dirty no. We were in darkness that night. We missed *Scandal*. I don't give a shit who t'iefs and robs from his shop.'

I didn't have the energy to even look up and see who was raging with Mr Dagthorn. All I could think was: Nesta had been arrested and he was gonna be parking in a cold cell at the fed station for the rest of the night. Once, Bit's sis told me about the dungeons at the fed station – it proper messed her up. I had no idea what he'd be charged with. *What do I tell Dad?* I knew Nesta would never forgive me if I didn't keep my beak sealed. *Damn! What am I gonna do?*

I felt a hand on my shoulder. It was Boy from the Hills. 'You'd better get Collie's bike before someone jacks that too,' he suggested.

I stood up and went over to the bike. I picked it up and sat on the seat.

'Do you know where he lives?' asked Boy from the Hills.

'Funny enough I just found out today,' I answered. 'He lives off the Heath Road. He's got an older sis, Yvonne. She ain't gonna be chanting hallelujah when she hears what went down.'

'Shit happens,' said Boy from the Hills. 'What are you gonna tell your old man?'

'I'll have to spill the whole score,' I said. 'The fed did lick him with the car door and there were nuff witnesses who saw that. But let me get the bike back to Collie's fam first.'

'Do you want me to step with you?' Boy from the Hills offered.

I paused and took a good look at him. I had known him

for more than three years but we had never had any kinda proper conversation or gone on any missions together, didn't ever park next to each other in class or step home together. Now and again we swapped jokey lyrics in the corridors at school but that was about it. Just banter. But since I'd helped him beat off the crew who tried to jack his tablet a few weeks ago, there was this unspoken bond between us. I wasn't even sure why I saved his ass. I felt sorry for him, I guessed.

'Yeah, I could do with the company,' I finally answered.

My phone vibrated in my pocket when we reached the Heath Road. I thought it would be Dad but it was Liccle Bit.

'What's going down with your bro?' he asked. Bit was all hyper, chatting really fast as if his credit was running out. 'Someone texted me it's all kicking off outside Dagthorn's. Is Nesta OK?'

I explained what had happened.

'You're with Boy from the Hills?' he asked, nuff surprise in his voice.

'Yeah, what's wrong with that?'

'Didn't I tell you that he'd be all over you like a mummy's bandages cos you saved his hide?'

'He ain't that bad.'

'Your bro better control his mad fever when the feds question his ass,' Liccle Bit said after a while.

'He'll be cool,' I said.

In truth I was shitting pillars about Nesta being interrogated by the feds. But Bit didn't need to know that.

'You're not gonna flop out of our mission tomorrow, are you? What with your bruv and all?'

'No, man,' I said. 'I've got your back. I'm on it.'

'You sure?' Bit wanted confirmation. 'Cos if you flop out then Jonah will definitely follow. You know what he's like. I need all the Chewbaccas I can get. This Sergio bruv ain't no Ewok. And I ain't too tall.'

'Bit, hear me on this one. I'm *not* gonna flop out. I'll be rolling with you to Notre Dame.'

'OK ... thanks. *Don't* tell Boy from the Hills about our mission.'

'I won't. No problem. We'll chat later.'

'OK, I'm gonna ding Venetia and tell her that we're all ready.'

'Cool.'

I killed the call. Boy from the Hills was giving me a messed-up look. 'You guys are cruising up to Notre Dame?'

'Er, yeah. Bit's got something to do for his mum and he don't wanna step up there on his lonesome.'

'You'd better steer clear of North Crong estate – remember your bro had an issue with Festus Livingstone – and Festus Livingstone's got the backup of Major Worries. And they're still shouting and splitting gums with the General Madoo thing. And Major Worries is still hunting for Manjaro—'

'You don't need to remind me,' I interrupted his flow.

'—*and* you and your bro really look alike—'

'I *know*! Just drop the score, will you?'


After two wrong turns, I finally found Collie's green door. I slapped the letter box. Yvonne answered it after looking out of an upstairs window. She clocked Collie's bike and read my face in an instant. 'What's happened?' she asked.

'Nesta,' I started. 'Nesta reported the jacking of his bike to the feds.'

Yvonne crossed her arms. There was a biro wedged over her ear. 'What else happened?' she pressed again. 'Just give me the endgame. Not interested in once upon a time.'

'Collie and Nesta both got arrested,' I spilled.

Yvonne closed her eyes, raised her hands to her head. 'Why? What did they do?'

'Collie jacked a tonic wine bottle at Dagthorn's store but he ran into feds on his way out,' I answered. 'Nesta was trying to reason with the feds to let him go, but they licked him with a car door and Nesta lost it.'

'What did he do this time?' Yvonne wanted to know.

*This time?* I thought. *What other madness has he done that I don't know zero squat about?* 'He headbutted—'

We heard footsteps descending from inside the house. A woman appeared. She was wearing a smart sky-blue trouser suit but the big fake eyelashes looked all wrong. A cigarette burned between her fingers. Her feet were going solo – her big right toe had a bitch of a bunion. 'What's going on?' she demanded.

'Simon's been arrested, Mum,' sighed Yvonne, her voice hushed.

'Can't say I'm surprised,' said Yvonne's mum. She pulled hard on the cigarette, glanced at Boy from the Hills and then me. 'It's the people he moves around with but does he listen to me? No, he bloody doesn't! Was he nicking again?'

Yvonne nodded.

'From where?' Yvonne's mum demanded.

Boy from the Hills and I swapped frantic looks. The brutal reality was that I didn't want to get into exchanging lyrics with this woman. She looked like she could give a cuss attack as good as anyone – even Liccle Bit's mum, which is saying something.

'He t'iefed a bottle of tonic wine from Dagthorn's shop,' Yvonne said.

'Just like his dad,' Yvonne's mum remarked, throwing her hands up in the air. 'He loved his liquor too! Tonic wine? He could've at least made it all worth it and stole a bottle of champagne! This is all I need. I go to work, try to earn enough to put a roof over our heads, and all Simon can do is spend hours in the bloody bathroom putting toothpaste on his spots, ride around on his bike and get himself arrested. I haven't got the time for it!'

'I'll go to the police station, Mum,' Yvonne offered.

Yvonne's mum sucked hard on her cigarette again. She glanced along each end of the street before she looked down at her feet. I had to stop the grin that was racing to my cheeks.

'When they let him out, tell him that if he's caught stealing again, not to bother coming home,' Yvonne's mum said in a raised voice. 'I'm tired of it! And tell him to stop leaving cereal bowls in his bedroom!'

She flashed Boy from the Hills and I another tough look, then turned and rolled back inside her castle.

'Sorry about that,' said Yvonne. 'Hold on to the bike for a minute. Just gonna put on my sweats and I'll ride up to the station and try to find out what's going down.'

# 8

## Mug Punter

We only had to wait two minutes. Yvonne had changed into a grey tracksuit. A black hairband had her frizzy hair on lock. 'Can't believe the both of 'em got arrested,' she said. 'I've had better freaking days than this! Thanks for coming down to our ends and bringing Simon's bike. Appreciate it. I don't know what I'm gonna do with his tiefing self!'

Boy from the Hills and I watched her wheel away. Before she reached the end of the road, she cycled back. She took out a biro and a piece of paper from her pocket. 'Here's my mobile number,' she said, writing it down. 'Call me if you hear anything. The feds won't allow them to keep their phones.'

She gave me the piece of paper and I banked it in my back trouser pocket. 'Let's step home,' I said to Boy from the Hills. 'Where's your castle?'

'On Crongton Heath,' replied Boy from the Hills.

'You live on Crongton Heath?' I asked. 'Not on the streets but the heath itself?'

'Er . . . yeah,' replied Boy from the Hills. 'We're on the other side of Ripcorn Wood. It's quiet up there. Mum likes it that way.'

'You're lying,' I charged.

'Not lying, bruv.'

'What do your parents do?'

'Oh, er . . . my pops is a barrister and my mum is a psychologist – she sometimes works with the feds.'

Boy from the Hills look proper embarrassed. I stopped walking. *Blinking shrinks!* You learned something every day. At least that explained what his muddy, mad-haired self was doing with a top-of-the-range tablet in the first place . . . Maybe his mum could clip-clop down to our castle and counsel my fam on a discount. What was he doing at our school? He should be going private. Maybe they didn't take him cos of his hair.

'If you've got nothing better to do,' Boy from the Hills said, 'why don't you step up to my place and we can watch a box set of *Boardwalk Empire* or something. Or you could give me advice on what sites I should use to download films on to my tablet. My dad's away and Mum's always late home every freaking day. I think there's gonna be some lamb for tea. After five I'll be there on my lonesome – I'm kinda always there on my lonesome. If you want I can get a bottle of wine from the cellar. Could do with the company. Can you play pool?'

Lamb! I was seriously tempted. But I didn't know a sweet

digital about downloading films. Boy from the Hills baffled me to the max. He had a pool table! He had the green light for wine! He lived in a palace! So why couldn't he wash his damn hair, and why did he wear such no-brand everything-must-go sale shoes? It didn't make sense.

'Maybe next time,' I finally answered. 'My dad will be wondering where my ass is – I told him I was watching some balling up the heath.'

'OK, I hear that,' said Boy from the Hills. His head dropped. He looked proper disappointed.

We parted ways at the Heath Road. He still looked pissed off but he should be hugging his blessings – I'd rather play pool on my lonesome than tell Dad that Nesta had been arrested.

I arrived back at my slab about twenty-five minutes later – I always walked up the stairs of our block slowly cos I didn't want to bump into the debt brothers. It was all clear. I pushed my key into my front door and entered. I kicked off my shoes and hung up my blazer.

'Is that you, Nesta?' Dad called out from the front room.

'No, it's me.'

I stepped through the hallway and found Dad at the dinner table, drinking a can of Coke. He was wearing a white vest, black jeans and his cockroach-crusher boots – the laces were undone. Stubble manned-up his chin. Bills, bits of paper and envelopes were strewn in front of him. He looked like he had been parked there for the longest time. Maybe he was trying to decide which bill he should pay first. He took another swig from his can and looked at me. 'Has Nesta got in touch with you?'

I placed my schoolbag on an empty chair. I filled the seat next to it.

'I asked you a question!' Dad raised his voice. 'Has Nesta called or texted you?'

'He's been arrested,' I blurted out.

The stress lines on Dad's forehead seemed to deepen as he drank the news.

'What for?' he asked.

'He was trying to help out one of his bredrens—'

'*What for?*' Dad repeated.

'He headbutted a fed in the chest,' I spilled. 'But they smacked a car door into his leg. I saw them! Nuff peeps saw it all too – up by Dagthorn's shop.'

For the next half an hour or so I told Dad the whole score. He didn't say much. Instead he just stared and sipped at his drink until he finished it.

'So you *lied* to me!'

'About what?'

'When I called you I asked where Nesta was and you blatantly *lied*.'

'He told me I had to rest my lips, or else!' I tried to defend myself.

Dad stood up, went to the kitchen to drop the empty can in the bin and fetched another from the fridge. He pulled back the lever and sunk about a third in one go. He seemed more hurt that I had lied to him than about Nesta getting himself arrested. 'I'll better go up there and see how he is,' he said. 'He's still a minor but you know what he's like – he'd rather they chop off his fingers than ask them to contact me.'

I watched Dad tie his laces then pull on his Bruce Lee T-shirt. Mum had bought him that top along with some old-school kung fu DVDs for his birthday three years ago. She'd managed to squeeze the T-shirt into his sandwich box to surprise him. Mum had loved doing things like that.

'When I leave the police station I'll head straight for work,' Dad said. 'You'll be all right on your own?'

I wanted to say, no, I wouldn't. I had just watched my big bro being arrested and if that wasn't bad enough, Festus Livingstone and the other North Crong hood-rats were intent on savaging his ass. It might be safer in prison than on the streets. So no, actually, I didn't want to be on my lonesome. In fact, it would've been nice if Dad kept his miserable self in the castle and told me that tings were gonna be OK, whether he believed it or not.

What I actually said was, 'I'll be good.'

He shuffled all his papers into a neat pile before placing them in a large envelope. 'Are you going to get yourself a takeaway?' he asked.

'No, Dad. I'm gonna stir-fry those chicken pieces you left in the fridge.'

'Do enough for three.'

'Yeah, course.'

I think we both hoped that Nesta would soon be back in our castle but I couldn't remember the last time all three of us parked at the dinner table and sunk a meal at the same time. Mum always used to insist that we eat our dinners together.

'And I haven't forgotten your birthday,' he added. 'It's why I've been working overtime.'

'You don't have to kill yourself for me, Dad. I know things are tight.'

'That's what parents do,' he said, switching on his serious face. 'Every day! If things work out I was thinking we could all go out for dinner. Go to a steakhouse or something.'

He collected his work bag from his bedroom before stepping up to me and placing his right hand on my cheek. A quarter of his face smiled – just half a cheek and part of his mouth. The rest of his expression looked like he was going off to war. In a way he was. Nesta wasn't gonna love my dad appearing at the fed station. *'Don't* answer the door,' he reminded me. 'If you're worried about anything, just call or text. Have you got enough credit?'

'Yes, Dad.'

'Good. Go to your bed at a decent time.'

He pulled on his thick black anorak from a peg in the hallway, opened the door and closed it behind him.

Home alone. Again. I parked for a while and thought about this crazy day and everything that had happened. I thought about Boy from the Hills and his lamb dinner. Then I went to the kitchen, switched on the radio and started to prepare my stir-fry. I found a tomato at the back of the fridge and I sliced it up and added it to the mix. Nearly an hour later I was sitting in front of the TV, watching a DVD of some foot-clumping fighting from Hong Kong, and sinking my food greedily. I didn't wanna brag but my stir-fry could've won *MasterChef*. My fam were blessed that I was so sick in the kitchen!

The kung fu was brutal – a bruv was getting the kidneys banged out of him by a guy covered head to toe in step-away-from-me tattoos – but at least it kept me from fretting about Nesta in a fed cell. It was past eleven when my phone dinged. I thought it would be Dad with news, but it was Jonah.

'Sorry to hear about your bro,' he said. 'Everyone's saying the feds nearly broke his leg when they smashed the car door into him.'

'Yeah, everybody saw that,' I replied. 'The feds won't get away with it.'

'He could sue them,' suggested Jonah. 'Yeah, take the feds to court. Tell your bro to say that he was traumatised by the whole damn experience. He can say he gets nightmares. What's that thing that soldiers get? Post-traumatic stress something? Also, make sure he says his vision is all messed up. He'll get nuff dollars for that.'

'My dad went up the fed station about two hours ago,' I said. 'I just wanna see Nesta back here.'

Jonah paused. I sensed the call wasn't all about Nesta's issues with the feds. 'About tomorrow,' he said.

'What about it?' I asked.

'Are you still going?'

'Yeah, I'm on it,' I replied. 'We got to have Bit's back.'

'Don't you think Venetia should step to the feds and report that this Sergio bruv napped her phone?'

'But if she goes to the feds she'll have to tell her fam,' I reasoned. 'And you know what Bit said about them, how strict they are about this stuff . . . Can you imagine what they'll say when they find out about Venetia giving it up for an older guy? Older bruvs don't just wanna hold hands, watch the moon rise over the slabs while listening to Little Mix songs, trust me, and when Venetia's dad sees the photos . . . man, he'll probably fling her over her balcony with a church organ tied to her leg.'

'But aren't we in enough worries already with the Manjaro situation?' Jonah reminded me. 'We're Bit's bredrens and who knows when he might jump out on us like the living Predator.'

'As I've always said, Jonah – why would Manjaro wanna maul us?'

'Because he's a psycho!' Jonah was quick to reply. 'He might not want to savage Bit cos he's Elaine's bruv but he might want to terminate us to get back at Bit.'

'Stop fretting, Jonah,' I tried to reassure him. 'No one's sniffed Manjaro's hide for six months. And he's hardly gonna be hiding his crazy self in North Crong or Notre Dame.'

A long silence. Jonah thought about it.

'So we're gonna do this for real?' he said finally.

Jonah didn't sound too sure and truth be known I wasn't too sure about the whole thing either. But we couldn't let Bit down, so I had to ignore the dread in my stomach and sound positive.

'Bruv, we *are* gonna roll up to North Crong and we *are* gonna get Venetia's phone back. "Eye of the Tiger".'

'OK,' said Jonah.

'I'll be round tomorrow morning before school.'

'Yeah, yeah. Me and Bit will wait for you.'

I deleted the call. As I washed my dish I wondered how Venetia was feeling. If I was stressed out to the max with my fam situation she must be suffering even more. I didn't have the vibe for violence any more so I switched off the DVD and crashed out on my bed. My eyes closed, and in the silent darkness, I saw Mum so clearly. Memories came to me in a rush. I could almost feel her raising my chin with her fingers as she adjusted my tie before my first day at South Crongton High. I could see her playfully slapping some cake mix on my nose in the kitchen. I remembered her giggling when I tried to flip a pancake for the first time. She was always smiling and laughing, even when the rest of us had our Grinch on.

I opened my eyes again and switched on the lamp beside my bed. I looked around my room. Mum's cookery books were on my shelf alongside my manga mags. On the shelf below were my *Lord of the Ring* DVDs sitting next to my *King Arthur and the Round Table* stories. Mum bought me most of them. I turned off my light. Tears filled my eyes as I drifted off to sleep.

I was woken up by someone entering my dungeon. I slapped on my lamp. My alarm clock read 3.20 a.m. Nesta parked at the end of my bed. I sat up. For the longest time he just glared at me with his good eye, not saying a skinny zero. Eventually, he spoke.

'You told Dad.'

'I ... I had to.'

'I told you not to tell him a damn ting ... but you did, like a proper snitch.'

'But you were arrested,' I managed.

Nesta stood up and pulled my curtains apart. He peered out of the window. We were on the seventh floor so he had a decent view of our estate and Crongton Park. I stared at Nesta's back.

He was my favourite person in the world. My heart started to gallop.

'I told you. I can look after myself. I don't need Dad's help. When Mum died it was me and you versus the world. From now on, I'm on my lonesome on that one!'

He pushed his hands into his pockets but he didn't turn around. I couldn't kill the tears.

'I can't trust you, McKay.'

'But I done the right thing,' I protested. My brain felt toasted and a world of rejection was moving in my belly. I wiped my face.

'No, you didn't!' Nesta suddenly raised his voice and turned around.

'But the feds took you away. I was fretting. You're not eighteen yet.'

'You think Dad can sort everything out?' he raged. 'He *can't*. He messes up too, just as much as me.'

'What do you mean?' I asked.

Nesta set himself up to spill something major but he checked himself, shook his head and sat at the bottom of my bed once more.

'What are you trying to say, Nesta?' I asked softly. 'Why can't you and Dad tell me stuff? *I'm* part of this fam too!'

He caught me in that mad one-eyed stare of his for a long minute. I managed to stop the tears.

'We can't rely on anyone, McKay. Not even Dad.'

'What do you mean?' I pressed again. *'Don't* shut me out.'

'You think I'm the only one messed up by Mum's death?'

I shook my head, not understanding what Nesta was trying to get at.

'Dad gambles,' Nesta finally leaked. It came out in almost a whisper.

'On what?' I wanted to know.

'Remember the Christmas after Mum died? Remember Dad saying he wanted us to have an extra-special Christmas? I got a computer and you got your PlayStation 3 and all those games. Dad even paid Bit's grandma for a rum cake?'

'Yeah, course, I remember that. Dad tried his best cos Mum wasn't around any more. Didn't we both rate him for that?'

Dad was a superhero to me, protecting me and my bruv through hard times.

Nesta stood up again and peered out of the window – since Mum passed he never slept with the curtains pulled. I could never work that out.

'He won most of that Christmas money in the bookies. He told me to my face, bro.'

'So all the presents, all the cake and niceness … It wasn't overtime?'

Nesta turned around and shook his head.

In an instant Dad's superhero cape loosened, fell off and landed in a moat.

'It wasn't overtime,' Nesta said. 'The only overtime Dad

does in the damn bookie shop. I saw him in there a few weeks ago. He told me some jackanory about putting on a friend's bet but he was gambling the rent money.'

I shook my head, not wanting to believe it, but it all made sense. Sometimes I arrived home to find Dad watching horse or greyhound racing. He had a world of swear words for slow dogs and lazy mules. Now and again he would leave messages on the kitchen table saying he was checking a bredren of his in the bookies. I never thought anything of it. Dad loved his sport to the max.

'Why'd you think I've been so vex with him lately?' Nesta added. 'I can look after myself, but what's gonna happen to your ass if you get flung out of here cos Dad can't pay the rent? You gonna raid the scout place at the end of Wareika Way and jack a tent?'

'That ain't funny. Where's Dad now?' I asked.

'He went work. He sat in on my interview but I didn't say zero nish to him.'

Nesta suddenly stood up and left. I found him in the kitchen getting himself a glass of water. I parked myself at the kitchen table in my Chicago Bulls vest and Barcelona football shorts – it was my bed-wear. 'What happened at the station?' I asked. 'Did the feds charge you?'

Nesta lifted up the foil that was covering the frying pan and inspected my stir-fry. He was impressed enough to take out a plate and serve himself a generous portion. He scooped out some rice and put the meal in the microwave.

'It was agreed that the fed who licked my leg with the car door apologise and I get a caution.'

'So you don't have to step to the court or anything?'

'Nope. As the sergeant said, the matter has been laid to rest. They warned me about my future behaviour. That's when Dad decided to spit some lyrics.'

'What did he say?' I wanted to know.

'He said the fed should get a warning about *his* future behaviour too. He made a big drama about it but by then I was getting bored and just wanted to get out of that damn place – the cells really stink and, trust me, you don't wanna know about the crap hole in there.'

The microwave bleeped. Nesta took out his dinner. I felt an overload of pride in my chest as Nesta scraped the plate clean. He washed it all down with another glass of water – we had run out of blackcurrant juice and Dad hadn't been shopping. He probably lost our food money on a go-slow hound, I thought bitterly.

'Are you staying?' I asked.

I wanted him to say *yes.* I wanted him to sort out his issues with Dad. I wanted him to talk to me more and keep me company. I needed him.

'I'm heading out,' he said. 'I don't wanna buck into Dad cos we'll probably start warring again.'

'Where're you gonna go?' I asked. 'Yvonne's castle?'

Nesta nodded. 'If you tell Dad about *her* then me and you will have *serious* issues.'

I followed him into the hallway. I watched him pull on his denim jacket. He turned around and grinned. 'The feds gave me a caution but I told 'em they still better find my friggin bike! Remember the lady fed who served us the coffees?'

'Yeah. I thought she was kinda cool. What about her?'

'She saw me when they brought me in – she tried to pretend she didn't recognise me. Stupid bitch! They're all the same. Their politeness is all a front.'

Then he was gone.

# 9

## Jonah's Family Beef

I went back to bed for a couple of hours or so but my snooze wasn't a blessed one. Nuff tings were fizzing through my mind. My alarm screamed at six-thirty on the dot. I got up and took a shower. I just stood in there stone still, letting hot water bounce off my fro and trickle down my body. This was it: the day of our mission. My heart jabbed hard even thinking about it. I wondered how Liccle Bit, Jonah, Venetia and Saira were feeling.

I boiled two eggs and roasted two slices of bread for my breakfast. I was on my second egg when I heard the letter box have a fit. *Thwap, thwap, thwap!* I looked towards the hallway. *Thwap, thwap, thwap!* The debt brothers. *God! This is all I need!* The kitchen light was still on. I got up and switched it off. I sat back down and took another bite of toast. *Thwap, thwap, thwap!* A deep voice followed it. 'Mr Tambo! Mr Tambo!'

I closed my ears and tried to ignore it but ... *Thwap, thwap, thwap!* I began to chew my toast softly, suddenly worried they'd be able to hear the crunch. I got up and crept to my dungeon. My phone was resting on my bedside cabinet. I texted Dad. In my head I raged at him. He should be here to deal with this shit.

The debt brothers are here! What shall I do? DON'T CALL!!!

*Thwap, thwap, thwap!* 'Mr Tambo! Anyone home?'

I felt vulnerable so I returned to the front room, collected my breakfast and went back to my dungeon, closing the door behind me. If I was gonna be deleted I wanted my full breakfast first! My phone vibrated. I checked Dad's text.

Still at work. Don't answer the door!

I replied super-fast.

Answering the door wasn't top of my to-do list!

I sank another piece of toast. My phone shook again.

Stay calm. DON'T OPEN DOOR. Illegal to break an entry.

It took me twice as long as usual to eat my breakfast. I drank two glasses of water. The door had been quiet for a while. I checked all the windows to see if they'd gone but I couldn't remember what colour or type of van the debt brothers drove. I slowly started to breathe easier and I gathered all the books I needed for school.

Eight o'clock. Time to leave. I pigeon-stepped towards the drawbridge. Carefully, I pulled back the bolt, placed my fingers on the latch and turned it in slow motion. My heart raced. Trickles of sweat rolled over my cheeks. When the drawbridge was ten centimetres ajar I peered out. I couldn't see anyone on the landing but I could smell cigarette smoke. I listened hard but all I could hear was the bleeping of a rubbish truck reversing on the ground below. In a flash I opened the door, stepped out, closed it, locked it and bounced down the stairs like a rabbit being chased by a T-rex. I didn't stop running until I reached the forecourt outside Liccle Bit's and Jonah's.

I was out of breath when I climbed the steps leading to Jonah's castle. I rested a while outside his door – I didn't want Jonah making jokes about my sweaty pits. As my heartbeat returned to normal I could hear loud voices coming from inside. They weren't singing songs to celebrate Jonah's ratings at school, that was for sure. I rat-a-tatted the letter box. Eventually I recognised Jonah's silhouette through the wire-meshed window in the drawbridge. He opened the door. 'Hold on,' he said. 'Just gotta attack the plaque.'

I stepped inside the hallway and waited there. Square-shaped marble tiles sexed up the floor. Framed pictures of long African women carrying jugs on their heads niced up the walls. Jonah disappeared into the bathroom, second on the right. After that was the kitchen and that was where the voices were coming from.

'I've been trying, Amaka.' Jonah's dad's voice was deep but kind, like a voiceover on a TV quiz show. 'I have an interview today for a job reading gas meters.'

Since Mr Hani got deleted from his job, Jonah's castle had turned into a place of stress and sadness.

'Reading gas meters?' said Jonah's mum, Amaka. 'And how much does that pay? And why do you have to go for a job like that? You worked for seventeen years in the council's housing department, with plenty of stress and strain too. Doesn't that count for anything?'

Mrs Hani had this *tone* – all high and screechy. I'd never tell Jonah but, damn, a bruv would not want to get cussed out by her.

There was an awkward silence. I could feel the tension from a distance. I felt guilty for overhearing truth be known – this was their fam's private business.

'I can only go for what's available, Amaka,' Mr Hani finally said. 'The housing department was hard knock, yes, but you think I can list the number of times I was assaulted on my CV? It doesn't work like that! This job is better than nothing, Amaka. It'll help pay the bills and God knows we need something.'

Silence again, only interrupted by the sound of Jonah's electric toothbrush.

'OK. Then you'd better get it,' Mrs Hani said. 'We can't keep going on my part-time bakery money.'

Jonah emerged into the hallway with spots of toothpaste around his cheeks. I pointed at my mouth and he understood the score, wiped his face with his sleeve, and we breezed out.

As we stepped up to Liccle Bit's floor, I asked Jonah about the beef between his mum and dad. 'They hardly chat to each other now,' Jonah answered, staring at his feet. 'And when they do, they just rage. Dad sleeps on the couch most nights. Dinner times are so quiet you can hear the goldfish taking a piss. *Believe it!* Why you think I don't invite you and Bit over to get our gaming on any more?'

'That's rough,' I said, feeling sympathy. 'And what's even

more tragic is that your mum doesn't bake her cupcakes any more.'

'Tell me about it,' Jonah said. I was sure he missed his mum's cupcakes as much as I did. I couldn't count the number of times Bit and I had emptied her cake tin. Man! Her baking was the real lick. 'And how am I gonna invite a chick up to my yard with Mum and Dad warring?' Jonah added. 'It's embarrassing.'

'Don't think you have to worry about that for untold years,' I joked.

'Screw you!' Jonah spat. 'Watch and learn! That Saira chick is gonna be *mine*. Before you know it, I'm gonna have her under lock and she'll be calling me *sweet cheeks* in my Valentine's Day cards.'

'She'll be calling you the mad stalker who lives on the third floor!'

'Watch me, McKay. In the next week or so I'll be linking with her, sampling her kisses in the playground, Crongton Park and Movieworld!'

'You'll be eating her fists in the playground if you try any moves on her.'

Jonah pushed out his chest. 'Nah, man. After the drama tonight goes down, she's mine – guaranteed!'

'If we *survive* Bit's mission this evening.'

Jonah paused. He sort of shivered, like he didn't want whatever was in his head to be there. 'Let's get Bit,' he said.

We arrived at Liccle Bit's door. 'Don't slap the letter box too hard, Jonah,' I warned.

Jonah gave it a delicate tap. No one came. Jonah smacked

it again, louder. We waited. 'Screw this!' Jonah said, frustration chewing his ass. Holding the letter box firmly with his thumb and forefinger, Jonah blitzed it like he wanted to wake Dracula's grandma. I glanced at Jonah. 'You're just calling for a bredren,' I said, 'not starting the war of the Five Armies!'

We heard footsteps. Suddenly, Bit's mum appeared in the door frame, her arms folded tight across her chest. She looked at the pair of us like we had dug out her earwax with a rusty sword. I could smell bacon and scrambled eggs – I made a mental note to slap something similar on my frying pan for a celebratory fry-up tomorrow morning when the mission was over and done with.

'Take time with my door, we're not deaf, you know. And use the freaking doorbell!'

'Sorry, yeah? I forgot,' said Jonah.

'*Lemar!* Your friends are here!' Man! Bit's mum was loud. She turned to us and smiled. 'Be good at school today, boys.'

Rope ladders on fire! I didn't know how Liccle Bit could live in his castle twenty-four-seven with his mum's ranting. His sister Elaine wasn't shy when it came to blasting people's eardrums either. My nerves would be mauled.

Bit finally emerged. His mum kissed him goodbye on the forehead and Jonah and I had to kill our giggles. 'Where're you going this evening again?' she asked before Bit closed the drawbridge.

Our mission could be grounded before it got going! Bit handled the pressure well. 'I'm gonna help Venetia with her dancing after school. She's . . . what you call it?'

'Cororographing?' said Jonah.

Bit's mum smiled. 'Oh yes. You're helping Venetia with her choreography. I'm working late this evening so you won't see me until after ten. Enjoy ... but make sure the both of you walk Lemar home. You hear me? You know why. You all got credit on your mobiles?'

Jonah and I nodded. We both knew why. Manjaro was still out there somewhere.

It licked me hard that all of us had to lie to our parents. I felt bad. I actually felt like Mum was watching and shaking her head in disappointment. I couldn't think about it too much though. Deep down I knew this mission was on point. How could we ignore Venetia's distress? We had to fix it. We had to make things proper. We had to get that phone back!

# 10

# A Strange Assembly

'I've got something to show you,' said Jonah as we were heading out of the slab to school.

'I'm not in the mood today, Jonah,' I said. 'Besides, I told you, we're just good bredrens; and I forgot my magnifying glass anyway.'

Bit laughed out loud but Jonah was North-Korean-soldier serious. He checked to see if anyone was watching us. Satisfied, he crouched down and zipped open his bag.

'What have you got in there?' Bit asked. 'A blow-up doll? A pic of Saira Aslan in the school showers?'

'Bit, you are one serious, three o'clock in the morning, messed-up perv,' Jonah replied. 'You need proper help, bruv. You want me to chat to the school counsellor for you? Off-key bruvs say she's a good listener.'

'Screw you!'

A glint of something shiny caught my eye. 'That a mirror? Gonna slap on some lipstick before games?'

'Funny – *not*. No, bruv, it ain't no mirror. I'll show you . . .'

He checked around again then carefully moved aside some books. I took in a gulp of air. Lying there, snug in the bag, was a bread knife. It had a black wooden handle and a sharp serrated edge. It was about the length of a ruler.

'*Bloodfire!*' spat Bit.

'For protection,' explained Jonah, zipping the bag back up, 'in case this Sergio bruv tries to shank us. You know he ain't gonna be happy to see us in his ends.'

I shook my head. 'Jonah, what's wrong with you, bruv? You can get nuff years in prison just for carrying a blade. Fling it away now!'

'*No, man!*' Jonah insisted. 'What are we gonna do if he comes at us with serious arms? I don't know about you but I wanna bust my virginity one day, drive a nice car, win gold in the Olympics, and I won't be doing any of that good shit if this Sergio bruv paralyses me.'

'If you're gonna carry that thing,' Bit raised his voice, 'you ain't stepping nowhere with us. I mean it! Stay in your yard if that's the way you wanna play in this programme. And I hope your mum licks you in your head with her cake mixer when she finds out.'

'She'll do more than lick you in the head,' I added. 'You'll be on lockdown forever and you won't be getting no more cupcakes till you're fifty, bruv. I wouldn't wanna wish *that* tragedy on anyone.'

'What about that guy who got burst some months ago

down Remington Walker Way?' Jonah reasoned. 'He was in foreign ends. He tried to stop some hood-rat mauling his girl and look what happened to him.'

'He had mental health issues,' I said. 'My dad read it in the paper. You can't cruise with a blade, bruv. There's too many feds around.'

'But say this Sergio bruv—'

'We are *not* going in like Rambo,' said Bit. 'Waste the blade.'

Jonah thought about it. I could see the fear in his eyes. In Crongton, not too many bruvs our age went to war with each other fist to fist. Three weeks ago some bruv in Year 11 got laced in his face with a football boot – hood-rats in school joked that he had trouble saying *Mississippi* now he had three nostrils. That was messed up, but trodding with blades was entering a different league.

Jonah opened his bag again. He looked at the knife and plucked it out. It glinted in the weak sunlight.

'Fling it away, bruv,' I urged. 'Or soon you'll be saying hello to a crusty man's balls in a stinking cell.'

'OK, OK,' Jonah said, 'but I can't put it back now, with Mum and Dad there – I'll have to take it to school and do it later.'

'*No,*' I cut in. 'You take *that* to school and they'll expel you quicker than diarrhoea from a baby's batty-hole.'

There were a couple of big metal bins outside Neville Enchanter House. Jonah threw the knife into one of them and we all breathed a little easier as we heard it land among the rubbish bags.

We continued on our way. Today had already been in*tense* and we hadn't stepped anywhere near Notre Dame yet . . . We all needed to chill, big time, or else our mission would crash before we even got started.

I patted Jonah on the back. 'Don't worry. When Sergio sees us all tonight, he'll probably just give Venetia her phone back without any drama.'

Jonah gave me a long look.

'He might, though!' I said.

'Yeah. Or he might not.'

Our form tutor, Ms Rivilino, told us that we had to attend a special assembly before class. I couldn't remember ever having assembly on a Friday morning. It took nanoseconds for the hype to start.

'The feds wanna lecture us again.'

'A bruv I know wants to blaze Dagthorn's shop. Maybe they're gonna warn us about getting involved?'

'Some hood-rats are planning to riot tonight. Nobody's loving the feds these days.'

'It's cos of what happened to McKay's brother – they snapped his leg in four places and they had the front to arrest his broken bod on his hospital bed.'

This was Kiran Cassidy. I couldn't let that go.

'No, they didn't,' I said. 'I was there. His leg isn't broken. My bruv's all right. Stop piling up the drama.'

'They *never* sink oats for any shit they do,' someone said.

'Can you all *be quiet*!' Ms Rivilino raised her voice. 'And the next person who swears will get a *double detention*!' She had a soft tone but when we got rowdy she could spit as loud as anyone. 'Now, please make your way to the drama hall, where Mr Maplebeech will talk to you.'

We stepped out of the classroom and made our way through the corridors. On our way we spotted Saira and Venetia. Jonah just about managed to kill his drooling. 'What's going down?' I asked them.

They shrugged. 'Our form tutor didn't tell us a damn thing,' replied Saira.

'Are we still on for this evening?' whispered Venetia, looking a bit nervous.

'Of course,' I said.

Jonah nodded and grinned a weird wonky grin.

Venetia smiled in relief. 'Six at my yard, yeah? Then we'll call for Saira.'

'Move along now,' ordered Mr Jenkins, Venetia's form tutor. You could see the skinny blue veins in his bald head. 'Stop clogging up the corridor!'

Saira, Venetia, Bit, Jonah and I parked ourselves in the back row of the hall. Boy from the Hills was four rows in front of us. He spotted me and waved. I felt a bit embarrassed so I kinda half-waved back. I wondered what the others would think if I told them he was a new bredren of mine.

There was a hyper buzz in the place – everyone was wondering what was going down. Mr Maplebeech rocked to and fro, his hands behind his back. He didn't look like he was in the mood for any rib-tickling. He had a world of creases on his face but his hair was blacker than an oil slick – we all knew he dyed it. Graffiti in the boys' toilets read:

Maplebeech thinks he's all peach,
But good looks are well out of his reach.

His forehead's sucked dry by a leech.
He dyes his hair with black bleach!

In his wake he leaves more toxins than an oily
    beach,
No way should HE be allowed to teach ...
All those who agree say PREACH!!!

Underneath, any number of bruvs had scrawled their approval in shades of biro.

Maplebeech was wearing a greenish-brown suit with a yellow tie. He cleared his throat as the last students took their seats.

'Good morning, everyone,' he started. 'Thank you for taking your seats and settling down quickly.'

'What's this all about?' shouted someone at the front. 'We finally finding out who keeps clogging up the boys' toilets with monster—'

'Let me stop you there, Ellison,' said Maplebeech.

'It's Dennis Mason!' shouted Raul Ramos. 'His farts could fracture the gents in a prison block!'

'It better not be another lecture on the feds,' yelled another student.

'Burn the feds!'

It was getting rowdy.

'*Please!*' Mr Maplebeech lifted his head and tried to locate who was interrupting him. The hum faded. He started again.

'There was a break-in at the school last night. The school kitchens, to be precise.'

'*Hooray!*' roared a skinny girl in the middle. '*No school dinners today! Hooray!*' When she realised that no one was joining in with her, she sank back into her seat.

Mr Maplebeech ploughed on. 'The intruders stole four hundred sausages, three hundred and fifty chicken and beef patties, four hundred chocolate muffins, five oranges and two apples.'

'That is one seriously peckish burglar,' joked Kiran Cassidy. 'Who would wanna jack food from the school kitchen? That's messed up!'

Everyone collapsed into giggles and even a few teachers had to cover their mouths to kill their grins. It took a couple of minutes for everybody to compose themselves. Mr Maplebeech wasn't impressed. His face went proper red with frustration. 'If *any* of you know something about this matter, *please* inform a teacher or any other member of staff. What you tell us will be treated in confidence. The playground area near the back of the school kitchens is now out of bounds. The police are still conducting their investigation there so *please* keep out of their way.'

'Tell the feds to keep out of *our* way, sir,' someone shouted from the corner.

'That's *enough*!' Maplebeech fumed.

Jonah gave me a funny look. 'McKay!' he hissed, just loud enough for everyone to hear. 'Don't tell me it was *you*.'

Around us, nuff people turned to look at me and a few of them started giggling. It was at times like this I could feel my tubbiness. I suddenly felt like a circus elephant wearing a Barbados beach bikini in front of a laughing crowd.

Saira reached over and squeezed my shoulder. 'Leave *him* alone,' she said to Jonah, Bit and everyone else.

Kiss my shield! *That* was a pleasure overload and a half.

'Any more interruptions and the time will be taken out of your break,' warned Maplebeech. Everyone hushed. 'To recap, anyone who does have any information *please* see a teacher, a teaching assistant or any other staff. *Please* leave quietly, starting from the back row.'

I blew out of that hall like I was blessed! We all regrouped near the girls' toilets. Venetia spoke in a whisper. 'As I said, we're linking at my yard at six and don't spill about our mission to anyone – not even parents. Especially not them. Stick to that programme.'

'Did you hear that, Jonah?' Liccle Bit warned pointedly.

Jonah scowled in return.

'Cos you've done it before,' I added.

'Leave it, bruv! I get it!'

'And *don't* get a detention,' warned Venetia.

They all looked at me.

'I haven't had a detention for two weeks!' I said.

'You totally deserved that last one,' said Bit. 'What you said to Alan Cummings was well beyond the trouser zip.'

'What did he say?' Saira wanted to know.

'That Alan was so Goddammit ugly, they should've left him under the bridge when he was born,' Jonah said. 'That his mum wanted to take home the afterbirth instead of him.'

'That's proper cruel,' said Venetia.

'But he called me Jabba the Gut!' I cried. 'And he said that when I run around the track, the hurdles fall over.'

Saira was trying not to laugh. It did all seem kind of stupid now.

At the end of the corridor, Boy from the Hills was watching us. It troubled me that he knew we were rolling to Notre Dame later; even if he didn't know why, I still knew it wouldn't go down well if I told Bit or Jonah or the girls. I had to keep my beak sealed on that one.

I was on my way to maths when I crashed into Ms Penn, my food tech teacher.

'McKay!'

'Good morning, miss.'

She was wearing black trousers, a long red shirt and her sleeves were rolled up as usual. Her brown hair was done up in some kinda bun thing that looked like a birds' nest. There wasn't much meat on her – I once joked in class that she'd have to run about in a monsoon to get wet. She was a good egg though. When she found out Mum passed she cried, hugged me and gave me a Bakewell tart to take home.

'Have you thought any more about joining the after-school cooking club?' she reminded me.

'Er . . . no, miss. I've been busy.'

The truth was that it was embarrassing. There weren't *any* guys in Penn's cooking club. It was all chicks, and I could just imagine them teasing the living piss out of the fat bruv in an apron. I didn't want them studying my wobbly butt when I took a Victoria sandwich out of the oven. I had asked Jonah and Liccle Bit if they'd join with me but they gave me the 'are you freaking serious?' look and that was that.

'You have a great flair for cooking, McKay.' Penn clapped her hands. 'Did your family enjoy your shepherd's pie?'

I thought so, but the night I'd served up the shepherd's pie was the night the debt brothers started battering our draw-bridge, so dinner was sort of forgotten about. Not that Penn needed to know the score.

'Er, yeah, they loved it to the max.'

'Then why don't you join us?' she insisted. 'Last week we baked cupcakes and next week we're making chocolate fondants.'

Chocolate fondants! Mum baked them once. For a short second, standing there in the corridor, I had a pleasure over-load. The smell of that chocolate was locked in my memory for ever. My taste buds' greatest moment, my tongue's finest hour. I replayed it all, that creamy chocolate ooze rolling down my throat, that smooth, blessed choccy texture ...

But no, I couldn't go there.

'I'm too busy, sorry.'

Before Ms Penn could reply, I hot-stepped away.

Nuff students had to report to Maplebeech's office for deten-tion after school that day but I managed to stay out of trouble. I didn't even take part in making fart noises at the feds at break time when they were checking out the broken window at the back of the school kitchens.

At lunch, Venetia and Bit had a change of plan – they decided that we should link at the main exit after school. I think they just wanted to check that everyone was all good and ready. I was on my way there when I bumped into Boy from the Hills.

'Can I come with you?' he asked.

'Where?' I replied.

'That mission you're going on, to Notre Dame,' he said. 'I can help. Maybe I can be a lookout? I don't wanna step home yet and be on my lonesome.'

'But it's not *my* mission,' I said, moving on.

'Can't you ask Bit then? It's always good to cruise in those ends in numbers. Word on road says that peeps in Notre Dame are well weird.'

I shook my head, apologised and walked away. I felt bad – the bruv just wanted to be involved and to have some company – but it was probably best that he didn't get caught up in our episodes. I was doing him a favour when you thought about it.

I met the crew and we rolled away and parked on a low wall near the school car park. It was the end of the week and teachers were racing to their cars with the look of hood-rats escaping from career advisors.

'How far does this Sergio bruv live from the bus stop?' Jonah asked.

Venetia looked proper nervous. Her fingers were locked together and she was staring at the ground. Saira had an arm around her shoulders. 'It's about a ten minute step,' she answered.

'Is there anybody living with him?' I asked.

Venetia shook her head.

'So, everyone ready?' Saira said. She checked our eyes.

'There's . . . there is just one more ting,' I cut in.

'No, we are *not* gonna stop at the Hot Rooster takeaway before we leave,' said Bit.

'No, it's not that,' I said. 'I need to top up my Travelcard but my budget is proper sad.'

'No worries,' said Saira. 'I've got some change to put into your pocket.'

She took her purse out and handed me a few coins.

'Thanks,' I said, my heart melting a little at her kindness.

We all headed off our separate ways.

I felt like a knight getting ready to mount his horse and head off to start warring with a fire-breathing dragon. I could feel my heartbeat behind my ears.

# 11

# Dad's Dinner

The lift in my slab was now working but I decided to climb the stairs – I had a messed-up fear of being trapped in a lift with the debt bruvs – nowhere to run, nowhere to hide. That would be a trauma overload.

The smell of lamb filled my nostrils when I arrived back at my castle. Dad was in the kitchen checking on the boiled baby potatoes in his black vest, blue jeans and snail-crusher boots. (I made a mental note: if I managed to save any cash before Christmas, I'd buy Dad a pair of slippers.) He had a big smile on his face, the same smile he wore when he gave you a birthday present or something, but he was tired too – and I could sense stress was licking his forehead.

'I've done your favourite today, McKay. Lamb shanks, boiled potatoes and runner beans.'

'Thanks, Dad. You didn't have to—'

'Yes, I did!' he insisted. 'Just felt bad that you were home alone when the debt collectors called.'

'I didn't let them in,' I said.

'I know. But I'm gonna sort it out,' Dad said, pointing a finger to my face. He didn't look convincing. 'I'm working on it. I don't want you to worry about anything – it's all in hand.'

He grabbed the oven gloves from behind the microwave and took out the tray of lamb shanks that were covered in foil. 'Come and have a look,' he invited me. 'I think they're not too bad. Smells all right anyway.'

I peeled back the foil and I had to admit that Dad wasn't wrong – they didn't look bad at all. Three of them. Dad had cooked one for Nesta. The steam releasing from the meat warmed my face and I took a couple of sniffs. 'Did you season the lamb, Dad?'

'Er ... I put some black pepper on it?'

I would've thrown some garlic, maybe spun some curry powder and slapped some Jamaican jerk seasoning on it to sex it up a bit. He didn't slice any onions or peppers to cook with it either. But at least the lamb was ripe. The last time Dad roasted beef, the meat was so damn raw I thought the cow might rise up from my plate, moo a serious moo and hot-trot away. I had to explain to him that all because the meat was brown on the outside it didn't mean it was all *MasterChef* on the inside.

'Did you buy any mint sauce?' I asked.

'Er, no, sorry,' replied Dad. 'I forgot.'

We sat down at the table and Dad watched me closely as I took my first sample of lamb. It was edible. I flashed my molars. Dad was proper pleased.

'I was thinking maybe we could go bowling after dinner?' Dad suggested. 'We haven't done something fun together for ages. What do you say? Fancy taking on the old man at some ten-pin bashing?'

'I-I can't,' I stuttered. 'I'm doing this dancing thing with friends at school.'

'Dancing thing?' Dad repeated. 'Didn't know you were interested in dance?'

'I'm just going to give support, you know, help out if I'm asked. It's more my friends' ting. They're working on a routine.'

'Oh, I see,' replied Dad. He looked proper crushed but I couldn't pull out of Bit's mission now.

'Maybe we can go tomorrow,' I suggested. 'Maybe ... maybe Nesta can come with us?'

Dad stared at his dinner. My question was dumb. Nesta was more likely to be playing Santa at the feds Christmas party than giving the smack-down to skittles in a bowling alley with us. Dad got up from the table and fetched a vodka-lemonade bottle from the fridge. He pulled the lid off and sank a few drops before he answered. 'I tried to call him today,' he said. 'But he wouldn't pick up. I left a message. Don't know what more I can do.'

'He'll come around,' I said. 'You know Nesta. He's proper moody.'

Dad sliced off a big chunk of lamb and mauled it. Hog on a platter! I wished I had a square jaw like that. 'Do you know where he's staying?' he asked me.

I thought of Yvonne with her blonde, frizzy hair and her

cool-stepping cat. I remembered Nesta's threat if I spilled any info about her.

'No, I haven't got a clue.'

The rest of the dinner was sunk in silence. Nesta's talk of Dad's gambling crashed through my mind. I didn't want to believe him, tried to convince myself that he was just angry with Dad and made it all up out of spite. But I couldn't deny, somewhere deep down, I knew he was on point. Still, I couldn't believe Dad would put us in danger. Couldn't believe he'd risk losing the slates over our head.

I had a sudden urge – from God knows where – to man up and ask him if it was true. Straight out, blunt, right there and then. What was the worst he could do, cuss me? Nothing he could do would be half as traumatic as being home alone with the debt brothers blasting at the door.

'Dad,' I started, 'Nesta said, he said to me that you, er, well, he kinda hinted to me that you lost a world of money gambling?'

Dad put his bottle on the table. He looked at me like I had grown another nose before picking at a slither of lamb trapped in his front teeth. He cleared his throat but his eyes never left me. My cheeks started to burn. My heartbeat started to bruise my ribs.

'Your brother's right,' Dad finally admitted, his eyes now gazing at his empty plate.

There was a long pause. I didn't know whether to stare at Dad or look away. Mr Embarrassment was mauling his ass.

I felt sorry for him.

'It got out of hand,' he said quietly. 'And when you lose a lot you try to win it back. But you can't beat the freaking bookie or the freaking *machines* they put in there! Those machines are *fixed*! I've learned that much.'

I didn't know what to say. I had to give Dad ratings though, manning up with his honesty.

'I'll never walk into a bookie shop again,' he continued. 'Yes, I've got loads of debt but I'll get us through it.'

'How much?' I asked.

Dad thought about it. He smiled but his eyes didn't smile with him. 'I'll get through it,' he repeated. 'The council has been writing me red letters but we're *not* going to lose this place.'

He stood up, collected my plate and his and took them to the kitchen. I followed him in there but he ignored me as he ran the taps and squirted washing-up liquid into the sink. I parked myself down at the dinner table again, feeling like crap cos I had made him face up to his nasty truth. I was just about to leave for my dungeon when Dad appeared under the kitchen door frame. He was drying his hands. His gaze was hard. 'Your brother was right to get mad at me,' he said. 'I let you both down. As I said, I'll deal with it. I just wish Nesta could deal with his own guilt.'

This was new.

'What guilt?' I asked.

Dad stepped back into the kitchen, pretending he didn't hear me.

I hot-toed after him. 'What's Nesta guilty of?'

'Oh, ignore me, it's nothing,' Dad replied.

'But you just said . . . ' I said. He grabbed the tea towel and started to dry the plates. He wouldn't look at me. 'Hey! Dad! *Stop* shutting me out! I hate when you and Nesta do that. I'm nearly *fifteen*!'

He dodged my stare. 'It's no biggie,' he said. 'All I meant was, you know, he gets himself in trouble, says things in a rage that he doesn't really mean … you know what he's like … Just let it go. Hey, you need any money to top up your Travelcard this evening?'

I know I should've just let it go, but it troubled me to the max. Dad was clearly trying to avoid my question – and that meant there was something he wasn't telling me. It all had to do with this guilt thing with Nesta, I just knew it. I couldn't stop now.

'It's just that … I mean, if Nesta's got guilt, how can I help him if I don't know what it's about?'

Dad slammed the plate in the cupboard and sucked in a long breath, trying to control his brewing rage. Obviously I had stomped on a raw nerve. 'Just *leave* it, McKay,' Dad raised his voice. '*Leave it!* It doesn't concern you. It's between *me* and *him*. If anyone's guilty of anything *it's me*!'

'Sorry, Dad.'

I decided not to push my luck.

He turned his back on me and continued drying the knives and forks.

'Have a nice time with your dancing thing,' he said in a quieter voice. 'Perhaps we'll go bowling tomorrow then?'

'That'll be cool,' I replied.

I went off to my dungeon. God! I missed Mum. She would've sorted this crap out.

I took off my school uniform and headed to the bathroom to wage war with my armpits – I didn't want Saira Aslan sniffing something toxic under there. I took a long shower and niced up my pits and my chest with roll-on deodorant. I even changed my socks. *If Jonah thinks he's gonna get the Holy Grail with Saira he'd better review the situation. I think she likes me.* I pulled on my baggy *Hobbit* T-shirt and hoped Saira wouldn't clock too much of my belly.

Dad was sitting on the sofa watching a wildlife documentary in the lounge when I emerged. A lioness was savaging a deer-type thing. Dad took a swig from his bottle.

'I'm off now, Dad.'

'What time will you be home?' he wanted to know.

*Who knows if we'll ever return?* 'Before ten,' I answered.

'Walk safe,' he advised. 'And call me if you have to. I'll be working till eight tomorrow morning – overtime.'

'All right, Dad, I'll see you then.'

# 12

# Team God

Liccle Bit and Jonah were waiting for me outside their slab. Jonah was wearing a black anorak, a Dallas Cowboys cap and black gloves – which was cool. But his trainers didn't look too sweet. I could tell funds were tight for him and his fam. Liccle Bit was rolling in a blue hoodie and brown gloves. Clean, white trainers niced up his feet.

Bit checked the time on his mobile. 'You're late, McKay. And what's that smell?'

'I had to bless my armpits, innit,' I replied. 'Don't wanna roll up to Notre Dame with the ladies with BO hanging round me, did I.'

Jonah looked at me like I was a rasher of bacon short of a fry-up. 'We're bouncing through North Crong and up to Notre Dame – NOTRE DAME! – and all *you* can think about is nicing up your armpits to impress the chicks?

This ain't no joke, you know! We could get mauled tonight.'

'Sprinkle your fire,' said Bit, trying to calm us down. 'What's important is that you're here for me. I appreciate it to the max. Let's roll.'

Liccle Bit led the way, stepping towards the southeast corner of our estate. We passed Dagthorn's store but he was closed for the evening, the shutters pulled down.

There were more hood-rats around than usual for an early Friday evening. They were cruising in their threes and fours towards central Crongton. Others were loafing on corners, chirping chicks, smoking rockets and sinking bottles of tonic wine.

'Something's going down,' observed Jonah.

I was about to reply when I spotted Kiran Cassidy and three other brothers rolling north. 'What's happening?' I asked.

'I think something might kick off in the High Street,' Kiran replied. 'And if it does I wanna bag myself a new phone.'

We moved on.

'I wanna get myself a new phone too,' Jonah said. 'I'm using Mum's old mobile now and it's as ancient as thick TVs. Can't we put this mission on pause and see what sparks off in the High Street?'

'*No!*' Bit roared. Some spittle flew from his mouth and landed on Jonah's nose. Jonah wasn't impressed. 'Venetia's expecting us – we can't scramble to the mouse's hole now.'

'I *need* a new phone,' complained Jonah. 'It's proper embarrassing. Come to think of it, I need new trainers too!'

As we trod on Bit and me had to listen to Jonah bitching on

about how sad his pockets were and how his parents didn't understand how the so-called poverty licking his family's ass was stressing him out.

Ten minutes later, we arrived at Somerleyton House. It was the tallest slab in this part of South Crong. It was famous in our ends for two reasons. Number one, some four-year-old girl managed to climb over the railing of her fourth-floor balcony and drop to the ground. She survived that fall with only a busted arm but her mum was still warring with social services to get her back. And number two, one of the prettiest, ripest girls in our year lived there.

'What floor does Venetia live on?' I asked Bit. 'Shall we come with you?'

'The fifth floor,' Bit answered. 'I can't see why it would be a problem if you bumped along.'

'Let's bounce then,' said Jonah.

'Hold up for a sec.' Bit checked us with his serious face.

'Stop fretting, bruv,' I told him. 'We'll behave ourselves in front of Queen Venetia.'

'It's not that,' said Bit.

'Then what is it?' Jonah wanted to know.

'Remember your promise,' Bit reminded us. He scanned our eyes. 'Please, *no* spilling about Manjaro.'

'What do you take us for?' asked Jonah, like he was proper offended. 'We're your bredrens! All that drama happened months ago, bruv. Don't stress out yourself.'

Bit stared at me. He still wanted our promises to be on lock. 'I'm with Jonah,' I said. 'Nothing's gonna leak from my mouth, believe it.'

'OK,' Bit said.

'He still might be out there though,' said Jonah, fear stroking his forehead. 'It might be him who's behind this riot.'

None of us wanted to think about that right now.

We stepped into the lift. Oh my days! It was honking something chronic! Whatever it was that had made that pong in the first place, it was school toilets, end cubicle evil. We all pinched our noses tight, shut our eyes, and hoped we'd make it to the fourth floor before we passed out. When the doors opened, we all burst out fighting for air! Bit led the way to Venetia's drawbridge. The walkways were scrubbed a lot more than the ones in my slab. Obviously the cleaner here did his work rather than smoke rockets in the garbage outhouse. 'No swearing,' Bit warned us. 'And no farting, McKay.'

'What do you take me for?' I defended myself. 'I don't roll into people's castles and bust farts.'

'Five words,' Jonah said. 'Jennifer Beckles and her mum.'

'A word to the fartable,' laughed Bit. '*Never* bounce into a chick's yard when you're desperate to let loose a dump.'

'Oh yeah,' I remembered.

'Be polite,' Bit advised as we stood outside Venetia's gates. 'Remember, Venetia's fam are all in Team God.'

Jonah looked for a doorbell but couldn't find one. He tickled the letter box. I think we were all wondering what the mum of one of the fittest girls in our school looked like. We didn't need to think too hard about Venetia's dad . . . we had all seen him, a walking tower block of a man.

The drawbridge opened and a sweet smiling face welcomed us. She was wearing a black headscarf and tiny gold crosses niced up her ears. Freckles dotted her nose. I couldn't tell whether she was Asian, African or Caribbean. I guessed she was about thirty-five, no older than thirty-eight. It was obvious where Venetia got her pretty looks from – Jonah had to make a serious effort not to slobber.

'Hi, Lemar,' she greeted Bit.

Liccle Bit did this I'm-a-nice-boy-and-I-never-smoke-rockets smile. Twang the arrows! Even I thought he looked cute.

'Hi, boys,' she greeted us. 'You all working on this new dance routine at the school this evening?'

'Er, yeah,' replied Bit. 'We're rehearsing.'

'Nice that you have found an activity that you can all enjoy,' Mrs King said. 'It keeps kids off the streets. Please come in – Venetia's in her room getting her things together.'

Bit took off his trainers and left them on the mat by the door. Jonah and me copied him. I was proper glad I changed my socks – they had a world of holes in them but at least the smell wasn't toxic. Mrs King led us along the hallway. Hanging on one side of the wall was a framed picture of Jesus suffering on his cross with a bed sheet covering his bits and opposite that was the 'Lord's Prayer' done all in fancy writing. We reached the lounge where Venetia's younger sister, Princess, and her liccle bro, Milton, were watching a Disney cartoon (a love-injected fish was singing to a mermaid). They both looked proper bored.

'Hello,' Princess greeted us like we were teachers or something.

'Hi!' we all replied.

Behind me was a dining table laid nicely with all the knives and forks neatly in position beside folded napkins. A basket of fresh French bread sat in the middle. The smell of polish was tickling my nose – it reminded me of Mum on a Sunday morning. Hanging on the wall overlooking all this was a framed painting of Jesus and his bredrens sinking their last supper. I had a sense that if someone spilled a swear word here in this castle, God Himself would lick them with a fist the size of Solomon's Temple.

'Would you like something to drink?' Mrs King offered.

'No, thank you very much though,' Bit answered in his most polite English.

Jonah and me both shook our heads. Mrs King disappeared into the kitchen. We heard a deep voice, like someone calling from the bottom of a manhole. Mr King! He was at home! He stepped into the front room and we all flinched. His arms were big enough to carry Jesus's cross and Muhammad's mountain. His neck was as chunky as the base of a pyramid. He was wearing this black boiler suit that could've doubled up as a circus tent. Raptors could've nested in his beard. Plain, blue slippers looked all wrong on his Jurassic Nine feet. I was proper terrified. If Bit ever managed to persuade Venetia to marry him, he'd better get his short ass to the church on time – cos if he didn't, by the time Mr King was finished with him there'd be no love-action happening on their wedding night!

'Evening, boys,' he said to us in that deep tone. 'Would you like a biscuit or anything?'

'No, thanks,' we all replied.

'You will be walking Venetia home after your dance rehearsal, won't you?' Mr King asked. 'Her mother believes God walks with her but I'd still prefer if she had some company on the way back – there's too many roughnecks around here.'

'Of course,' Bit replied.

'If you like I could pick you up after you finish,' Mr King offered.

'*No!* That's all right, Dad,' Venetia said, emerging from the hallway. 'We'll be OK.'

We all stood up. Venetia looked well pretty in her blue jeans, white crop top and denim jacket. Sky-blue coloured trainers sexed up her feet. A blue rucksack was strapped to her back. I totally got why Bit was willing to risk getting us all mauled to get back her mobile, but I couldn't help thinking that if Mr King asked Sergio for his precious daughter's phone, he'd get it back in a serious hurry.

We didn't want to stay another minute in Venetia's castle of nerves, and made our way towards the front door as politely as possible.

'Lemar,' Mr King suddenly called out. 'I saw your grandmother in church two weeks ago. Don't you ever accompany her?'

Bit's complexion is milk-chocolatey but I swear I saw his cheeks switch to the dark side of red as he thought of an answer. 'My mum's teaching me how to cook on Sundays,' he spluttered eventually.

I had to kill my grin – it was such a blatant lie! Bit couldn't even roast his own toast!

'Oh, I see,' Mr King said. He turned to Venetia. 'Don't be too late, V, remember I want you to help Princess and Milton with their Bible study tomorrow.'

'I won't, Dad,' Venetia replied.

No offence intended but the truth was I was proper relieved when Venetia closed her drawbridge behind us. Mr King was well polite and everything, never heard him raise his voice, but he had something of a gone-wrong Hulk about him.

'Thanks for coming, guys,' Venetia said before she hugged Bit. 'And being there for me.'

Bit didn't let Venetia go. I had to kill my grin as embarrassment slapped her cheeks. 'We'll go down the stairs,' Venetia suggested, peeling off Bit's arms. 'I think something crapped in the lift this morning. Disgusting.'

# 13

# Lambs Bread Lane

'Sergio knows I'm coming,' revealed Venetia as we bounced down the steps.

Jonah stopped dead in his tracks. 'He knows we're coming? Why'd you spill that? He'll probably have the whole of Notre Dame waiting for us in his yard!'

'No, no,' explained Venetia. 'He knows *I'm* coming. I didn't spill the whole score about you guys backing me up.'

'There's gonna be drama, V,' I said.

'I had to make sure he'd be there,' reasoned Venetia. 'I didn't want us to trek all the way up to Notre Dame and Sergio's not in his yard.'

'So how did you let him know you're coming?' wondered Bit.

'I used Saira's phone to text him,' explained Venetia. 'He thinks we're getting back together.'

Saira. Jonah grinned at the mention of her name and I have to admit I did too – I couldn't wait to bounce up to her place. 'So we're rolling up to Saira's castle?' I said casually. 'Where does she live?'

'Lambs Bread Lane,' replied Venetia. 'That row of small yards behind Black Rose Avenue.'

I could see that Venetia was proper nervous but she was hiding it well. Jonah kept on glancing up to the sky, as if he was asking for some kind of divine intervention to sabotage our mission.

'Do we actually have a plan for what we're gonna do when we crash into Sergio's yard?'

We all looked at each other. I had told myself not to think about that part. I didn't *want* to think about that part.

'We ask him politely for V's phone back,' said Bit.

'And say he turns round and says, "Screw you, short-ass," and cracks up laughing at a crew of schoolkids asking him for so much as the time of day – what then?' returned Jonah.

It was a good point. Venetia looked at us, hoping we'd come up with an answer. My heart started to pump. Nobody said a word. Until—

'We'll just have to *take* it from him,' Bit finally answered.

We all knew what he meant. Grease the knuckles! I hadn't had a fight since Year 8 when we were playing basketball. Nobby Starling said I looked like the fat blue genie in some Disney film. He forced me to eat fists, but when I got a blow in, he dropped to the ground like a drunken hobbit falling out of a tree. I got nuff ratings for that move, enough that I didn't hate the untold detentions I got as well. Mum minded though. No TV or games for a week. (It was worth it.)

'There're five of us,' added Bit. 'No one can tell me we can't handle this Sergio bruv. Who does he think he is, jacking V's phone? Freaking liberty!'

Lambs Bread Lane was a twenty-minute trek to the west side of our estate. On the way we noticed more hood-rats, G-girls and others all heading towards central Crong. Jonah couldn't hide how desperately he wanted to be stepping with them rather than with us.

'I've been hearing that the High Street is gonna get blitzed tonight,' said Venetia.

'We're not on that,' replied Bit. 'We're on our own agenda. *Believe* it.'

I was trying to believe it but the little voice in my hard drive was telling me it wasn't gonna be as easy as jacking a kid's dinner money.

I had never really trod in these ends before. The castles here were small. Each one was fronted by a grey, waist-high fence set around a tiny front garden barely big enough for a fox to do a cartwheel.

'You guys wait outside the front gate,' advised Venetia when we arrived at Saira's. 'I'll call for her.'

'Can't I roll up with you?' asked Jonah.

'No,' insisted Venetia. 'Saira's mum switches when brothers slap on her gates.'

So we hung back and watched Venetia step up to Saira's drawbridge. A small dog was barking at the end of the street.

Venetia pressed the doorbell and seconds later Saira poked her head out, her black hair sexing up her shoulders. She smiled at Venetia and looked over at us. 'One sec,' she said.

She disappeared but left the drawbridge open. I could smell lamb cooking. Someone was raging inside Saira's castle. A girl's voice with a bit of an accent. 'You're *not* going out tonight!'

'Yes, I am!' roared Saira.

'You're always going out! Why can't you stay in for once on a Friday night? You know Fridays are family days.'

'I told you why!' Saira shouted back. 'Cos I'm helping out a friend. Isn't that what you and the fam are always telling me to do? I'm *helping people!*'

Saira slammed the drawbridge behind her.

# 14

# The Magnificent Six

'You're all here!' Saira said excitedly, looking at us all up and down. 'Even you, Jonah! I thought you were going to mouse out.'

'Nah,' Jonah replied, rebooting his bravery. 'Not gonna miss this! You have to step up when a bredren needs help.'

Saira shut the gate behind her and she and Venetia led the way towards Black Rose Avenue. Saira was rocking this black tracksuit with red, gold and green trims. Pink trainers blessed her feet. Jonah and me were watching her flow from close behind.

'There's ...' Venetia started to Saira, 'there's enough of us to deal with Sergio. I don't wanna blitz things with your mum.'

'My mum?' Saira replied. 'She's more worried about what my family spill behind her back than fret about me on road.

I'm *coming*! This Sergio bruv better start realising he can't just jack phones off girls and get away with it. He needs two dents in his head!'

'Thanks, Saira,' Venetia said before giving her a quick hug again.

'What's the bus that rolls up to Notre Dame?' Saira asked.

'159,' I replied. 'We call it the ghetto bus cos it goes through all the ends.'

I wondered which one of us would deliver the two dents to Sergio's head. My budget wasn't on Jonah that was for sure – for me, Saira was the blatant favourite.

The 159 bus stop was a five-minute step away, not too far from our school. Once we were on that bus there would be no going back – a bruv can't get halfway and then run home wailing. If we bolted now, we would never live it down. Any rep we might have scored with the chicks would be dust. Any street cred we might have gained would be gone for good.

It was mad, I know, but in the midst of all the craziness, all I could think about was how delicious that lamb dish had smelled at Saira's yard ... I wanted to ask her for the recipe but it didn't seem like the right time. I decided to save that one-on-one for later.

There were about ten Crongtonians waiting at the bus stop when we arrived – some old, some young, some with shopping trolleys and a young couple who were sampling each other's tongues. Then I saw someone I recognised. Peel my eyeballs! Boy from the Hills, still in his school uniform, was waving at me as we rolled up to the back of the queue.

'What's happening, McKay?' he hailed me. 'Been waiting

for you for the longest time. I ain't got sweet nothing to do so I thought I'd roll with you on your mission.'

'You waited all this time?' I wondered. 'Is your hard drive missing some wiring?'

Venetia stopped in her tracks. She looked at me like she wanted to pull out my teeth and drill my tongue. 'You told Boy from the Hills about me? About our mission?'

'No, no!' I defended myself. 'Course not! I mean, yes, he knows that I'm rolling up to Notre Dame tonight – but that's all! Believe me!'

'Of all peeps to tell.' Bit shook his head. 'Why?'

Saira gave me an evil sideways look.

'I didn't tell him!' I said. 'Trust me on that.'

Boy from the Hills sidled up to us. The girls stepped back.

'I don't know a fat nothing about your mission,' he said to Bit. 'I just heard that McKay was rolling up to Notre Dame. It's not good to plant toes in those ends on your lonesome too much. So I'm just offering to bounce with you. That's all.'

'Who else knows?' Saira wanted to know.

'No one else,' I said.

Saira crossed her arms. I could feel her eyes lasering into my brain. *Damn!* I hadn't even picked up the bat let alone got to first base with her. 'You sure?' she said.

'He ain't wrong,' said Boy from the Hills.

Venetia pointed her finger at Boy from the Hills and said, 'I don't wanna be rude but I don't even know you too strong, none of us do. So don't get yourself involved in *my* drama. You hearing me?'

Boy from the Hills stared at the ground. 'Just wanted to help,' he said. 'That's all. McKay saved my skin so I thought I could repay the favour ...'

He tailed off, turned and stepped away to sit on a low wall that ran along the pavement. He hung his head like an unruly kid.

'He doesn't know about what's on my phone, does he?' Venetia whispered to me. 'Cos if he does I'm gonna deal with Sergio and *then* I'm gonna deal with *you*!'

She jabbed me in the chest. Out of the corner of my eye I could see Jonah getting his chuckle on. Bit just shook his head. Shame was licking my cheeks.

My bredrens didn't say anything more to me until the bus arrived. When it did, we paid our fare, bounced upstairs and parked in the front seats.

'This is it!' said Bit.

'Michael Jackson said that and look what happened to him,' said Jonah.

As the bus rolled off, a reflection in the window caught my eye. Boy from the Hills had hopped on to the bus behind us, and was making his way down towards the back seats. I shot up from my seat and hot-toed after him.

'What you *doing*?' I asked him.

'I ain't doing sweet zero,' he replied. 'Just taking a ride.'

'Sweet zero?' I repeated. 'You are following us. Why? They already think I spilled the whole score about the mission.'

'C'mon, McKay. Can't I help you?'

Man, this bruv was a sad sight, with that hair of his

sprouting untold nastiness. I swear dust flew off it every time he moved his head.

Out of the corner of my eye I could see Jonah, Bit, Venetia and Saira were watching us.

'I owe you one,' Boy from the Hills continued. 'I might be useful. You know, be a lookout or something? Or be a backup.'

'Step off at the next stop!' I demanded. 'I am not having your wild-haired ass follow us. How many times do I have to lay that down for you? It's *not* your mission! It's *not* your fight. Go back to your castle and play some pool or something.'

'Fight?' Boy from the Hills repeated.

He yawned and stretched out his arms. I think he found me as intimidating as a sardine laying it down to a shark. 'As I said, I'm just going for a bus ride,' he said, half-closing his eyes. 'Ain't no law against that.'

'So you're not getting off?' I was kinda pleading at this point.

'No,' Boy from the Hills replied.

'Please yourself.'

I didn't know what to say any more. All I could do was return to my seat.

'Don't tell me bush-head is coming with us?' remarked Jonah when I sat down. 'This is what you get when you help lonesomes – he thinks he's your best bredren now.'

'He's *not* coming with us,' I insisted. 'He says he's just taking a ride.'

'Maybe he'll get off at central Crong,' said Bit. 'Every other young head is stepping that way.'

Bit wasn't wrong. By the time we reached the centre of

town, hood-rats, G-girls, drama-lovers and the curious were jamming the pavements along the High Street. In the space of two bus stops I spotted three parked fed vans. Feds were prowling in their threes and fours in their yellow Day-Glo tops. Others were chatting into their radios.

We heard sirens in the distance. A tall guy was filming everything with his tablet. In the flats above the shops, peeps gathered at windows to watch the show. Shopkeepers were slapping down their shutters. The Footcave store was already shut and boarded up. A middle-aged woman with a shopping trolley was about to get off the bus but changed her mind. The bus moved on a block and when we stopped again we could see four feds searching the pockets of some guy wearing a Denver Broncos cap. On the other side of the road, five brothers watched on.

'I know him!' said Venetia. 'That's Linval Thompson! He used to go to my church – haven't seen him for ages.'

'He's gonna get his ass slapped in confession,' I said.

'Trust me!' added Venetia. 'Knowing his mum he won't make it to confession.'

We all looked out of the window as Linval Thompson was handcuffed. Another officer jacked something from his pockets as the hood-rats on the other side of the road launched a world of swear words. No one could say Crongton was ever boring.

We heard the doors close but the bus couldn't move cos of the traffic ahead. I felt a tap on my shoulder. It was Boy from the Hills.

'You again?' I roared at him. 'You said you wanted a bus ride, so get your ass back to your seat and enjoy the view!'

'I think you better see something,' Boy from the Hills replied. 'This is definitely not good,' he added.

I swapped glances with my crew. Boy from the Hills shuffled to the back. I followed him. Through the back window I could see seven or eight hood-rats hot-stepping towards the bus. Boy from the Hills pointed at one of them. He had a white patch slapped on the side of his head. 'That's Festus Livingstone,' he said. 'The G from Major Worries' crew who napped your bro's bike.'

'You sure?' I asked, hoping the answer would be no.

'Yep, double sure.' He gave a big nod. 'I saw him and his crew once doing wheelies on Crongton Broadway. Another time I saw them rolling into the Crongton Fitness Suite.'

The dinner I'd sunk earlier now made rapid progress down my chest to my belly. Dread stroked every rib and ran a sharp fingernail down my spine. 'I . . . I thought he was busy having brain scans,' I said. 'Or he was being kept under observation or something?'

'They must've sent him back to his yard,' Boy from the Hills guessed. 'And he ain't putting his feet up and begging his mum for cocoa and a bedtime story.'

They caught up to the bus and were running by the side of it. I was thinking of all the damn buses that had passed along this road in the last hour or so, Festus Livingstone had to jump on mine.

'What you gonna do?' Boy from the Hills wanted to know. 'Call your bro?'

My heart started to bang so hard I was sure it was picked up by Q at MI5 headquarters. I glanced over my shoulder.

'What is it?' Liccle Bit asked.

'It's ... '

I started to answer but I couldn't finish.

The bus started to move. I almost lost my footing. I regained my balance and made my way back to my seat.

'What is it?' Liccle Bit repeated.

I was sure everybody saw the dread in my eyes.

'F-Festus. Festus Livingstone's outside,' I stuttered.

Everyone looked out of the left-side window. Festus Livingstone and his bredrens were still hot-toeing alongside and slapping the side of the bus. The bus stopped. They smacked the bus again. I heard the swish of the doors opening. The bus tilted as a battalion of feet bounced on. Boy from the Hills shot from his seat and parked immediately behind us, terror in his eyes. *Kiss my knights! After they've finished with me, Dad will have to peel me off the seat. Nesta will probably kuff me for getting on the bus in the first place.*

'Sit in the front corner and *don't* show your face,' ordered Saira.

'We're all gonna get wasted,' said Jonah. 'I knew this mission was bad.'

'Just stay cool,' said Bit. 'Act like nothing's happening.'

Easier said than done.

Saira nudged up next to me and squeezed my left shoulder. 'If we don't do anything stupid we'll be OK,' she said. 'Trust me on that.'

Jonah stood up in a mad panic but Bit pulled his ass back down again. Eight pairs of name-brands scrambled up the steps to the upper deck – sounding like a crew of orcs on a mad night out. I couldn't help myself – I turned and looked over my shoulder. Festus Livingstone was the first to emerge at the top of the stairs. He was in black, taller than I expected, and he had a bit of growth going on below his nostrils. Two plasters kept the white dressing on his forehead in place. Judging by the size of his arms, he'd be able to throw me like an American football ball. He headed for the back seats, followed by seven of his bredren. They were proper rowdy and also dressed in black right down to their trainers. Boy from the Hills looked out of his window and I wondered if his heart was banging as wildly as mine.

'*Don't look back,*' hissed Saira.

The bus picked up speed. Saira kept squeezing my shoulder. None of us said a squeak. I tried to concentrate on listening to Festus's crew.

'Too many feds around.'

'We'll slide down later.'

'Someone must've spilled that something was going down tonight.'

'I bet it was a South Crong brother. There're always spilling to the feds. Freaking *pussies*!'

'Don't fret, the feds won't be there all night. And when they roll away, there's a fifty-inch TV with my gloves on it!'

'There's a new smartphone with my fingerprints on it!'

'But at least you've got something already, Festus. You've got those new mudguards!'

'I would've jacked a helmet if that assistant hadn't clocked me.'

I had this crazy urge to turn around again. Saira dug her nails into me so I wouldn't. I glanced at Jonah – horror was blasting his face. Venetia had her eyes closed. Her lips were moving. I think she was muttering a silent prayer. I hoped she included my name in it.

'That helmet would've been sweet!' Festus laughed. 'Don't wanna get stopped by the feds for not wearing one!'

We had just passed the old Crongton Bingo Hall and were now approaching the Crongton Green roundabout – Liccle Bit's pops used to live around here. A street sign indicated that North Crongton estate was two blocks away.

My phone shook in my pocket, making me jump half out my seat. I fumbled around, my fingers licked with nerves, and nearly dropped it when I saw who was calling: Nesta. *Damn! This mission is cursed.*

'Who is it?' Saira asked.

'My bro, Nesta.'

'Don't answer,' Bit whispered softly.

'I wasn't about to.'

The call ended. Ten seconds later I received a text.

Where r u?

Chicks in long towers! *What do I tell him?*

I'm with my bredrens. They're rehearsing this dance ting for school.

Liccle Bit and Jonah?

# The Magnificent Six

Yes.

Bit and Jonah? Dancing? You're not jackanoring me???!!!

No, on the level, it's funny to the m-a-x.

It's all booting off in the High Street. If you don't want me to kuff each side of your head don't let me hear that you're rolling up there.

I won't. I'm in school.

Keep your dancing feet in South Crong!

I'm not dancing.

You know what I mean!

I will.

Get your ass straight home after. No bouncing up the High Street with ur bredrens – unless u wanna double kuff and a half.

I hear you, bruv.

I put the phone back in my pocket and looked out of the window, still feeling guilty about my world of lies. We were on Elm Park Lane. The bus pulled up outside a row of shops. One of them was a spicy chicken takeaway with a pack of hood-rats hanging around outside it. I imagined a hot chicken wing sliding down my throat. There was a pub called the North Crongton Arms. I willed Festus and his crew to hop off the bus. But they didn't. I trained my ears on their chatter again.

'I'm telling you, bruv, he's in hiding. Just like that other pussy, Manjaro.'

'He ain't gonna show his butt on the road.'

'He's the living chicken.'

'He'll never slide up to our ends again.'

'If he does we'll shank him up and let the paramedics sew up his throat!'

I wondered who they were talking about. And then it licked me.

I turned to Saira and tweeted in her ear. 'I think they're chatting about Nesta.'

'Could be,' she said. 'But don't let all that macho pussy talk trouble you. After all, who's the one riding a bus with a white patch on his head?'

I noticed Jonah was giving me a messed-up look but I continued my conversation with Saira. 'Wish I knew where Nesta's bike was,' I said. 'I'd jack it back.'

Saira laughed. 'It's pure cradaziness us rolling up here to get V's phone back. But to get his bike back from somewhere in North Crong estate? Do you have a SWAT team to help our backsides?'

'Not exactly,' I replied.

We both laughed. The tension eased a little.

At the next stop, Festus and his crew jumped off. I think my sigh of relief rolled on for about a minute. Venetia had her eyes open again. Jonah was staring straight ahead and keeping his ass very still like he had crapped his pants.

'That was close!' he remarked.

The boy wasn't blessed with brains but, for once, he wasn't wrong.

# 15

## The Flying Lobster

Notre Dame was just four K away now. Our bus puffed uphill towards Fireclaw Heath – I remembered my dad telling me once that back in the day some old school North Crong G singed a South Crong bruv on his bits up there. The thought of it made me cross my legs. I wondered how long ago the original beef between South and North had kicked off. When Dad's bredrens came around they often talked about wars back in the day. I still recall some of the names: Louis Offkey, Stepping Razor, Double Shanks and Split-Ribs McKenzie. From what I heard it always seemed to be about some hot chick from a kick-ass fam linking with a G who lived on the wrong side of town. Or it could be a pissed-off rogue who napped whatever drugs or goods his old crew were selling. Someone would get carved and revenge would get passed down like family photographs. By the time a brother stepped back to see how much blood had been spilled, no one could remember what booted it off in the first place. All the posses knew is that they *hated* each other. How long had this fight been going on? It felt like for ever. I mean, North and South Crong were just two grimy council estates where most fams had a gas card, an electric key and they didn't want their kids to end up in the biscuit factory, stacking shelves in the supermarket or selling extra-large colas down the bowling alley. So how were they so different?

Through the back window, we could see the yellow lights of Crongton shining. It was almost pretty from a distance. My mum had always wanted to escape these ends. *'It would be nice to live in a house and have a little pond and flowers in the back garden,'* she would say. *'I would put a TV in the garden shed so your father could watch all the damn sport he wanted!'*

If I was gonna realise my ambition of running my own brand of chicken restaurants, I'd have to get out of Crongton. But although it was all bonkers living there, what was outside scared the living kidneys out of me. I wondered if my bredrens felt the same.

'Guys? I don't wanna be the one who's always asking awkward questions,' Jonah said, *'but* ... We never really came up with a plan for when we get to Sergio's gates. And I gotta say – we're getting damn close!'

I wished Jonah would gum his lips. I was trying to pretend none of this was happening ... The others, however, could see his point.

'He lives on the second floor, right?' Saira said. 'We need

to keep close, but out of sight. V should slap on his gate and when he opens it – we rush his backside!'

'*Rush* him?' I repeated. 'Ain't we gonna ask him to give back the phone first?'

'Oh, yeah,' chuckled Saira. 'But if he doesn't wanna give it back – THEN we go all *Gladiator* on him.'

'Everyone on the level with that?' asked Bit. 'Venetia?'

Venetia didn't look too happy about it at all. I guessed for her it must have been a bit messed up. I mean, one second you were making out with a guy and taking pics of it – of it *all* – and the next minute you were rushing his drawbridge with a crew in tow. I felt for her, and then I thought about Nesta and Dad, and suddenly, reality slapped me round the cheeks.

*Shit! I'm in Notre Dame!*

Mr Woo Kang's Chinese Kitchen was the first takeaway on the short High Street of Notre Dame. I stood up expecting to hop off the bus there, but Venetia stopped me. 'Two more stops.'

Two stops felt like a lifetime. Nobody said much. I peered out of the window at Notre Dame. I saw a brother walking two dogs. The roundabouts were little islands, with flowers and a nicely trimmed lawn in the middle – we never saw that in Crongton. A shopkeeper was locking her door after her last customer walked out with a bag of cupcakes. We strolled past some pretty castles with neat front gardens, just off the High Street. Mum would've loved it to the max to live in one of those.

Eventually, at Venetia's say-so, we bounced off the bus. Saira went first, then Jonah, then me and Bit and Venetia.

And then Boy from the Hills who just parked himself on a seat at the bus stop as if he wasn't really linking with us.

At the end of the High Street was an open green space, with tall slabs rising up behind it like the Estate at the End of the World. In the distance beyond was wilderness – the odd tree poking up here and there. Darkness began to boot out the daylight.

I rolled up to Venetia, pointed at Boy from the Hills and said, 'We can't leave him on his lonesome in foreign ends. He only wants to help.'

'I don't want him knowing my business,' she protested. 'Before you know it, every bruv, sister, hood-rat and dog will know about Sergio's pics of me.'

'He can be a lookout,' Saira suggested.

'I can do that!' offered Jonah.

'You're gonna be with *us* and have our back!' Bit insisted.

'OK.' Venetia nodded. 'He can be a lookout. But tell him to keep his distance.'

I went over to Boy from the Hills and told him.

'How much of a distance?' he asked.

'I dunno. Just keep in sight of us.'

'I told you I can be of use.'

'Then don't mess up,' I said. 'Just tell us anything that looks dodgy and we'll be cool.'

Boy from the Hills saluted me, *Full Metal Jacket*-style. I didn't find it funny.

I returned to the others.

'This way,' said Venetia.

We followed her without making a sound. Boy from the Hills held back until we'd established a decent lead. Then he set off, tracing our steps.

Venetia stopped and closed her eyes. A tear rolled down her cheek.

Saira put her arm around her shoulders. 'Are you sure you want to do this? If you change your mind, it's OK. We'll just step on a bus back to Crongton and treat ourselves to a strawberry cheesecake from the Cheesecake Lounge.'

Venetia thought about it all as she wiped her face.

'Not too late to roll back,' said Jonah, obviously excited at the prospect of a last-minute change of plan. 'Those cheesecakes are the bomb!'

Venetia opened her eyes. No tears this time: she looked proper determined, angry even. 'No. We've come this far. We'd be cradazy to turn back. Let's do this! He jacked my freaking phone!'

She led the way, stepping more quickly than before, with a fierce bounce in her pounce. We quick-stepped along a pathway through the Green. We passed a tramp sitting on a bench digging out his nose with a small twig – Venetia didn't even notice him. I looked behind. There was no sign of Boy from the Hills. *So much for our lookout!*

The street lights were switched on. We crossed a road and entered the Notre Dame estate. It was like any other estate I had seen. Satellite dishes fixed to walls looked like sad, grey umbrellas. Kids playing football. Pop music blaring out from high above. Same crap patchwork of bricks.

A signpost hanging high on the side of a block listed all the different towers with a crude map for directions: Sam Sharp House, Ella Baker House, Garvey House, Paul Bogle House, Emmet Till House and many more.

'Which slab?' I asked.

'Gloria Richardson,' replied Venetia. 'It's not too far.'

'How'd you get up here, you know, when you were seeing him?' asked Jonah.

'He'd pick me up on his motorbike,' replied Venetia. 'Never rolled up here by bus before.'

We stepped along the estate road before veering off through a forecourt. The odd brother or sister gave us an eye-pass, wondering who we were. One bruv got off his bike to take a closer look. A guy in a woolly hat sat on the hood of his car, watching us like an undercover fed. I swapped glances with Bit and Jonah. This wasn't good.

Gloria Richardson House was four storeys high and about the length of a football pitch. There were no lifts. Led by Bit, we started to climb the steep concrete steps leading to the upper floors. My heart started to pound again – and not just cos I wasn't exactly in gold-medal shape. This was proper scary now. When we reached the second floor, Bit stopped. 'Everyone good?' he asked.

Me and Jonah nodded yes, but what we both meant was, *ARE YOU CRAZY?! OF COURSE NOT!*

Saira linked arms with Venetia and said, 'Course.' She was one brave chick – my heart even stopped drumming for a second. I took in a big gulp of air.

Venetia didn't answer. She simply stepped ahead of us and

made her way along the balcony. She moved like an Olympic gymnast. Graceful. Her trainers didn't make a squeak. We followed in single file.

I started to flex my fingers. Bit crunched his fingers into fists. A car revved in the forecourt. I caught a whiff of someone nearby cooking fish. Reggae music was playing from one of the flats above. We had almost reached the end of the balcony when Venetia slowed down, stopped outside a blue door, closed her eyes, breathed in, breathed out and said: 'We're here.'

'You still wanna do this?' asked Saira.

Venetia nodded. 'Step back a bit,' she advised. 'I'm gonna ask him to give me back my phone on the level. I don't want any drama.'

'OK,' said Bit.

'Of course!' said Jonah.

We drew back about three metres.

Venetia slapped the letter box. She shuffled her feet as she waited. She stretched her fingers. She took in another breath. She said a silent prayer. My insides were flinging custard pies at each other. The reggae music blared out – the bassline was solid – then there was a noise at the door. The drawbridge opened.

'You're here!' said a voice with an Italian accent. 'So glad you made it! I would've picked you up like usual on my bike.'

'I've come for my phone,' said Venetia bluntly.

'Can we talk first?' said Sergio. 'I just wanted to see you again so we can settle things. Please hear me out, V. I'm so sor—'

'We're done, Sergio! End of! *Finito!* There ain't anything to chat about or to settle. I'm sorry, but . . . Just give me back my freaking phone!'

'Can you just come inside and talk? Let me say sorry properly. We can get through this, V. It'll be different from now on. We'll go out more. I'll take you to that theatre place you're always talking about. I'll come to your dance performances. I won't be so – what do you say? Demanding?'

Suddenly, Bit burst forward, barged past Venetia and pushed Sergio back into his castle.

'Give V back her phone!'

Saira and me rushed in after him.

The scene inside was *Rocky X*: Sergio pummelling Bit on the ground; Venetia clawing at Sergio's face.

*'Non mi rompere i coglioni!'*

It was bonkers. I wasn't sure what came over me but, without thinking, I rushed up to Sergio, pulled my fist back and detonated the left side of his face. Sergio rocked back in the hallway, half-turned and fell on top of Bit. My knuckles screamed.

*'Figlio di puttana!'*

Venetia looked at me like I was the fat kid in the playground that had suddenly turned into the heavyweight champion of the world. I wasn't sure what to do after that but Saira had it covered – she jumped on Sergio, grabbed his ears and started yelling: *'Where's my friend's phone?!'*

I saw that Bit was struggling to get back to his feet so I pulled him up. His soul was willing but his legs might as well have been made of pasta. I caught him before he dropped again, helped him out of the flat, then hot-footed it back.

While Saira was still mauling Sergio, Venetia bolted down a lino-covered hallway into a room to the right just before the kitchen. It was clearly Sergio's bedroom – I noticed a framed picture of Fabio Cannavaro hanging on one wall, and a photo of the Italian football team on another.

*'Where is it? Where is it?'*

This was Jonah. He had finally found his courage and came in screaming this Zulu warrior cry before jumping on Sergio like he was in *WrestleMania*. Sergio tried to fight back but Jonah held his legs down in a lock so tight that I thought he'd break them into small pieces of ravioli. Still, he kept struggling like a koala bear trying to hold on to an elephant's foot, and I could see Jonah was getting tired.

*'Fanculo!'*

So I took a mad run up and dropped my ass hard on to Sergio's chest – it seemed the thing to do. Sergio let out an airy grunt like 'Gnhhhhnh!' His eyes popped out like someone was playing pinball with them.

For some reason I felt hungry for chocolate cheesecake.

I sat there for a second, thinking of creamy-gooey-velvety-tangy-sweet deliciousness, but my daydream was interrupted by the sound of Venetia hollering down the hallway.

*'Got them!'*

She hurdled past us and out of the castle. Jonah, Saira and me swapped a glance, and in unison we released Sergio and foot-slapped it out of there, slamming the drawbridge behind us.

*'Dio dannato!'*

Outside, Bit was sort of sliding down the wall so I grabbed his arm and dragged him with me. I knew Jonah was rapid but he zoomed along that balcony like his bits were on fire – he even overtook Venetia. Bit was starting to find his feet as we bounced down the steps.

'What happened?' he asked. 'What happened?'

'Sergio licked you in the head,' answered Venetia, helping me sit Bit down when we reached the bottom. 'You sort of made a mad dash into his fist . . . '

'Did you get your phone?' Bit asked.

Venetia held up two mobile phones in front of Bit's messed-up eyes. 'I sure did – and I got his, n'all!'

'Come on!' cried Jonah, looking over his shoulder. 'He could come out of his yard at any second! He might be calling his bredrens right now! We could still all get mauled! *What are we waiting for?*'

'Look at the state of Bit,' said Saira. 'He can barely walk. V, give him some water.'

Venetia took out a bottle of water from her rucksack, cradled Bit's head and smeared water over his face. I couldn't work out if Bit was moaning cos he was proper hurt or cos V was caressing his chops. Jonah and me kept watch on the steps. I decided that if Sergio showed his ass once more, we could double-team him again – me launching myself on his chest and Jonah, the flying lobster, strangling his legs. One thing I was sure of: Sergio could NOT have been expecting our Ninja moves . . . I have to admit, I wasn't expecting them, either. And what's more, I felt proper proud.

'He'll survive,' said Venetia, kissing Bit on his cheek and helping him to his feet. 'Now come on, I know where we can hide for a bit. I ain't leaving till we've checked the phones.'

'Why can't we check them on the bus?' Jonah said.

Jonah wasn't wrong but Venetia ignored him.

We stepped behind the back of the slab. There were parked cars and smelly dustbins all around us. It smelled toxic, but it felt less exposed.

'You know Sergio's code?' Saira wanted to know.

Venetia grinned and nodded again.

The two girls' fingers were a mad blur of activity as they deleted what had to be deleted.

'I can help,' said Jonah. 'I know a lot about smartphones. I used to have one.'

The two girls glanced at Jonah like he'd been stealing underwear from a washing line.

Man! He was as subtle as a rhino in a field of baby chicks.

I slapped him on the side of his head.

'What's wrong with you, bruv?' I cussed him. 'You think they want you perving over this stuff? When will you learn? *Kill* the drooling!'

Jonah scowled and held his hands up as if to say, *Fine, whatever!*

As the girls worked, Saira seemed shocked, her mouth and eyes wide; Venetia, however, looked proper relieved. I was fretting about Sergio. It had been a while now and we weren't anywhere near the bus home.

'Can't you delete as we roll?' I asked. 'Don't wanna stay here for too long.'

'Almost done,' said Saira. 'One sec. Just checking his folders.'

Darkness had finally killed the daylight. I felt my forehead and it was covered in sweat. My armpits were leaking too – that deodorant I slapped on earlier wasn't strong enough to combat the kind of evening we were having . . . The light was weak, but I could still make out Jonah's eyes darting around, watching for trouble. And Bit looked messed up – the bruises on his face were coming up proper ripe now – just like Nesta.

Thinking of Nesta began to tip the shit for me. We needed to get out of here now.

Just then we heard footsteps approaching but not from the balcony or the stairs. 'Get up,' I whispered to the girls. 'Someone's coming.'

My knuckles throbbed like crazy, but I was full of adrenaline and ready for more drama.

And then I glanced at the crew.

Bit, a ball of pulp on legs; V and S, looking like they'd sacrifice us all in order to save a couple of mobile phones; Jonah cowering – actually cowering! – behind the *girls*.

The least intimidating posse ever. A six-year-old could have licked us!

But we were where we were. And the footsteps were close now. Like it or not, this was it . . .

When Boy from the Hills emerged from around a corner I didn't know whether to hug him or launch myself at his ass, and bring him down with my signature move.

'Where the foreign ends have you been?' I barked at him.

Boy from the Hills didn't say a word. Instead, he looked at each of us in turn. The mood turned dark.

'I think you guys better get moving,' he warned.

'Why?' Saira wanted to know.

'Why? Look at you. And I'm guessing Sergio ain't looking too pretty either. You have to get away from these ends – this estate, the brothers who prowl here, they're seriously off-key.'

'*Done!*' announced Venetia. She had been too busy deleting pics to listen to Boy from the Hills. She looked up and finally saw him. 'Hey! Where has your bushy self been?'

'Doing my job,' Boy from the Hills said. 'There's a brother in the forecourt who's been watching your movements since you got here.'

'Just one?' Venetia wanted to know.

Boy from the Hills nodded.

'How old?'

'About our age,' Boy from the Hills replied. 'But he was dressed funny, looked well weird. We should get our skins out of here.'

'I'm on that,' agreed Jonah.

'We have to give Sergio's phone back first,' Venetia insisted.

'Are you nuts?' I said, speaking for us all. 'What do you want us to do? Slap on his drawbridge and say, "Sorry for mauling your ass but here's your phone back"?'

'No, no!' Venetia shook her head. 'Just fling it through the letter box. We can't keep it.'

'Why not?' asked Jonah. 'I could do with a new phone. I'll have it. I'll even give you ten notes for it. *Damn!* I'll even give you fifteen – I'll give you three pounds a week for the next . . . ' God, he was rubbish at maths. ' . . . five weeks? Yeah, five weeks!'

'No you won't!' confirmed Venetia. 'I don't want us to keep anything of his and I don't want to give him any reason to come hounding for my ass again. This has to be finished. No baggage. One of you has to run upstairs and do the right thing – one of you has to be *the* man!'

We all looked at each other in the dark. Smack the shields! I didn't want it to be me! The pride I'd felt at dropping my bones on to Sergio's ribcage drained away. *He'll probably take that into serious consideration before he savages my ass.* Bit looked like he couldn't climb a stair let alone bounce up to Sergio's drawbridge again and deliver his phone. We all turned to Jonah, as if we'd all reached the same conclusion at the same time.

'It'll have to be you,' Saira said. 'Don't peeps call you *Rapid*?'

Something went wrong with Jonah's face. I thought he was either gonna faint or blast his pants a different shade of brown. 'Me?' he said, pointing at his own chest. 'But he might be waiting for me! With a baseball bat! Or an axe! Or an AK47! He's gonna *Game of Thrones* me!'

'Out of all of us you're the fastest runner,' I said. 'They don't call you *Rapid J* for nothing.'

'Yeah.' Saira nodded. 'Lily Thomas calls you that. I think she fancies you.'

'I can't outrun a freaking bullet!' returned Jonah, his dread overriding any chick fancying him.

'Stop fretting,' said Venetia. 'He hasn't got a gun.'

'McKay's not wrong,' added Boy from the Hills. 'He's not gonna catch your skin. He'd definitely catch McKay though.'

I wasn't offended. It was the truth.

'What about Bit?' argued Jonah. 'It's *his* mission.'

'Are you serious?' asked Saira. 'The state he's in we'll be lucky if he reaches the top of the stairs let alone posts the damn phone through the right letter box.'

Jonah thought about it. We all gazed at him once more.

'I'll come with you,' offered Boy from the Hills. 'I'm pretty quick – nowhere near as rapid as you though.'

It wasn't such a bad idea. At least Boy from the Hills was fresh and unmauled. Maybe his hair or what lived in it would put Sergio off.

'I'm on that,' said Jonah. 'I still think you should give the phone to me though. I'm having to use my mum's brick.'

Venetia shook her head. Jonah closed his eyes. I guessed he was trying to boot up his courage or maybe he suddenly found a God to pray to. He reopened his eyes and reached for Sergio's phone.

'You sure everything is deleted?' asked Saira.

'I've checked all his galleries and documents,' replied Venetia. 'We blitzed them all.'

'Let's hope he hasn't sent them on to his bredrens,' remarked Saira. 'Guys do that kinda stupidness to show off.'

'Not me!' said Bit. 'I wouldn't even take the pics in the first place.'

Venetia handed Sergio's phone to Jonah. He looked at it like it was a nuclear bomb to get rid of. He breathed in hard then turned to Boy from the Hills. 'Ready?' he asked.

'And primed,' Boy from the Hills replied.

They climbed the concrete steps slowly. I followed them to the top. Boy from the Hills seemed well happy that he was playing a part in our mission. I glanced behind and Venetia was stroking Bit's forehead. Saira was looking here and there.

Jonah began to creep along the balcony like he was a proper commando. Boy from the Hills was right behind him. I had to admit, I was with Jonah on the whole phone thing – *Why didn't Venetia let him keep Sergio's phone?* Maybe it was one of them things you had to do if you were in team God. Mind you, we had savaged Sergio before he'd had a chance to negotiate.

Jonah stopped, like he was having second and third thoughts about this new mission. He glanced back at Boy from the Hills. Boy from the Hills tweeted something in Jonah's ear. They started moving again and stopped at number seventy-two. My heart boomed. I had no idea whether Boy from the Hills could fight or not but I knew I'd have to step up if they needed help so I prayed he was a secret Shaolin fighting monk.

Standing outside Sergio's drawbridge, Jonah lifted the letter box with his left hand and with his right he posted the phone. Without wasting a second he was off down the stairs before you could say *chocolate cheesecake with a bit of raspberry sauce*, leaving Boy from the Hills trailing in his slipstream.

'He's done it!' I said to the girls.

As Jonah bounced down the steps, Venetia said, 'Thanks. I owe you one.'

'Can you tell me more about Lily Thomas?' Jonah asked. 'She linking with anybody?'

'Later,' replied Saira.

As soon as Boy from the Hills joined us, Jonah urged, 'Let's shift! We're going to Cheesecake Lounge whether it's been blitzed or not! Vanilla with a strawberry milkshake . . . Crong, here we come.'

'I'm feeling that,' agreed Saira.

Now they were speaking my language!

Boosted by his letter-box triumph, Jonah led the way with Boy from the Hills. We stepped behind a tower block before cutting back on ourselves to join the main estate road. Bit seemed brighter in himself, but his left cheek looked like he had tried to eat one of his mum's dumplings. (I'd had a plateful for tea at his once; I came away feeling like I'd been chewing the street kerb.)

I don't know why, but something felt off. Too many windows opening, faces glimpsed in curtain shadows, the sound of feet running down stairs. Someone was whistling, too. It wasn't the kinda tune that Santa Claus whistled before he rumbled down your chimney. And it was more than one person, like they were responding to each other.

Nerves ping-ponged through me. My face heated up. My blood ran cold. We stepped quicker and closer together. The girls linked arms.

'Is . . . is there another way out of the estate?' asked Jonah.

'I don't know,' replied Venetia. 'We always came in at the front. The estate's big. It goes all the way back to the hills beyond.'

'Something's definitely going down,' said Boy from the Hills.

He wasn't wrong. No one wanted to say it but it was the cold reality.

Then we spotted a still figure standing in the middle of the road. We stopped dead in our trainers. I heard someone – I don't know who – draw a sharp intake of breath. Jonah was about to burn his soles away, but I put my hand on his shoulder.

*'Stay together!'*

# 16

# The Hunchbacker Crew

The figure was blocking the main exit of the estate. It was a boy. He looked about seventeen, maybe eighteen. A grey beanie hugged his head. He was wearing a black duffel coat, dark jogging bottoms and black trainers. He had his hands in his pockets, and he was staring at us, casual like. We turned around. Two more guys had cruised in behind us, dressed in exactly the same garms. We heard a car door slam off to the right and turned to see another four brothers climb out of a rusty old Mini – one of them was *oh my God* ugly, another had tattoos inked all over his neck. To our left, we heard more feet bouncing down steps.

My body had become one giant pulse. Venetia hugged Bit tight and buried her head into his chest. Boy from the Hills just stood still in total disbelief as to what was going down.

Jonah was looking for a place to run. Saira grabbed on to my arm with both hands.

The beanie-rat, who it seemed was waiting for us at the estate exit, began stepping slowly towards us. It reminded me of the showdown scene in one of those ancient westerns that Dad still liked to watch on a Sunday afternoon when there wasn't any sport on. I prayed he didn't have a gun. I noticed for the first time now that we were standing directly under a street light. Our shadows were short.

'Shall we make a run for it?' whispered Jonah. 'There's an alleyway near the garages to the right.'

'*No!*' said Venetia. 'Bit's still dazed and we are *not* leaving our wingman.'

Jonah shook his head but I was glad to hear that. I didn't think my big butt would get too far anyway.

'What do we do?' asked Jonah. 'Can't just stay here and let them terminate us.'

'We stick together,' I said. 'Together we're a team, but on our own? Who knows what they'd do to us then.'

We were blatantly outnumbered. All we could do was be knights together, not easy bait apart.

I glanced to my left and then to my right. Beanie-rats were converging on us from all angles. We squeezed closer together. Sweet Merlin! *Deleted by brothers wearing stupid hats and duffel coats! What a messed-up end. Here lies the body of McKay Tambo – the Big M – savaged by a beanie-rat in some slab jungle at the end of the world.*

The chief rat spoke first.

'Who gave *you* permission to pollute our ends?' He was

pointing at us with his right thumb and forefinger, like a gun.

'We ... we weren't,' I managed, pathetically, not really knowing what I meant.

'We're not in any gang,' Venetia was quick to say. 'We don't step with bad-boy crews. We're not into that game. We just rolled up here to see my ex.'

'You *don't* just stroll into *our ends* like you own 'em!' he shouted. He moved closer. He was only three or so metres away now, close enough to see what he looked like. He had a rough goatee. Red spots sprouted on his nose and bred like angry germs around his nostrils. He stared at Venetia and seemed to be momentarily distracted by her. For a second he looked almost calm but not for long – rage soon shaped his face again. 'This is *Hunchbacker ends*,' he roared. 'Don't you know who we are? We *control* tings round here. *Everything.*' He emphasised that last word looking Venetia up and down in a way that I could tell made Bit want to holler. Saira gripped me tight. I could feel her nails clawing into me.

I tried to think of all the G-crews Nesta had ever mentioned to me: Mo Baker and the Folly Ranking crew, the Hash Posse, the Poverty Driven Orphans – PDO for short – but Hunchbackers didn't even tickle my bell. I had never heard zero nish about them. I swapped rapid glances with Jonah, Bit and Boy from the Hills. I didn't think they knew anything about the Hunchbackers either.

'No!' Venetia answered. 'We don't know anything about your stupid freaking gang! We haven't come up here for any drama. As I said, I've just seen my ex and now we're leaving.'

The beanie-rat with the pussed-up nose stepped three paces forward. He took out a blade from the pocket of his duffel coat. It glinted under the yellow street light. Venetia had dissed his crew and he didn't love it. I felt Saira flinch. We all retreated a step – all except Venetia.

*What is she thinking?*

'You think you can pollute our ends at night!' the brother screamed at us. 'Do you think I can allow that? You think I can allow any pussy to stroll in our ends. Do you? *Answer me!'*

He raised the knife to eye level. The blade was about twenty centimetres long. The tip of it was stained brown. The handle was curved and wooden. I reeled back a zillion years to this morning, back in South Crong with Jonah, his school bag and his mum's bread knife. His instincts were on point, I guess. But standing here now, facing this ugly crew, I knew we were right to leave it behind. Cos if we pulled a blade, every one of these Hunchbackers might've pulled one too. We'd be minced.

I sensed movement from all sides. We were trapped. Saira's nails mauled my arm once more.

'You'll have to pay the tax!' the G-leader barked. 'For taking the liberty! Hunchbackers can't allow peeps from foreign estates strolling through our ends at night like they own it!'

*Tax?* I thought. *He's gonna be well sad when he looks in my pockets. The remains of well-used tissue isn't going to buy our freedom.*

'How . . . how do you know we're foreigners?' asked Bit.

'We just know!' came the answer. 'Now *pay the freaking tax!'*

'We ain't got any money,' I said. 'Our pockets are dry.'

'Your phones then,' roared the G-leader. He waved the knife in front of us. *'Now!'*

Jonah was the first to take his mobile out of his pocket. He placed it on the ground in front of him. By the look on his face he was glad to be rid of it. Saira was next – I saw her arm shake as she dropped her phone on the road. *Robbing the hood!* It wasn't a good week for me and Nesta – he'd had his bike napped by a North Crong G and now I was about to get my mobile stolen by this Hunchbacker posse. I placed it in front of me. Boy from the Hills and Bit did the same.

We all glanced at Venetia. She had her eyes closed. Her lips were moving. I guessed she was whispering another prayer. It licked me that she didn't want to give up her phone – she'd only just got it back. At least she had blitzed the pics.

Bit gazed at Venetia, no doubt silently pleading with her, begging her to give it up, let it go. Venetia stood her ground, pushing her chin out.

'You. Where's your phone?' demanded the G-leader.

Venetia ignored him, turning her head to look at the tower to her right. The beanie-rat was brewing. He took another step towards her. I saw the desperate panic on Bit's face but he couldn't do a damn diddly, especially as he wasn't yet recovered from eating Sergio's fists. I had this sick feeling in my stomach. I could barely watch.

'So you think that just cos you got a pretty face and look all sweet that I will squeeze you out of the tax?' shouted the G-leader. He stared at her again. He hated her cos she wasn't as scared of him as the rest of us were. A girl! It wasn't in the programme.

'Do you think we give a shit about how pretty your hair is? For real. *Give me your freaking phone!'*

Venetia didn't look up. She didn't move an eyelash. She just shook her head: *No.*

Suddenly, the G-leader punched her in the mouth. She rocked back, holding her face.

Bit raged but the beanie-rat held him off with a flash of his blade right in front of Bit's eyes.

*'Don't let me ask you again!'* the G-leader warned, glaring at Bit but directing his lyrics at Venetia. *'Drop your phone or someone's gonna go home with a blade-sketch tonight!'*

Venetia's face was a picture of pure contempt that promised some kinda *Kill Bill*-style revenge. Finally, she took her phone out of her pocket and hurled it on to the ground. It bounced past the beanie-rat. The back panel broke off. With rage that fierce, Venetia could've taken on Sergio on her lonesome. And won.

The G-leader signalled to one of his crew and this brother, dressed in identical black duffel coat and beanie hat, picked up the phones.

'Where're you from?' the G-leader wanted to know.

Venetia refused to answer. She wiped her mouth. Her bottom lip was swelling up.

'What's it to you?' Saira replied.

'Are you from North Crong ends?' the beanie-rat raised his voice again. 'Think you could casually stroll through our ends cos you're from North Crong? *You're wrong!'*

None of us replied.

'Wherever you're from,' the beanie-rat continued, 'tell your peeps that Hunchbackers don't fear *anyone*. Tell them G-Gore told you. Tell them, you mess with the Hunchbackers, you pay the cost to the boss!'

I had never heard anyone in Crongton mention they wanted to roll up to Notre Dame, ever.

At last G-Gore put his knife back in his pocket. He nodded to the members of his crew like he was some kinda military general – I half-expected them to salute his ass and perform some kinda crazy goose-step. I guessed we were the only young-heads his crew had jacked for the longest time.

G-Gore gazed at Venetia again. 'You're freaking lucky you're just getting taxed tonight,' he said. 'We could've done more … a *lot* more. But I'm on the level; I'm giving you a squeeze.'

Venetia looked at G-Gore like he was something that wouldn't flush down the school toilet.

'Hunchbackers!' G-Gore called, still staring at Venetia. 'Let's stroll.'

They all followed him as they marched ahead of us. We watched them disappear into the darkness. We didn't move a toenail until they were completely out of sight. When they were, I looked to my left and saw Venetia had dropped to her knees. She covered her face with her hands. 'I'm so sorry!' she cried. 'Really sorry! I never thought this would happen! Didn't think he'd go that far. So sorry!'

Bit and Saira tried their best to comfort her but Venetia was shaking her head, shivering, tears freefalling down her cheeks, her nose dripping. And all she could do was apologise, over and over.

'I've never seen those Hunch ... those brothers before,' Venetia managed as Bit and Saira helped her back to her feet. 'Maybe cos I was with Sergio, I didn't notice them.'

'We're alive and breathing, aren't we?' said Jonah. 'All that's happened is a bit of a rough-up and a phone-jacking. It could've been a whole heap worse! Our parents could've been reading about our gored-up bodies in tomorrow's papers. Flowers outside the school gates. Teachers with collection buckets. A special church service and—'

'We get the score!' snapped Saira.

'I was just saying we could be, you know ... dead,' returned Jonah.

'Since when did you turn into the Grim Preacher?' I snapped at Jonah.

Venetia started bawling again, this time proper loud, like a howling animal. This pain wasn't just because of G-Gore beating her down; it came from somewhere deep. None of us really knew what to say. Instead, we all kinda gave her a group hug. Even Boy from the Hills joined in. Venetia didn't seem to mind. Eventually her wails became sniffles. Time stood still, only Venetia's sobbing and the whoosh of distant traffic to be heard until, very gently, Saira softly spoke to her.

'It's not your fault, V,' she soothed. 'Listen to me. It's his fault – if he hadn't taken those damn photos, we'd never have set off on this mission in the first place; we'd never have ended up here and we'd never have had the bitch luck of meeting the worst-dressed, spottiest G-crew in the whole entire world! Man did you see them zits? Ugh, I swear! I just wanted to give them a Boots voucher!'

Venetia started chuckling. Boy from the Hills joined her. And one by one we all joined in. It was messed up! We had just been jacked, couldn't tell anyone where we were cos we didn't have our phones, were stranded nuff Ks from home, our parents would probably delete us when they found out we'd rolled up to Notre Dame – and here we were, laughing like someone was swatting us with the world's most tickly feather.

'And they think they're bad but they are such pussies,' continued Saira. 'I know. Our fam has moved around a lot. I've crashed into untold so-called G-leaders – and not one of them would hold up fourteen- and fifteen-year-old kids with a blade. So they're straight-up, whisker-licking *pussies!*'

'And duffel coats?' remarked Boy from the Hills. 'What's that all about? Maybe it snows up here more than anywhere else.'

'If they wanna tax something they should make sure it's fashion sense!' joked Jonah.

Everybody laughed again. It made the trauma of losing our phones and seeing Venetia beat down not so bad.

'Right,' I said, as we stepped away from each other. 'Let's get out of this sad-no-hope, end-of-the-world estate.'

# 17

# Lamb Kofta

'I never thought I would say this,' said Venetia when we were back at the bus stop, 'but I'll be well happy to be in South Crong ends again.'

'You're not wrong,' said Jonah. 'Home's starting to look like a palace in my head.'

'Anyone know what the time is?' asked Saira. 'My mum will probably send for the SAS if I'm not back before eight.'

'I don't know,' answered Bit. 'Must be after nine.'

'The neighbours are gonna be well entertained when I finally breeze in,' Saira joked.

I spotted a Costcutter on the other side of the road. 'All that drama has made me feel peckish – can anyone give me a donation so I can get some biscuits or something?'

'Can't you wait till we get to the Cheesecake Lounge?' asked Bit.

'No, bruv,' I replied. 'I feel the need to feed.'

'Your dad should gum up your mouth,' said Bit.

'And your mum should send you to height school,' I cut back.

'Here,' said Venetia, 'this will help. I could do with a biccy too.' She gave me fifty pence.

Bit moaned and groaned but grudgingly handed me seventy pence. 'That should be enough,' he said. 'And once you get them, *share them*!'

I thanked them and started off across the street.

'If you see a bus coming,' called Jonah, 'just forget about your belly and move your ass to catch it. I for one ain't gonna wait for you.'

'I, for two, will not wait for your butt either,' agreed Bit.

I waved to let them know I'd heard and entered the store. I picked up a packet of custard creams and some bourbons. The woman behind the counter gave me a strange look as I passed her my funds. She kept staring at me until I left the shop.

The bus clearly hadn't carried anyone away in my absence. I crossed back over the road and shared the biscuits out.

'Has *anybody* heard of this Hunchbacker crew?' I asked.

'Nope,' replied Liccle Bit. 'They may well be pussies – but I thought for a minute there we were all graveyard-bound.'

'So did I,' said Jonah. 'We should've run for it.'

'Run where?' asked Saira. 'We might've ended up somewhere worse.'

'I can't think of anywhere worse than that estate,' remarked Jonah. 'And if we had burned away we'd still have our phones at least.'

'You can always get another phone,' said Venetia. 'It's body parts that don't grow back.'

'Then why didn't you give up your phone straightaway?' I wanted to know.

Venetia thought about it. She shook her head. 'I messed up,' she admitted. 'I thought he was trying to scare us, you know, acting all big in front of his crew. I thought he was putting on a show, acting all hardcore but then laughing and making jokes about it all, then giving us our phones back. I didn't want to give him that pleasure. I can't stand guys like that.'

'You got that wrong,' cut in Jonah. 'We could've all been nibbling worms!'

'Sorry,' she managed. 'I just ... I just *hate* G-leaders and anybody who follows them.'

'Don't make her feel bad,' said Bit, raising his voice to Jonah. 'It wasn't V's fault we crashed into the Hunchbackers.'

'And I still haven't ever heard of them,' remarked Boy from the Hills, trying to steer the conversation away from Venetia. 'They were some weird, off-key gang.'

'But we risked our asses coming here to get *her* phone back,' Jonah said, raising his voice and pointing at Venetia. 'And then *she* plays hero with her damn phone like it's more precious than anyone else's!'

'You didn't have to come!' shouted Bit.

'But I did!' yelled back Jonah. 'And you lot don't seem to appreciate it anyway. Didn't I rush into Sergio's yard and jump on his legs?'

'After you moused outside when the rest of us rushed him,' raged Bit.

'I wasn't mousing outside,' spat Jonah.

'That's what it looked like to me,' challenged Bit. 'If you weren't mousing outside then what were you waiting for? Maybe you stopped to put on your freaking superhero cape!'

I couldn't believe the way my best two bredrens started warring against each other. It kinda reminded me of Nesta always calling Dad a pussy or worse.

Jonah wasted no time in his retaliation. 'Why don't you go and fu—'

'Time out!' called Saira, placing her left palm on top of her right fingers. 'Time out! The mission was successful! So what do you wanna do now? Cuss and maul each other on Notre Dame High Street for the whole world to hear? Create another drama? Or jump on a bus and wheel down to Crong to the Cheesecake Lounge?'

Jonah thought about it. Bit's chest was heaving with rage. Looking awkwardly at Venetia and Bit, Jonah mumbled, 'Sorry, OK.'

'I'm sorry too,' added Bit.

'Brothers like G-Gore, Manjaro and Major Worries,' Venetia mentioned, 'they're the cradazy *shit* of the world. I *hate* them to the core! All they do is mash up people's lives and they don't give a freaking damn. Brothers like that killed my cousin Collette. So I'm sorry, but I didn't want to give in to that G-Gore prick. And I'd do the same again any time.'

Venetia's eyes filled up with tears. Saira gave her a hug. As Bit placed his hand on Venetia's shoulder, Jonah hung his head. Boy from the Hills looked proper awkward and

I was feeling the same vibe – I sunk another couple of biscuits without thinking. I knew what it was like losing a close family member. Mum's death was always with me. No matter how hard I was laughing, if I was telling jokes to my bredrens, or rolling on missions and cooking up a world of treats to please my stomach – that grief was always there; it never left. If my memory was on point, Collette was only twelve when she lost her life, taken out by a stray bullet in some G-crew madness. It was a proper tragedy. No one should expect a sister or brother to stop feeling that pain, however many years passed.

As if to spear the tension, an old woman crossed the road towards us in a motorised wheelchair. As her chair climbed the nearside kerb I noticed she had a big bottle of brandy and a box of Maltesers resting on her lap. It wasn't that cold but she had a long pink knitted scarf wound round her neck so it almost covered her mouth. Her top lip was a map of creased lines that made her pink lipstick look all wrong. Her fingertips were covered in melted chocolate. I guessed she was at least eighty, or maybe a hundred and five.

'Are you waiting for a bus?' she asked in a croaky voice. It was kind of a dumb question to ask a teenage crew standing at a bus stop. What did she *think* we were waiting for? The Hunchbackers to jack us again?

'Yes, we are,' Venetia finally replied in her Sunday school voice. 'Hopefully one will come soon. We've been waiting a while. We all want to get home.'

The old woman shook her head.

'The buses have stopped running, I'm afraid,' she said.

'There's all sorts carrying on in Crongton – is that where you live?'

'Yes,' I said. 'South Crong.'

'I thought so,' the ancient said. 'I've been listening to the local news on the radio. I suppose the authorities don't want any more young-uns going down there.'

Half a custard cream stuck in my throat. I swallowed hard to get it down. *What am I hearing?* Jonah shook his head, swore under his breath. Saira started studying the bus time-table. Boy from the Hills just sat down casually on the kerb.

'Oh dear,' said the old woman. 'There's a cab station at the top of the road though. It's not far, just a ten-minute walk – probably five for you young-uns.'

She then clicked a button on her wheelchair, something whirred under her seat and she was off rolling down the street, probably going back to her castle to sample her big bottle of brandy and download more Maltesers. I didn't know why but I imagined her place was full of cats.

'Thanks!' Venetia called to her.

The lady didn't look back. Instead, she just raised a hand and waved.

'*Great!*' Jonah shouted in mad frustration. 'Just freaking-deaking *great*! I can't freaking believe this! How're we gonna get back to South Crong?'

We all looked at each other.

'Cab,' said Boy from the Hills. 'Didn't the old woman say there was a cab station at the top of the road?'

'You're not wrong,' recalled Bit.

'But have we got enough funds?' asked Saira.

I didn't have a dirty cent and now I felt proper guilty for begging funds for biscuits. I ate another custard cream. Boy from the Hills dug into his pocket and came out with three pound. Bit did the same and revealed sixty pence. Venetia had a pound fifty. Jonah only owned thirty pence and Saira counted a pound eighty from her purse.

'How much is that altogether?' I asked.

'Put it this way, I don't think we would've had too much joy in the Cheesecake Lounge,' said Boy from the Hills. 'That could probably just buy us two and a half slices.'

'Seven pound twenty,' said Venetia, ignoring Boy from the Hills. 'Not enough to take us all the way to South Crong. Not even enough to get us as far as North Crong.'

'It'll take us part of the way,' said Bit. 'McKay, you sure you haven't got at least ten pence in your pockets?'

I shook my head. 'I had to get charity from Saira just to get the bus here. Sorry, bruv, my pockets aren't singing today.'

'Maybe we can pay the rest of the fare when we get back to South Crong,' suggested Saira.

'That might work,' I agreed.

'Or the driver might look on our asses and tell us to trod the rest of the way,' said Bit.

'He might not,' argued Saira.

'We have to try,' I said. 'What have we got to lose? I don't know about you guys but my legs are killing me and I haven't had enough Shredded Wheat to make the distance.'

'As the worm crawls it's about eight K,' Boy from the Hills guessed. 'At least most of it is downhill. Mind you, we have to pass Fireclaw Heath and that ain't a place to be at nightfall.'

'Yeah, Fireclaw Heath – the scene of the legendary burned seed bags . . . ' said Jonah.

Venetia and Saira winced. I wanted to change the subject.

'Eight K is still eight K,' I said. 'My toes will never forgive me.'

'Let's roll to this cab station then,' said Bit.

We walked along Notre Dame High Street past a couple of phone shops, a charity shop, a restaurant named Hugo's, Alex Dumas's book store, Esmerelda's coffee house, a pub called The Four Bells, one of those gaming arcades and a Footcave. The cab station was located beside a bakery. The window display showed cakes in all kinds of different colours, flavours, shapes and varieties. The one that alerted my taste buds was a perfect cupcake, shaped into a heart with a piece of choccy flake on top. I closed my eyes and imagined that nice smooth chocolate texture nicing up my tongue and running smooth and blessed down my throat.

As I enjoyed a daydream attack, Bit continued into the cab station. There was a short, dusty hallway with a door to the right that led into the office. Straight ahead a flight of uncarpeted stairs climbed into darkness. The whiff of cigarettes polluted my nostrils. On the other side of the office window, a skinny guy was sitting on a stool with a phone stuck to his ear. He was rolling a cigarette and a steaming mug of coffee was on a table in front of him. Behind him, pinned to the wall, was a large map of the local area. Notre Dame to the north, Crongton in the middle, Ashburton to the west and the wilderness to the east. I didn't realise how much green space there was around our ends.

# Lamb Kofta

'It'll be half an hour,' the guy on the stool said into his phone. 'That's the best I can do. Take it or leave it. Why? There's a bloody riot going on in Crongton, that's why! The minute I put down the phone it rings again. All my drivers are out. Will ya wait? You can try somebody else if ya want, it's a free country last time I looked. I'm not being rude, I'm just telling ya the way it is ... OK, as I said, it'll be half an hour.'

He killed the call and looked at all of us. He lit his roll-up with a match before he spoke to us. 'And where are ya going?' he asked. 'I can't guarantee a cab for at least forty minutes.'

'We're ... we're going to South Crong,' said Bit.

'South Crong?' repeated the guy. He puffed out some serious smoke towards the light bulb that hung above his head and studied us again. 'Ya know they're going crazy in Crongton right now, do ya? Ya know that they're tearing up the place, looting and allsorts?'

'We know,' Saira answered. 'But we live there and we need to get home.'

'So do a lot of people,' said the guy. 'By the sounds of it ya might find ya haven't got much of a home when ya get back. Anyway, if ya want to wait the driver will have to take the long way around. The police have cut off the main roads into Crongton. Your driver will have to take the ring road and approach Crongton from the south – from the Crongton Heath side.'

'That's where I live,' said Boy from the Hills. He had been listening near to the entrance but when he heard the brother mention Crongton Heath, he had joined the rest of us. The man studied Boy from the Hills's hair like gorillas were making out in it. 'Maybe I could get dropped off first,' Boy from the Hills suggested.

'But do you have the fare?' the man asked, searching our eyes. 'As I said, the driver will have to take the long way around so that'll cost ya about twenty-five notes, maybe thirty.'

I could see the panic in Bit's eyes but Saira stepped forward, all confident and cool. 'We have it,' she said. 'Why wouldn't we? We'll all chip in.'

The way Saira said it, Buddha, Jesus and Muhammad would've believed her.

'And that's another thing,' the man said. 'There're six of ya. Ya'll have to wait for Edwin – he's the only driver I've got working tonight who's got a seven-seater. And he won't be back for about an hour – he's on an airport run.'

'An hour!' Bit repeated.

'Take it or leave it,' the man said. He pulled on his roll-up, blew his smoke towards the ceiling and sipped again from his mug. He had a bit of a grin curling his lips as if he loved the situation we were in. His teeth looked like he had been chewing tobacco as well as smoking it. I just didn't like him. 'So ya can either wait for Edwin or start hitch-hiking,' he chuckled. 'Your call.'

'We'll wait for Edwin,' said Saira, outstaring the man. 'No problem – we realise that everything is messed up cos Crongton's going all Gaza.'

'OK,' said the man. 'I'll let him know you're waiting.'

He sucked on his roll-up once more before making another call. Saira still glared at him. Bit and Venetia were swapping frantic looks. Boy from the Hills had disappeared outside into the street again.

'I need some fresh air too,' said Saira. She bounced along the short hallway and I decided to follow her.

Outside, Boy from the Hills was sitting under a lamp post. Saira stood near him with her arms folded.

'Don't fret,' I said to her. 'We'll get back soon enough.'

Saira didn't turn around to face me, instead she continued to look across to the green towards the estate. I wanted to ask her so many questions. *What's Turkey like? Where did you live before coming to Crongton? Is your dad around? How do you feel about a brother who breathes like Darth Vader after hot-toeing for a bus? Would you like to link up? I could come round and stir up something nice and tasty and I'm not just talking about my cooking.*

'Getting home will be the easy part,' Saira finally said.

'Why's that the easy part?' I said.

Saira shrugged. Boy from the Hills looked up, taking an interest.

Saira glanced at me before switching her gaze to the green again. 'I still have to deal with Mum,' she said.

'She doesn't seem that bad,' I said. I wanted to be on point, say the right thing. I sensed Jonah's eyes drilling into my back. 'She's just looking out for you.'

'You don't know her,' she said. 'She thinks we're still in Turkey. *Don't do that! Don't do this! Make sure you're in by early o'clock! Remember your prayers! Don't talk to any boys! Don't let them touch you!* It's a freaking wonder that she allows me to go to school and watch TV after eight.'

'My dad doesn't want boys touching me either,' I joked.

*Did I detect a chuckle? Kiss my knights! If only we were out in different circumstances!*

'My mum might as well live in Timbuktu,' laughed Boy from the Hills. He turned to Saira. 'She's never there to tell me what time I have to be in or what I can and can't watch. At least your mum's *there* for you.'

I thought of my mum. She was no longer *there* for me. Never would be again. That was the cold hard deal. I remembered her funeral. Nesta couldn't watch – he rolled away and Dad had to hot-toe after him. It was the first time I had heard Nesta cry – he was bawling the cemetery down. I'd never forget the sound he made. It came from somewhere deep. I couldn't even look at him. The soil we flung over her coffin was damp, heavy. It took the longest time to dig it out from under my fingernails. I didn't know why but the most important thing for me was to go back to the castle with clean fingers. I didn't think I could ever pot a plant or dig up turf with my bare hands again.

Nesta had sort of taken on Mum's role, checking up on me and stuff; he would go nuts on me if he knew I was stranded in Notre Dame on a Friday night, struggling to get home. Dad wouldn't exactly love it either.

Jonah, Bit and Venetia had all emerged now, and we joined Boy from the Hills on the kerb. Venetia took a small make-up mirror from her rucksack and started checking out the size of her swollen lip. Jonah sat next to Saira, Bit had his eyes on full alert across the green and I was killing the rest of the custard creams.

'Can I ask you something, Saira?' I said.

'As long as you're not planning to sneak into my yard at night and knock on my door,' Saira joked. 'My mum will kill you.'

'No, no, nothing like that,' I replied. 'Just wanna know what that lamb dish was that I sniffed outside your castle.'

'Oh, that's lamb kofta!' Saira smiled.

'Always thinking of his belly!' laughed Bit.

'How do you cook it?' I wanted to know.

'It's quite easy,' Saira explained. 'Mum taught me when I was about seven years old ... Go to the butchers, get some minced lamb – make sure it's off a shoulder joint. Take it home, nice up the lamb with parsley, coriander, paprika, black pepper and whatever else sweets up your tongue. I prefer to roll up the lamb into meatballs but you can shape it any way you like. After that you heat up a frying pan with olive oil, put the lamb in with some onions and peppers on top. Wrap some foil over it, let it cook in its juices. *Bitmis!*'

'What?' I asked. Man! She seemed as much into her cooking as I was.

'*Bitmiş* – done.'

'And what do you serve it with?'

'Pitta bread or rice.' Saira's eyes were alive now. 'I love it to the max!'

I decided then and there that when we got back home – if we ever got back home – I would *make* Dad and Nesta sit down at the dinner table at the same time, and I would feed them both nice big plates of Saira's tasty lamb kofta, and I would let them know that whatever was going down, however bad, we had to be in it together: Mum might be gone but we were still a family.

'Maybe we can come round your yard and sample this lamb thing,' suggested Jonah.

'I would invite you all,' replied Saira, 'but Mum wouldn't allow it. She's too ... she's too ... '

Saira couldn't finish her sentence.

'You can all come around to *my* yard,' offered Boy from the Hills excitedly. 'I can't cook to save my guts but if one of you can – my kitchen's massive, you could wrap on an apron and get your *MasterChef* on. My larder's full of stuff!'

Everyone stared at him in disbelief.

'You've got a *larder*?' Venetia asked.

Boy from the Hills shrugged. 'Yeah, by the side of our kitchen. Mum's always buying stuff – spices and jars of weirdness – but she hardly ever cooks! She only uses the kitchen when she's having a dinner party or something – the people she invites are proper boring, except one guy who was in politics or something. I caught his ass smoking a rocket in our shed! He gave me a game of pool – I beat him nuff times.'

'You've got a garden shed?' asked Venetia. 'And a *pool table*?'

'Yeah,' Boy from the Hills replied. 'My dad keeps his pinball machine, his golf stuff and his, er ... mags in there. It's kind of his crib. He's got a sofa and a TV in there as well. He banned my nosey self from going in, but I've got a spare key and he isn't around much anyway. The pool table's in our basement.'

Everyone was proper shocked apart from me. They all looked at his wild hair again. Jonah couldn't help asking the question they were all thinking.

'Are you rich?'

# 18

# The Bush Cabbie

Before Boy from the Hills could answer Jonah's question, we heard the blast of a car horn. We stood up and an estate car had pulled up beside us. The passenger side window was wound down and a man with a mad beard poked his head out – it looked like there were squirrels mauling his chin, his whiskers were so thick.

'That's not your dad, is it?' whispered Jonah to Boy from the Hills, noticing the hairy similarities.

Boy from the Hills didn't answer. The driver looked at us and smiled. He had one good eye but the other was what some would say was sleepy but I thought of as half-dead. He was wearing a wide cloth hat and a black leather jacket. His eyebrows joined in the middle and looked like a skinny vampire bat. 'Looking for a cab?' he asked.

We glanced at each other.

'I'll charge you less than what they'll charge you in there.' The man indicated with his forehead. 'Rip-offs, they are.'

My mum always told me that when I talk to people I must look in their eyes to show I'm respectful and paying attention. But with this brother I just couldn't help but stare at that jungle below his mouth. Tarzan could've swung in it.

'Where're you going?' he asked.

'South Crong,' answered Saira.

'No problem,' said the man. 'I've got some family living down there – a sister and an uncle. I'll have to go the back way though – they've blocked off the main road.'

'How much are you charging?' I wanted to know.

'Twenty notes will cover it.'

Venetia looked at me like she wanted to hammer rusty nails into my tongue. 'Hold up, hold up,' she said to the one-eyed driver. 'We just need to, er, chat about this.'

Venetia stepped along the street and beckoned us to join her. We huddled in close together just outside the bakery. I was thinking about a vanilla-strawberry special when Saira asked, 'What's the problem? He's gonna take us to South Crong for twenty notes. Ain't that good? We've only gotta find twelve pound something.'

'*Look* at him. He looks well dodgy,' said Venetia. 'He's probably got a few hood-rats hiding in that bush.'

'It has to be said the hair's not too lovely,' remarked Jonah, 'but if he can drive us back to South Crong I don't care if he's got the Masai Mara dangling from his chin. My mum's already gonna terminate me. Then my pops will waste me again after that. Don't wanna wait another hour.'

'We don't even know if he's legal,' put in Bit. 'Did anyone see an ID in his car?'

'I'm not worried about his beard,' Boy from the Hills said. 'I'm fretting more about his eye – can he see when he's driving around corners?'

Silence. I checked everybody's faces. No one seemed to want to step up to the one-eyed taxi driver. I leaned out of the huddle and glanced behind me. The cabbie was drumming his fingers on the steering wheel. He was listening to the news on his car stereo. He glanced at me. I barged back into the huddle.

'I'm *not* stepping into that man's car,' confirmed Venetia. 'No way! Let's wait for the seven-seater.'

'At least let's see if he's got ID,' argued Saira. 'I'm with Jonah – I really don't wanna wait in these ends for another hour if I can help it.'

'Yeah,' Jonah was quick to agree. 'The Hunchbackers might find us again.'

'We haven't got anything left to jack,' I said.

'Our trainers?' replied Jonah. 'Some Gs jack people's trainers – especially if they're brand spanking new. And if we have to step back to South Crong I don't wanna do it with my feet going solo!'

'Trust me, Jonah,' said Bit. 'No one's gonna jack *your* trainers.'

I was getting proper impatient. I just wanted to settle this thing one way or another.

'OK, this ain't getting us anywhere. Wait here,' I said.

I left the huddle and approached the one-eyed driver.

'Er ... have you got any ID? You know, to prove you're a proper cabbie.'

The man grinned again. His teeth looked strangely white in the middle of all the overgrowth. 'I work freelance,' he said. He showed me his driving licence. In his photo his beard was half the length it was now. 'People know me around here. Ask anybody if they know Mr Malloy the bearded cabbie. They'll tell you I can be trusted.'

I looked back at the others. Venetia was shaking her head. Jonah folded his arms and Saira looked impatient. Bit was peering across to the green and Boy from the Hills was staring at the kerb, dodging my gaze. I wondered what Dad would expect me to do. I turned to the cabbie once more. 'Sorry,' I said. 'We don't know you and you haven't got any proper ID.'

The driver checked his rear-view mirror, clicked his indicator and rolled away.

'*Great!*' spat Jonah. 'Freaking-deaking great! Say this Edwin guy doesn't turn up? Say he wants to drive back to his yard now after his airport run? Say he doesn't want to take some South Crong hood-rats in his car? Say the Hunchbackers come hunting for our asses again? What we gonna do then?'

'Enough!' said Venetia. 'The taxi's on its way back from the airport. The guy inside just said so. Stop fretting, we'll get home.'

'We've still only got seven pounds twenty,' Boy from the Hills reminded us.

Boy from the Hills sat down on the pavement again and the rest of us parked ourselves around him. Saira and Venetia took the remaining bourbons. Jonah stood up and went to look at the cupcakes displayed in the window. I decided to follow him. He had a face like someone had kidnapped his PS4.

'Who's pissed in your juice?' I asked.

Jonah looked at me like he wanted to deep-fry my balls in olive oil. '*You!*' he replied.

'What have I done?' I defended myself.

'*I'm* meant to be linking with Saira!' he snapped. '*Me!* Bit was gonna set me up neatly. *That* was the programme! But he hasn't had time to do that, cos you've been hogging her attention all for yourself! I can't get a look-in.'

'I have *not*!' I defended myself. 'What am I supposed to do? Blank her when she chats to me? If you really want to link with her, man up! Step up to her and do your hound thing. See if that gets you anywhere!'

'That's what I wanna do,' argued Jonah, 'but your fat ass has been in the way. *Oh, Saira! How do you cook lamb kofta?!* Stop being a cock-block!'

'You stop being a jealous drooler! It's like I said, if you wanna get to first base with her you're gonna have to fling away your shyness and step up!'

'I ain't shy!'

'And I can fit my butt into drain-pipe jeans!'

I left Jonah stewing in his own juices. Why should he have got a free run at Saira? It wasn't like he had her on lockdown or something. I was sick and tired of my bredrens thinking I'd never score with chicks. Why wouldn't I? And judging by his reaction, Jonah must have thoughts I was a player in this game. I was up for it, so *bring it*!

Venetia was interrogating Boy from the Hills. 'Your mum's a psychologist?' she asked.

'Yeah.' Boy from the Hills nodded. 'And a psycho-analyst, whatever that is. She's got a practice in Ashburton. All sorts of clippety-clop peeps want her to fix up their problems.'

'Why do they need her help if they're rich?' Venetia wanted to know.

Boy from the Hills shrugged. 'Because they can afford it? She sometimes works in Fort Augustus prison – don't know what she does in there, she don't chat about it. She doesn't get paid for that though.'

'So your mum's a psychologist and your dad's a barrister,' I said. 'I'm just gonna spill it out, bruv – why are you even attending South Crong High? Why aren't you in a private school where none of the kids stress about mobile phone credit or the feds stopping them or getting jacked for their tablets? Those schools are way nicer – they've got their own playing fields and stuff. South Crong ain't even got the greenery to fling a shot putt!'

While Boy from the Hills thought about a reply, Jonah returned and sat his sulky ass down.

'I went to a private junior school,' answered Boy from the Hills. 'But Mum said I should go to a normal secondary.'

'Why though?' Venetia wanted to know. 'Why come to South Crong dump? Your mum made a wrong move.'

Again Boy from the Hills took his time to answer. He took in a slow gulp of air and gazed at the dark sky. 'Because ... because my mum wanted me to mix with kids who were not as lucky as me.'

181

'Well, if that's what she wanted, that's what you got,' I said. 'Luck definitely hasn't blessed my ass.'

'Nor mine,' added Bit.

Jonah took it another way. 'So you're saying we're unlucky?' he challenged.

'*No,*' replied Boy from the Hills. 'She said that. I ain't saying diddly-squat about anyone. It's my mum who keeps telling me I'm lucky – every freaking day! *We don't have to worry about heating the house in winter. We never have to scrimp on food. Most kids' parents can't even get a pool table up the stairs of their block let alone afford one . . .* On and on she goes.'

'True. None of us lot got to choose the school we went to, either.'

I nodded. My ass was always going to South Crong High, no questions, no argument; that was how the strawberries crashed into my custard.

'I wanted to go to this girls' school in Ashburton,' admitted Venetia. 'St Cecelia Manor. They get really good results and they've got their own running track. They've even got a proper drama stage with all the lighting and everything. But Dad said it was too far.'

I wondered if Saira had any choice on what school she attended. *Hopefully, when the taxi arrives, I can sit next to her and swap more lyrics – Jonah's gonna have to deal with the competition.*

'No offence or anything,' Saira said to Boy from the Hills, 'but why do you have your hair so wild-like? You look like a gone-wrong Rastaman.'

'And why don't you wear nice garms?' Venetia put in. 'I

remember one school trip where you turned up in your school uniform when you didn't even have to. What's that about?'

Boy from the Hills shrugged. 'No biggie,' he answered.

'Tell us!' Venetia wanted to know. 'I'm not gonna go all Judge Judy on you.'

'None of us will,' I added. 'It . . . it's just well weird that you live in this big castle with rich parents and you come to school looking like you've been sampling food from the bins.'

'I *don't* sink food from dustbins!' Boy from the Hills raised his voice. I could sense he was brewing a head of steam but we still wanted an answer. If he wanted to be a proper bredren so much, he was gonna have to fess up about himself. Lord knows the rest of us had a whole heap of stresses to deal with.

'OK,' Boy from the Hills said as he momentarily closed his eyes. 'Do any of you remember your first day of secondary school?'

I went to the same primary school as Jonah and Bit so we rolled in together on our first day at South Crong High. I remembered it well. Jonah and me took the piss out of Bit's new school uniform cos it was too big for his tiny ass. Apparently, Bit's mum said he'd grow into it. I joked that he'd have to keep growing his bones till he was a hundred and eight if he wanted to fill it out. Whenever Bit moved you could hear a flapping sound so I christened him Flap-Flap. Bit didn't love that so after school that day he rolled back to his castle alone in a long sulk. Another thing I recall was Nesta seemed to be embarrassed by me. I tried to sit next to him at dinner break but he rocked away, telling me not to stalk him, insisting that I get my fat ass out of his face. When I got home, I told Mum, who gave him a proper cuss attack. That same night Nesta gave me a dead arm for snitching on him.

'I remember that week too good,' said Boy from the Hills. 'The weekend before, my mum bought me brand new everything, including a freaking briefcase that I didn't love – I wanted a rucksack like everybody else. She took me to have my hair cut on the Sunday afternoon – I looked like a bloody choir boy!'

'Whose class was you in?' asked Venetia.

'Mr Bolton's,' said Boy from the Hills.

'Wasn't Mad Vincent Chapman in Bolton's class?' said Jonah.

Boy from the Hills nodded. A sad look slapped his face and his eyes stared at the ground.

'I didn't want Mum to drop me off on my first day,' Boy from the Hills resumed. 'I wanted to step it alone. It was bad enough carrying my briefcase – God! I felt like a damn idiot waiting in the playground. Everyone thought I was well weird. I don't know who but some bruv called me *rich kid*. Anyway, after our first assembly, we went off to our form classes.'

'Oh yeah,' said Jonah. 'I remember that. Bit was upset cos he wasn't in my class.'

'Nah, I was raging cos you kept on taking the living piss out of my uniform!' returned Bit.

'Shut up, you two!' Saira said. 'Let him talk. What happened when you got to your classroom?'

Boy from the Hills kept gazing at the concrete pavement like it was the most fascinating thing he'd ever seen. 'I sat in front of Vincent. It was the last seat left. And he was cracking up. When I showed up he lost it. He jumped out of his seat and jacked my briefcase, thought it was all funny. Bolton told him to give it back but he just blanked him.'

'Chapman loved doing that kinda crap – showing off,' I said.

'Yeah,' Venetia nodded. 'He was an idiot.'

'Then he emptied my briefcase all over the floor,' continued Boy from the Hills. 'My sandwiches spilled out, and my pencil case, my protractor, compass, ruler, sharpener, calculator . . . every damn thing I had. It was all new. There was a note from my mum as well – there were little smiley stickers all around it – don't know why she did that. Anyway, Chapman started to kick it all around the classroom, laughing his freaking head off.'

'What did Bolton do?' said Venetia.

'He got him to stop in the end,' he answered, 'but Vincent refused to pick my stuff up or anything – I had to do it, hands and knees. Everyone was still laughing, of course. Can't blame them.'

'Did Chapman get detention?' Jonah asked.

'Nope,' Boy from the Hills replied. 'Cos it was the first day, he got a warning. On the way home I put my stuff in a plastic bag and threw my briefcase into the Crongton stream. I just didn't ever want to go through that crap again.'

'Did you tell your mum?' Saira wanted to know.

'Nope,' he replied. 'She wasn't there when I got home. Nor was Dad. They didn't even know my briefcase was missing till a couple of days later.'

I felt sorry for him. On my first day people were taking the living piss about my weight.

*Tambo the Gut!*

*Dough-Boy!*

*General Tyres!*

Maybe that was why I had Boy from the Hills' back that time. In some strange way, rich or poor, we were kinda similar in many ways.

Suddenly it licked me: I actually liked him. We were proper bredrens. It had taken me this long to realise it.

# 19

## Fireclaw Heath

The time seemed to move along fast as we swapped tales from our first day of school. We discovered that Venetia had a serious crush on a teacher but she wouldn't reveal to us who it was. (Bit didn't love that convo at all . . .) I was about to ask Saira about her first day of school madness, when a black car pulled up outside the cab office and a guy wearing black shoes, blue slacks and a white shirt stepped out of it. He was smooth-shaven *and* he had an ID card around his neck. He looked like someone who nine-to-fived in a bank. He slowed his stride to study our asses as he passed us, then he disappeared into the office.

'He doesn't look so dodgy,' Venetia whispered hopefully.

We all stood up. Half an hour and we'd be back on South Crong streets. Relief kissed my forehead. I hoped Nesta wouldn't be waiting for me with untold questions about where I'd been. It was hard to imagine he wouldn't though. Then there was Dad – he'd probably called from work by now to check up on me. *One way or another I'm gonna get mauled again before this night is over. And this time by my own fam!*

'Give me your budgets,' asked Bit. 'In case he asks for a deposit.'

Everyone gave their coins to Bit except for me cos I couldn't give a dirty cent. I was too ashamed to look anyone in the eye. We waited by the car. The driver reappeared. He studied us hard for a few seconds – I didn't think he loved the look of Boy from the Hills. He smiled at the two girls. 'You're all going South Crongton?' he asked. His eyes then locked on Saira.

'Yep,' answered Bit.

'That's where we dent our pillows,' added Saira.

'You realise that I have to approach from the heath side?' the driver said. 'And it'll be more expensive?'

'Yeah, we know the score,' replied Saira.

'OK,' the driver said. 'Step in.'

We bounced into the car – a people carrier. Bit and Venetia sat in the front. Saira and Jonah went to the middle and Boy from the Hills and me parked in the back. The seats were leather. Boy from the Hills clipped on his safety belt – I didn't bother with mine. A satnav thing rested on the dashboard. Some kinda sickly sweet scent was filling my nostrils – I think it was lavender, but fake lavender, made of chemicals. A tiny pair of British Bulldogs was hanging off the rear-view mirror. The car radio was on. Some chick was reading the weather. The driver switched the ignition and the engine rocked into life.

'My name's Edwin,' said the driver. He grinned at Venetia.

He had straighter teeth than the cabbie with the mad beard. 'Nothing against you guys but it's policy to ask for a deposit if we're driving teenagers, or anybody looking a bit, you know ... different.'

Boy from the Hills cursed under his breath. Edwin's *different* was aimed at him.

Bit dug into his pocket and counted out seven pounds. Blazing tyres! *Will he take our sad deposit or tell us to get our skins out of his car?*

'That's all the loose change we got,' said Bit.

*That's every damn penny we got, you mean.*

Edwin looked a bit dubious, but half-smiled at Venetia as he accepted the cash.

*Thank King Arthur for that!*

'Thanks,' Edwin said. 'Sometimes we have to be careful.'

Edwin indicated, checked his mirrors and pushed through the gears as we cruised along the High Street. It was good to finally leave Notre Dame (though I did want to come back another time when the cake shop was open – just to have a little try ...).

Within a few minutes, open fields, bush and wilderness stretched out on either side of us. It was proper dark, empty. I imagined wolves and bears munching little cute rabbits out there. On the road, cat's eyes replaced lamp posts. The moon was fat and juicy and cast a glow that gave me the living Death Eaters.

Every now and then, I checked Edwin in the rear-view mirror. He kept glancing at Venetia and Saira as well as the road ahead. I thought Venetia had noticed his attention, cos she was sitting as close up to Bit as she could. Saira, though, was too tired to notice anything much. Her eyelids kept drooping down-up, down-up, fighting sleep. Jonah was inching closer and closer, like the hound he was, wanting to make his move.

We cut through Fireclaw Heath in silence. I guessed weariness was licking all of our asses. The satnav glowed bright. The ride was smooth. I spotted a signpost that read *Crongton 7 miles*. The driver was slowing down. He parked up on a grass verge beside some bushes and shook his head.

*Kiss my knights!*

'What's wrong?' asked Bit.

'I feel very uneasy about this,' said Edwin. 'Just the other day I carried three teenagers to North Crongton and they legged it out of my car without paying anything.'

'We've paid a deposit,' said Saira, wide awake now. 'Trust me, we're not gonna split on you.'

'I should've really asked this before I set off, I know, but can you at least show me that you've got the whole fare? It'll be another twenty-three pound.'

Silence. Jonah and Saira fidgeted in their seat. Bit and Venetia looked at each other. I didn't know what to say. Boy from the Hills stared out of the window – there wasn't anything to see.

'I'll pay you a tip if you take me home first,' offered Boy from the Hills, suddenly switching his gaze to the driver. 'I live right next to Crongton Heath, beside Ripcorn Wood.'

'What do you take me for?' snapped Edwin. 'Have I got idiot printed on my forehead?'

'I ain't lying,' said Boy from the Hills. 'I'll give you forty.'

'By the looks of you I don't think you could find another forty pence let alone forty notes,' mocked the driver. 'As soon as I stop by the heath you'll all be gone. What do you take me for?'

'I ain't lying,' Boy from the Hills repeated. 'Forty notes. Trust me, I'm bona fide. My mum will give you it – she should be home by now.'

I didn't know what bona fide meant but I kept my beak sealed cos it was our only chance. Even if my dad was in I didn't know where he would find forty notes from. I knew Jonah had the same worry. If Boy from the Hills pulled this off, I might even ask if I could stay at his yard and play a few games of pool – anything to delay the drama of facing Nesta.

'Head to my yard first,' suggested Venetia to Edwin. 'My dad will give you the rest of the fare – the thirty though, not the forty.'

'You sure?' Edwin wanted confirmation.

'I'm sure.' Venetia nodded. 'My dad will be cool with it.'

Saira flicked Venetia a messed-up glance. She was thinking what I was thinking – Venetia's dad would not be cool with it.

Edwin turned the radio down, stroked his chin, thought about it, glanced at Saira in his rear-view then locked his gaze on Venetia again.

'I just can't trust it,' said Edwin quietly. 'I'm not gonna be played like an idiot again.'

'What do you mean?' asked Venetia.

'What do I mean?' repeated Edwin. 'I don't wanna be chasing shadows in the mud on Crongton Heath!'

'So how're we gonna get back?' Venetia wanted to know.

Silence again. I flexed my toes ready for the trod ahead. I glanced at Boy from the Hills and he was shaking his head. I looked at Saira and she was brewing. The red arrow on the satnav was on pause.

'I'll tell you what I'll do,' said Edwin, leaning towards Venetia. 'I can't drive all six of you back to Crongton – can't trust it – but as there are two girls—'

'But we paid you a deposit!' raged Bit.

'And *this* is as far as that deposit gets you!' snapped back the driver. 'Listen up! I'm prepared to take the two girls home – I don't think they can outrun me – but as for you guys? Sorry.'

*I'd have trouble outrunning a tortoise carrying a laundry bag!* I glanced at Bit. The lid of his kettle was whistling. He was about to say something but Venetia beat him to it.

'You think I'm gonna ride with you and leave my bruvs? We rolled to Notre Dame together and we're going back *together!*'

'That's my offer,' said Edwin, now gazing through the windscreen.

'Are you freaking serious?' challenged Saira, leaning forward. *'Siktir Ian!'*

'So you're some kinda saint for taking the girls home, but leaving four bruvs on Murder Heath is OK?' said Jonah. 'Why don't you just drive us to hell dot com and leave us there?'

Edwin ignored Jonah and grinned again at the girls. Venetia unbuckled her safety belt.

I heard a click to my left. Boy from the Hills was climbing out of the car. He looked at me. 'Are you coming?' he asked. 'Screw this guy.'

'You're a *prick*!' Saira suddenly shouted to Edwin.

Edwin turned around to face her. 'And you've got a foul mouth for a girl with a pretty face,' he said. 'Didn't they teach you any manners where you come from?'

Saira heaved something toxic up from her chest, sucked it through her throat with an ugly noise and launched it into Edwin's face. *Splat!* It wasn't pretty. A mess of spit and the gooey, half-digested remains of chewed bourbons crashed on to Edwin's nose. Some of it dripped off his nostrils. Edwin just sat there unable to move. His eyes Kermit-the-Frogging out of his head, his fingers stretched. He didn't know where to wipe first. I couldn't watch! There was a laugh somewhere at the back of my throat but I thought I'd better keep it on lockdown.

Bit and Venetia scrambled out through the passenger door. Jonah bounced out too. *'Anani avradini sikeyim!'* raged Saira. 'Planning to get us on our own and get all dirty, were you? I'm gonna report you to the feds, you fuc—'

Before Saira could launch a full-on cuss attack, I undid her seat belt, grabbed hold of her arm and yanked her out of the taxi with me. 'Get your ass out of the car!' I screamed at her.

Edwin wiped his face with his shirt sleeve, checked himself in the rear-view mirror.

'Freaking perv!' Saira yelled. 'I hope some brother stomps on your balls and gets biblical with your—'

'Move away from the car,' I stopped Saira's flow.

'Animal!' Edwin shouted at Saira. 'Freaking animal! Go back to where you come from!'

'Go suck on your gearstick, you prick!' she screamed.

He had a look of mad disbelief on his face as he climbed out of his car and slammed shut the passenger doors. He jumped back in. We heard the car locks crash down and watched as Edwin performed a rapid three-point turn, set his bonnet towards Notre Dame and screeched away.

'That was messed up,' remarked Boy from the Hills. 'Anyone get his number plate?'

'Messed up and a half,' added Venetia. 'First three letters were TRX – then there was a number four – didn't catch the rest.'

'Write those down anyway,' I said. 'Can't be too many taxi drivers with those first four digits.'

Venetia took out a pen and a notepad. Man! She was like a proper Hermione.

We watched the red tail lights disappear into the distance, the headlights lighting up the mist in the fields as it went. It rounded a corner and dipped away. The road was still, dark, silent. We were alone.

I turned to Saira. 'You all right?' I asked.

'I am now,' she answered. 'I wonder what that perv had in mind for me and V.'

I didn't want to answer that. I didn't even want to think about it.

We stood in the middle of the road. There was a cool breeze blowing that was nicely refreshing. It made it easier to breathe. The bushes rustled. The man in the moon looked on, probably chuckling at us.

I looked around and wondered out loud if there were any wild animals around here.

'Just deer,' replied Boy from the Hills. 'Maybe foxes too. There could be the odd snake.'

'And badgers,' added Venetia.

'What are badgers?' Saira wanted to know.

'They're sort of a cross between a fox and a deer,' I tried to explain. 'I wouldn't stir-fry one with my runner beans.'

'Whereas fox and deer you'd munch on without thinking,' joked Bit. 'Maybe even a side order of skunk!'

I glanced at Jonah. He wasn't joining in the tease.

'I just can't freaking believe this,' he repeated, still shaking his head. 'Do you know what my mum's gonna do to my ass? What am I gonna tell her? What time are we gonna get back to South Crong now?'

'The quicker we fly,' Boy from the Hills said, 'the quicker we land.'

# 20

# Stepping in the Dark

'Have you lot forgotten that we'll have to trek through North Crong?' Jonah reminded us. 'And there's a riot going on tonight. We don't know what the blazes is going down! South Crong could be burning. And you know what the feds are like. They'll be cuffing people everywhere – even if you're only looking through a shop window or sinking a bottle of water! And we know what the feds do to bruvs in cells.'

'Thank you, Mr Positive,' I said. 'That's made me feel a whole heap better!'

'Then what do you want us to do?' argued Bit. 'Stay here on Fireclaw Heath and fang a badger for breakfast? And I'm sorry I don't have a freaking drone hovering over Crong central to film what's going down!'

'I don't know why I listened to you about going on this mission,' returned Jonah. 'I could've been slayed ten times already, my phone's got jacked and no one's paid a speck of attention to my warnings about what craziness we're stepping into!'

'You *hated* your mobile! If we listened to you, we wouldn't have gone anywhere and Sergio would still have the pics on his phone,' said Bit.

'At what cost?' Jonah asked. 'It was a dumb mission! All for one girl's phone! If it was mine you wouldn't give a shit! But you know what? I came anyway cos you're my bredrens.'

'Calm down, guys,' Venetia pleaded.

'Calm down!' Jonah repeated. 'Are you serious? Because of *you* we're in the middle of nowhere dot com. Buses ain't rolling and ahead of us North Crong hood-rats won't just jack our asses. They're gonna beat us down, shank us and then fling us in some big North Crong bin.'

'You're a happy, clappy, optimistic kinda brother, aren't you?' I said to Jonah. 'And it's not Venetia's fault what happened.'

'And *you* didn't have to come!' Bit raised his voice to Jonah.

'But I did – to help your short butt!' spat back Jonah. 'And do I get a *yeah, Jonah, thanks for having my back*? No, I don't!'

'You should've stayed,' raged Bit. 'All you've done is complain in my ears the whole freaking time!'

'Cool your fever!' I said and stepped between them, arms wide to keep them apart.

'Complain?' repeated Jonah, pushing my hand away. 'Stop playing the hero in front of your girl! Stop going on like you're so freaking innocent! Anybody would think you've never done a major wrong in your life!'

'What do you mean by that?' Bit retaliated. 'Anyway, at least I don't mouse out! Don't think I didn't notice that you were the last one to crash into Sergio's. Even Saira and Venetia rushed in before you!'

Jonah's eyes narrowed. A slap of evil shaped his eyebrows. He seized Bit with a mad stare.

'Yeah,' he said, 'I might complain in your ears too much and I might've been the last one to crash into Sergio's yard ... but at least *I* don't hide guns for Gs.'

*Smoking barrels!* A world of shit had crashed down hard on the parachute, no question about it.

*Jonah, what have you done?*

Bit tried to speak but couldn't.

Tears filled his eyes.

There was a word for what had just happened: *betrayal.*

I don't know how long the silence went on.

Venetia stared at Bit, aghast.

Bit glared out Jonah – fury had taken over.

The barbarians were approaching the castle.

Suddenly, Jonah knew the dark side was coming. He backed away a step, put his hands up in anticipation, and before I could say or do anything, Bit let out a great roar and charged at Jonah, knocking him clean over.

Bit punched. He punched and punched and swore like a South Crong rapper.

'Stop it!' screamed Saira. 'Stop it!'

I managed to get my arms around Bit's waist and I dragged his ass away. We fell on the grass verge. He was still booting and wriggling, trying to get free. I didn't think he meant it but he headbutted me in the chin, trapping my tongue between my teeth. Pain filled my whole mouth and throat. Bit was small but he had nuff energy!

'I'm gonna kill him!' he raged. 'Him and his big mouth! I'm gonna mess him up bad!'

I tightened my grip. Boy from the Hills hauled Jonah away in the opposite direction.

I couldn't believe it! My two best bredrens wanting to savage each other. Why did Jonah have to go there? He could've said anything else – *anything*. But the gun was our secret. We had promised – we had sworn months ago – never to leak it. It was a soldier thing. I think it had kept us as tight as we were.

But with one crazy impulsive outburst, all that trust was dust. And if I'd learned one thing from watching Dad and Nesta since Mum died, it was that without trust any relationship could melt like a Cadbury's on a grill.

Bit kept struggling, but my weight and grip was beginning to tire him out. I could feel him breathing heavy. His cheeks were wet with tears. My face was leaking sweat.

'Let me go!' yelled Bit. 'I'm not gonna maul him. Get your fat ass off me!'

I released my hold gently and wearily got up to my feet. Bit was still puffing hard. For a second I thought he was gonna have an asthma attack. I didn't feel so glorious either – my chest was tight and I felt like it was about to go wrong. Thankfully he didn't find a second boost – no way did I have the energy to go another round.

I was resting my hands on my knees, trying to get my

breathing under control, when I heard soft footsteps. I looked up to see Saira. I stepped towards her. 'Your mouth,' she said. 'You're spilling blood.' She gave me one of her pocket tissues. I dabbed my tongue. It stung like crazy. I tried not to let Saira see I was suffering. I don't think she bought it.

Bit was still sitting on the ground, head down. Venetia was slowly walking towards him. Her arms were folded. Out of the corner of my eye, I spotted Boy from the Hills a little distance away with Jonah, chatting calmly to him. Saira watched with me watching them.

Venetia was standing directly over Bit. Bit leaned back, like he was expecting a cuss attack from his mum.

'I . . . I was gonna fess up,' he said. 'It was so messed up, V. In the end my sis threw the thing away . . . '

Venetia didn't say a word. Her eyes gas-ringed into him. Everyone knew what this was about: Colette.

Bit tried to explain. 'I know I messed up. *Big* time. Manjaro was blackmailing me—'

'You knew how I feel about Gs carrying arms and blazing up innocent people,' Venetia said, her tone low. Another pause. Her chest heaved up and down with the mad rage that was downloading inside of her.

'You *knew*!' Venetia repeated.

Bit's eyes flooded over. He loved Venetia to the core, but he'd never be able to undo this badness and make it up to her. It was proper hard to watch.

Saira was nibbling her fingers. Boy from the Hills was sitting on the side of the road with Jonah. Jonah was staring at the ground, willing it to swallow him whole.

I wished I knew what to say. Something. Anything.

Venetia turned to me, her eyes wet, red-raw and burning with betrayal. '*You* knew too, McKay? And *don't* lie to me.'

I backed away a step.

'Did you know too?!' Venetia shouted.

I took another stride back. I nodded.

Venetia turned to Jonah. 'And *you* too? You all freaking knew?'

'I . . . I didn't,' managed Boy from the Hills. 'I didn't have a clue.'

Jonah didn't respond. At that moment he looked more scared of Venetia than of all the hood-rats in North Crong.

'It wasn't all Bit's fault—' I said.

'Keep your tongue on lock!' Venetia warned me. She turned to Bit again. 'I told you *everything.* How I helped Collette's mum dress her so she would look nice in her coffin. How her mum still can't get over it. How around four o'clock in the afternoon she still expects Collette to come bouncing through her gates from school.'

'I know,' said Bit.

Venetia stepped closer to Bit, bent down, brought her face to his. 'Her mum can't even throw away her clothes – *they're still in her wardrobe!* Her school books are still in her bag in her bedroom. A gun, Bit? Serious? Are you one of them waste-life brothers who think they're hard core cos they're packed with guns? Collette was *killed* by one of them.'

'I'm so sorry,' Bit managed. 'I wanted to do the right thing. I know I fuc—'

'You knew what my fam went through. Why do you think

their faith is so important to them? I trusted you, I let you in; you saw live and direct what guns do to people and all that while you were ... You hid a gun for a G, Bit. And you let me believe you were all shiny – you're as grimy and wolf-hearted as the rest of them!'

'I'm not! If you just give me a chance to explain. I was—'

'*Don't chat to me!*' screamed Venetia. 'Don't pollute my freaking eyesight!'

Venetia turned around and stepped up to Saira. Saira gave her a hug. Bit didn't get up. I almost leaked tears with him. I stepped up to him, sat down and I placed my hand on his shoulder. I gave him a squeeze. He looked away.

Time passed. After a while, Bit stopped crying but he was totally beaten down. 'I'll be all right,' he said. 'Go on, you guys step on. I'll catch up with you later – maybe tomorrow maybe ... or sometime.'

'What are you talking about, bruv?' I said. 'I'm not leaving your ass here.'

'I'm not stepping anywhere,' said Bit. The tears started again. 'Just leave me alone.'

'Are you freaking serious? There's a peckish fox out there who'll look on your hide and see supper, with leftovers for brekkie!'

Bit didn't love my attempt at humour. I decided to leave him be for a while, and go check the vibes with Jonah and Boy from the Hills.

Jonah was shaking his head like he wanted to unscrew it from his neck. 'Tell him I'm sorry,' he said. 'The situation just got to me. I didn't mean to spill. Tell him ...'

*'Why?'* I asked him. 'What the freak did you put in your pumpkin juice today? Why?'

Jonah didn't reply. He stared at his trainers.

'When the shit has finally flushed down you should tell him sorry yourself,' I told Jonah. 'It's better that it comes from you.'

Jonah nodded but still wouldn't look at me.

'Is it true?' Boy from the Hills asked. Disbelief slapped his face. 'Bit hid a gun for Manjaro? *Bit?* Can't believe it! Does he know where Manjaro's hiding out?'

I thought about it. Boy from the Hills was one of us now. I wanted to trust him – perhaps, after what had just gone down, I needed to trust him.

'Of course he doesn't know! It was a messed-up situation. Manjaro was linking with Elaine, Bit's sister. They had a baby together. It's well complicated.'

Boy from the Hills's eyes widened.

I glanced behind me. A car was approaching. Its headlights showed Bit slumped on the ground. Saira was still hugging Venetia. For a moment I was thinking of hitching for a lift but thought better of it – for a start there were too many of us, and what would happen if Bit, Jonah and V kicked off again? The car raced by. Red tail lights faded into the distance. All was quiet.

'Look, this is mental and all – but we still have to get back,' said Boy from the Hills.

He wasn't wrong. We had to do a what's-her-name from *Frozen* and let go what just happened. We had to return to South Crong in one piece and as a crew, the way we started out. We could deal with the fallout and drama tomorrow morning. *But not now.* I downloaded some steel into my spine.

'Stay here,' I told Jonah and Boy from the Hills. 'Don't step off on your own. I'm gonna swap some lyrics with Venetia.'

'You sure?' asked Boy from the Hills. 'She's still simmering.'

'Yeah,' I agreed. 'She's switched big time but we have to step home *together.*'

I stepped up to Venetia and Saira. They didn't notice me at first so I cleared my throat. Venetia looked up. Her face was damp, her eyes full of pain. I wondered if that was all down to Bit. I turned to Saira. 'Can . . . can I have a few lyrics with her?'

Saira just glanced at Venetia who thought about it and then nodded. We both watched Saira walk away. Venetia wiped her face with her fingers.

'He didn't mean to hurt you,' I started.

Venetia gave no response. She glanced up at the moon.

'It was a freaked-up situation, you know. With Manjaro and his sis,' I continued. 'Bit's head wasn't thinking right. Believe me. He knows he done a major wrong. When Manjaro charged through Bit's gates, he slammed his gran into the wall – she could've died. Bit too. Manjaro had proper flipped. You saw her yourself at the hospital. On the night it all happened, Manjaro was hunting Bit down cos he didn't give the gun back – Bit *wanted* to fling it away. That's the stone-cold deal – trust me on that. In the end he *did* the right thing. And even now, six months later, he's still fretting buckets about bumping into Manjaro. He could've moved, but he and his fam wanted to stay. They didn't wanna lose touch with their friends.'

She was listening, I could tell.

'He's been sweet on you since Year 7. It was Bit who first noticed you doing dance after school in the gym. Who do you think he watches when we have athletics meets? He doesn't just come to see my big self flinging the shot putt. And yeah, he might shout on Jonah tearing up the track, but he really comes to watch *you*! Don't even say you haven't noticed the way he bounces up and down when you win a race? You know I'm not lying.'

Venetia's eyes flickered briefly towards me – I took it as a sign I was getting somewhere.

'Me and Jonah took the living piss out of him cos he wouldn't step up and say a damn word to you until Year 10. Not even a shy hello or a sweet morning.'

Again, Venetia made a slight movement. I guessed my lyrics were finally getting through and I wasn't talking a word of a lie.

'It crushed him when he found out about you and Sergio,' I went on. 'It cut him up bad – like his heart got dunked in a bath full of piranha fish. It was all he ever talked about. He had it bad.'

Venetia turned towards me. 'I didn't mean to hurt him,' she said. 'At first I didn't know he was on me like that.'

'Check out what he done tonight,' I said. 'To be honest, Jonah and me weren't really up for this mission, not to the max anyway. But Bit wouldn't let it drop. With my own eyes I saw Bit rush into Sergio's castle and try to beat down a bruv who's twice the size of him. A bruv who did you wrong and disrespected you. Bit's no Nelson Mandela – and he definitely owes you a big sorry – but he'd never do anything to hurt you or shame you in public. Not like Sergio.'

Venetia thought about it and nodded.

'He hated to see you stressing out cos of those pics. Don't hate him for his mad, stupid mistake.'

'I don't hate him,' said Venetia. 'Just disappointed in him. He's on point with so many things but this is just so off-key. How could he hide a gun for Manjaro? What was he thinking?'

'We all mess up,' I answered.

'I suppose we do ... You're not wrong – I shouldn't have got involved with Sergio in the first place. I ... can't believe I let him—'

'Hear me on this one,' I cut in. '*He's blatantly* in the wrong for threatening you with the pics. Man could get locked up for that shit.'

'I don't think I was ready for ... I wasn't thinking right,' V admitted. 'I don't think I've been thinking right since Colette ...'

'I know what it's like,' I said to Venetia.

'Know what's like?' Venetia replied.

'Losing someone close,' I said.

Long after Mum's funeral, I still expected her to be in the kitchen when I came home from school, stirring up something tongue-pleasing in her mango-jackfruit apron. She would smile at me as I walked in and then she would talk to me, just chatter away, and it was always so easy and natural. *'Have you got any homework, McKay? And fix up your bedroom before dinner! But before you do that, give your mother a kiss on the cheek!'*

After dinner she wouldn't rest until everything was washed up in the sink. Then she'd watch some TV – she was getting into this American series called *Scandal* – Dad had bought her the box set. She wouldn't go to bed without checking in on me first. I would feel a kiss on my forehead. Nesta always said he was too old for that – but I never once heard him brushing Mum from his room.

'It must've been terrible losing your mum,' Venetia said, soft and compassionate. She took a step towards me and gave me a hug – I hoped she didn't smell my leaky armpits. 'I wish we could've all done something to make you feel better.'

I stepped away from Venetia's embrace. We were raised differently but I felt we understood each other.

'Bit and his fam helped me a lot during that time,' I said. 'My dad was having issues. You knew about his breakdown, right?'

'Yeah, I heard,' she replied. 'Bit said something about it. There was nuff of us really feeling for you but we didn't know what to say.'

'Bit had my back, though,' I said. 'He even let me sleep in his bed while he crashed on the couch.'

'He's good like that,' Venetia admitted.

I felt confident enough to call her V now.

'Listen, V. I've still got the scars, sis. After a while people stop slapping on your drawbridge asking if everything's all right. And they finally stop asking if there's anything they can do.'

'I hear that, McKay.' Venetia nodded. 'I went through the same thing.'

'You collect all the *Sorry About Your Loss* cards and put them in a box. Then after a while you wanna tear them all up, cos you can't bear to read the messages. I even wanted to burn them.'

Venetia was now giving me her attention to the max. Her eyes were swimming. The ugly truth was I felt good offloading all the crap inside me.

'But you can't do squat. You can't fling the damn thing away, however much you want to,' I continued. 'You go back to school and everything is supposed to get back to normal, but the box is always there – just like the pain's always there. So, it's not normal, it's never gonna feel normal.'

'What do you mean?' Venetia asked. She wiped her face again and studied her fingertips.

'Well, I guess I mean it's never the same again,' I answered. 'Things go on, because they have to. But there's someone missing now. Someone you will keep on missing in your life for weeks, months . . . years. If you love someone for real it never goes away.'

Venetia thought about what I said. She nodded. She managed a quarter-smile.

'Chat to Bit,' I advised her. 'His mum, sis and gran will crush my bones if I leave him to peckish bears who haven't had their porridge.'

Finally, I got a laugh out of her.


Bit was sitting with his knees held against his chest. His arms were wrapped around his shins and his eyes were shut. Venetia slowly rolled up to him in that cool way of hers – like an Olympic gymnast stepping up to perform her floor exercise. She sat down beside him and rested her head on his shoulder. Bit opened his eyes. Nothing was said.

I thought I'd better leave them to it and bounced up to Saira, Jonah and Boy from the Hills.

'Are they gonna be OK?' Jonah wanted to know.

'I don't know,' I replied. 'Let's hope so.'

# 21

# Saira's Dad

We watched and listened to Bit and Venetia settling their differences for about twenty minutes or so. Sometimes Bit stood up to make a point and at other times Venetia would roll away, think about something and return for another round. Sergio's, Collette's and Manjaro's names were heard now and again.

'Which way will the crap bomb the bathtub?' I asked Saira.

'Not sure,' she replied. 'She's sweet on Bit but losing her cousin really messed V up.'

'Has she ever had counselling?' I asked.

'Don't think so,' replied Saira.

I was offered counselling after Mum died. I turned it down. I could barely chat to Nesta or Dad let alone a stranger. And if news leaked out that you'd visited the school counsellor, bruvs and sisters would laugh at you. It was cold but that was the way it was in Crongton.

'What do you think the time is?' asked Boy from the Hills.

'About midnight,' Jonah guessed. These were the first words he had said for a while. Remorse still stroked his face.

'V was there when Collette got blazed, you know,' said Saira. 'People forget that. One second, they were both queuing up to buy tickets for a concert, the next second Collette caught a stray bullet to her head. The other day, we were watching a DVD, and V freaked out when someone on screen fired a gun. It's the sound that gets to her. If you're thinking about asking her to watch the fireworks – don't even go there.'

The reality of it all stopped our flow. Silence. Collette's face downloaded into my visual memory. Cute girl. Always smiling. She and Venetia looked alike. I used to see them together in Dagthorn's shop reading the sports and celebrity mags. Collette was always sucking something minty.

I wondered if we all could've done more to help Venetia through that trauma.

Bit and Venetia finally rolled towards us. They weren't holding hands.

'You two good?' Saira wanted to know.

'OK for now,' answered Venetia – she clearly wasn't finished with Bit yet!

'Bit?' I asked. 'Everything good?'

Bit's nod wasn't convincing. He looked at Jonah. Jonah stared into the far distance. I couldn't bear to even consider trying to get them two back on the level – it would just have to wait.

'Everyone ready for the trek home?' asked Boy from the Hills. 'I reckon it's about three K to the Crong circular. We're gonna have to decide whether to roll through North Crong or take the long way around.'

'Isn't there a shortcut?' Saira wanted to know.

'The North Crong estate is *big*,' said Bit. 'But if we take the long way, the birds will be sinking their worms for brekkie before we reach back to our yards.'

'Can we decide when we reach the circular?' I suggested. 'Let's get there first.'

We set off. There wasn't any pavement so we had to step on the grass verge. We rolled in single file. Bit in front, Boy from the Hills second, me next, Venetia behind me, Saira and Jonah. Now and again a car or a truck drove by. Chill began to brush my cheeks. I could see the mist of everyone's breath in the air. It reminded me of Mum's power walks in Crongton Park. She liked to get her walking on in the winter. She had all the garms and apps and she would check her stopwatch every fifty steps or so. For some mad reason I'd volunteer to go with her.

'I think if we see a truck or something we should thumb for a lift,' suggested Boy from the Hills after a while. 'You never know, someone might stop and pick us up.'

'That's a big no!' snapped Saira. 'You think I'm gonna jump into another stranger's car or truck after what happened tonight? Delete that!'

We trod on for another half an hour or so. Eventually, we saw street lights in the distance which gave us an energy boost. We stepped up that bit quicker and we all made out the row of castles on the left side of the road. Relief blessed me as we marched under the first street light.

There was a tense silence between us. I decided to break

it. I bounced up to Saira. 'Saira, you always chat about your mum – what about your dad?'

The question caught Saira by surprise. She stopped in her tracks and gave me a messed-up look. She then stared at her trainers for a couple of seconds before gripping me with a hard gaze. 'He's missing,' she finally answered.

'Missing?' I repeated.

Everyone stopped. Venetia put a supportive arm around Saira's shoulders. Saira dropped her gaze to the ground. 'Let it go,' Venetia told me.

'Nah,' said Saira. 'It's all right. I can deal with it.'

Four cars flashed by before Saira looked up again. She searched all our eyes before she spoke.

'I might as well give you the score,' she started. She took in a deep breath and cleared her throat. A deep sadness filled her eyes. 'Our fam lived in Urfa, a town near the Syrian border. Nice place . . . or used to be. Dad had his own shop where he used to sell everyday stuff and he had put a few tables outside where people could sit down and drink coffee or smoke their shish on the pavement. Everyone knew us. Sometimes Dad would let me serve the customers their drinks on a Saturday afternoon.'

'You don't have to do this,' said Venetia, stroking Saira's back.

'It's OK, V,' Saira replied. 'I know all about you guys.'

We sat down on the grass verge with our backs to the hedgerows. It wasn't the time to admit it, but I was well happy for the rest. My legs were really feeling the miles. Bit parked next to Venetia.

'I was ten when I first noticed that Dad was sometimes missing from our yard at night,' Saira continued. 'I would creep into Mum and Dad's room and he wasn't there. On other nights I would wake up at stupid o'clock in the morning cos I heard arguing. I would get up and see Dad raging with a world of other men around our dinner table. They all looked *muhim* – proper serious. Mum would be in the kitchen making them snacks and hot drinks. They would smoke up the place, cuss and argue and smoke some more. I'd never see them during the day. Dad never spoke about it and if I asked Mum she told me to keep my tongue on lock. It was proper confusing.'

'What were they raging about?' Jonah wanted to know.

'Syria,' Saira revealed. 'You can't imagine the stuff that was going down there. Warring, blazing, rape, kidnapping, beatings, people trying to escape . . . It seemed like every other day, someone my dad knew was killed . . . I think he wanted to help the fam.'

'Sounds like a Friday night in Crongton,' I joked.

'McKay!' Venetia raged. 'This ain't funny!'

'You're not wrong!' Jonah agreed. 'It's not funny.'

I thought it was a valid joke. Nesta would sometimes bounce into my dungeon at night and spill to me all the beefs and issues that were going down between Crongton Gs. *Jonah's just trying to make me look bad in front of Saira. He needs a kuff.*

Saira paused. 'Soon after the arguments, Dad went missing,' she continued. 'No one knew where he went or they didn't wanna spill to us if they did. Our shop windows were blitzed. People stopped coming to buy things. In the end we had to shut down. People raged at me and threatened Mum on the streets.'

'Man. It must've been well rough,' I said.

'It was.' Saira nodded. 'In them days we had to rely on handouts from friends and fam. Life became a hard-lick. Mum was stressed to the max. She had to do what little work she could find. I had to look after my little bro and sister – that's when I learned to cook. I couldn't go school any more either. Didn't even have time to say goodbye to friends.'

'How ... how did you get to this country?' Jonah asked.

'That's a long one,' she said. 'Some man turned up at our yard one day looking well nervous. He had a gun hidden underneath his garms. He told Mum that we'd better leave Urfa. I asked him about Dad but he wouldn't spill a word. Mum was asked nuff questions but in the end he gave her a wad of money and then split. Two nights later we left for Ankara, where we have relatives – we're one of them Turkish fams that have a world of aunts, uncles, second and third cousins in Germany, Sweden and all over the damn place. We spent a week in Ankara before going to Istanbul.'

'Where's that?' Jonah wanted to know.

'One of Turkey's biggest cities,' Saira answered. 'The carpet to the West, Mum called it. You'd love it there. I did. When James Bond is hunting that bad brother on a motorbike in *Skyfall* you can just about see my uncle for half a second standing outside the Grand Bazaar.'

'That's a *sick* scene,' said Bit, 'especially when Bond chases the bad guy over the rooftops.'

'Mum was interviewed nuff times by people at the British Embassy,' Saira went on. 'One afternoon she came home with a heap of papers in her hands. She was bawling her eyes out but she was well happy. '

'So you got your visas and everything?' Boy from the Hills guessed.

Saira nodded. 'I wasn't too happy about leaving. I really miss Istanbul. From where we lived I could see the blue glow from the Blue Mosque at night – *guzel!* In the summer I used to watch the tourists queuing up to get into the Hagia Sophia and wonder what lands they came from. I used to take the tram after school to watch the big boats roll in and out from the bridge near the river. If there weren't any boats around I'd step into the tourist shop and look at all the postcards. Mum would get cradazy with me for coming home late but I always believed that if I waited long enough my dad would bounce off one of those boats ... Turns out I was wrong.'

'So you still don't know what happened to him?' I asked.

Saira shook her head. Her eyes flooded over. 'Mum won't say it, but I think he's dead.'

I felt bad for asking the question. We could hear birds singing in a nearby tree. I liked to think they were singing about Saira's dad. I liked to think they were chirping about my mum and Colette, too.

'Sometimes, if there wasn't anyone sitting down outside our shop, Dad would brew me an apple tea.' Saira wiped her eyes. 'He would sit down with me and teach me English and show me maps of the world from an old atlas he had. I miss those days.'

I couldn't help but think of Mum. I had to go to war with the tears filling up behind my eyes.

Venetia squeezed Saira's shoulder and Bit stood up. 'I can't imagine what it's been like for you, Saira, but I had a liccle dose of it when my dad left Crong with my liccle sis, Stefanie. At least I see them at some weekends and school holidays.'

'Yeah, I hear that.' Saira nodded. She got up to her feet and dusted herself down. 'We should get our asses moving again. You guys don't wanna park here listening to my sad woes 'til your butt goes numb.'

'I hope your dad turns up someday,' said Jonah. 'You never know . . .'

Tears dripped down Saira's cheeks again. 'So do I,' she said. 'But it won't happen.'

I wanted to give Saira a hug but she might've cussed me out – I didn't want to push it.

We crossed the road to step on the pavement.

Dad had his issues – he had a breakdown after Mum passed – but at least he hadn't left my castle never to return. Thank King Arthur for that.

## 22

# Madame North Leg and
# Queen Belly Blender

It was more built up now and we could see the traffic lights of the Crong circular ahead of us. I imagined falling asleep on a plush L-shaped sofa with a world of cushions supporting my head. In my fantasy, a fit, ripe nurse treated my wounded knees and sore tongue with nuff love and smiles.

We were crossing another street when I thought I heard something – it deleted the nice vision I had.

'What's that?' wondered Venetia.

We all stopped to tune in our ears.

'Music!' said Saira. 'That's definitely music. Someone's having a rave.'

'Let them rave,' said Boy from the Hills. 'The Crong circular is only about fifteen minutes away – you can see the traffic lights.'

'Don't we wanna have some nice vibes for once on this mad night?' suggested Saira. 'Let's check it out.'

We all looked at each other.

'It's worth a try,' Jonah said. 'Look, let's face it – I don't wanna step through North Crong ends and I'm guessing none of you guys are mad keen on it either. The night's been a drama overload as it is. I just wanna rest up somewhere and chill my toes.'

'Say it's not a party,' I said. 'It might be someone buzzing from smoking rockets, playing their music too damn loud.'

'Even if it's a smoked-out brother playing his tunes it'll only take us a few minutes to find out,' Venetia said.

'And then we'll step back on course,' added Saira.

'Are you cool with this?' Boy from the Hills asked, looking at me.

My head was saying 'roll on home' but my curiosity was chirping me to check out where the music was coming from.

'What do I have to do? Show you the blisters on my feet?' said Saira. 'Whatever we decide I need to chillax for a bit.'

That made up my mind. I guessed Saira wanted something to distract her thoughts from her missing dad.

I took the lead and the others followed along behind me. The castles on this street were smaller than the ones we had passed before and there weren't any front gardens. Ahead of us we could make out a few figures standing outside a four-storey slab. A stomping bassline rocked the road.

'Have you ever been down these ends before?' I asked Bit.

'Nope,' he said. 'I think my dad's girlfriend had friends around here though.'

'Remember,' Boy from the Hills warned. 'Our mission is to get back to our ends *safely*.'

By the time we reached the slab, everyone had gone inside apart from three brothers and a chick smoking rockets in a parked car – it looked too expensive to be owned by one of them. They were giggling like the world's funniest comic was in there busting jokes on them. A brother started revving a motorbike. For a second my heart jumped as I thought it might be Sergio, come to have his revenge. But it wasn't him.

Dirty paper plates littered the ground. The tunes were coming from an upstairs room. This was definitely a rave. We could hear the cheers, shouts and curses as silhouetted figures danced by the windows.

'Is this a good idea?' said Jonah.

'Jonah!' Saira mocked. 'For just a minute can you drop some backbone into your pumpkin juice!'

I didn't wanna mouse out so I kept quiet. I glanced at Bit and his tongue was on lock too. The drawbridge to the slab was being kept open by a broken brick. I could smell pork and chicken. That was it – my hard drive may have been unsure, but my belly wanted to check out the food.

'Let's go up,' said Saira.

Boy from the Hills looked at her like she asked him to dance 'Gangnam Style' butt naked. 'I'm not bouncing into that party in my school uniform!' he said. 'I'll look like a damn idiot!'

'We're not gonna be there for long,' argued Saira. 'Let's just see what's going down for a liccle while. Don't block our flow.'

'But I'll look like I haven't changed my garms since school,' protested Boy from the Hills.

'But you haven't changed your garms since school,' said Jonah.

Boy from the Hills thought about it. 'Shouldn't one of us stay down here and keep watch or something?'

'Best to stay together,' Venetia advised.

'OK.' Boy from the Hills nodded. 'I'll come, but if anyone starts laughing at my skin I'm out of there.'

'What's a matter with you?' Saira said to Boy from the Hills. 'Haven't you ever been to a rave before?'

'No,' Boy from the Hills said. 'The last party I went to was my tenth birthday and Mum forced me to wear a freaking paper hat! I didn't even know half of the kids who were there! The cake was all good though.'

My shameful dose was I had never stepped into a rave and I didn't think Bit or Jonah had either.

Saira led us. In a weird way, we were alike. I tended to want a dose of fun after I talked about Mum – I just wanted to smile again rather than be frozen on sad dot com.

Saira pushed through the heavy door and bounced up the concrete steps. My heart started smacking against my ribcage but at the same time excitement shot through my veins. The smell of chicken and pork was teasing me forward. On the second floor landing a few bros and chicks were standing outside a flat smoking cigarettes and weed, and sinking liquor from paper cups. I guessed they were sixteen or seventeen, maybe one or two were eighteen. I didn't recognise any of them. The guys were casually dressed in checked shirts, jeans and name-brand trainers. The chicks were garmed in jeans, T-shirts, short-sleeve jackets and whole paintbox's worth of make-up. The music made the entire slab vibrate.

I couldn't believe how thirsty I was.

'I could drain a big-ass bottle of Coke,' I said. 'Even water would work.'

Bit nodded. 'Me too.'

'I wonder if they've got any wine,' said Venetia.

We all gave Venetia a messed-up look.

'What?' she said. 'My fam sink red wine every Sunday with our dinner before we say Grace. What's wrong with that?'

'We don't know whose yard this is? It could be the neighbourhood G,' said Jonah.

'Stop being a drama king,' said Saira. 'Chillax yourself! Look at it like this – we're not gonna get a drink parked outside here, are we?'

'I dunno,' said Jonah.

'Look, if there's a riot going on, any bruv with any swagger's gonna be carrying their new goods home or playing tag with the feds. Come on, guys! When are we gonna get another chance of going to a rave? Come on. It'll be the bomb!'

Saira was well convincing and, to be honest, I didn't think anyone wanted to say no after what she'd told us about her dad.

Saira and Venetia linked arms and headed for the door.

The bros and sisters around us seemed friendly enough. One of the chicks smiled at me. The drawbridge was open. The brother standing next to it seemed a bit liquor-bombed.

Me, Bit, Jonah and Boy from the Hills shrugged and followed the girls.

Inside, the crowd was alive. People were bubbling, laughing and joking. Some were busting moves. I tried to strut like a cool brother. Wasn't sure if my bounce worked. Jonah's definitely didn't. I glanced behind and Boy from the Hills was still stepping in his Farmer Giles kinda way. At least he wasn't being fake.

'Is it all right if we go in?' asked Saira to the bouncer.

'The more the merrier,' he said before tipping the rest of his liquor down his throat. He definitely liked Saira. He started singing. '"Consider yourself one of us! Consider yourself, part of the family!" So, Your Royal Ripeness! You wanna lay down your digits so we can link up somewhere nice? My block ain't too far from here.'

Saira ignored him. We breezed in. The merry bouncer flung off his rejection and carried on singing behind us.

'"I've taken to you, so, strong! It's clear, we're, gonna get along!"'

Ravers were standing along the walls draining drinks or sinking chicken patties. The buzz of chilled conversation flowed neatly. Balloons kissed the ceiling. Paper chains blessed the walls. Dance music blitzed our ears. We reached a kitchen to our right. The chicks inside had gold and silver glitter on their faces shaped into hearts. They also showed off the world's longest eyelashes. Bright flowers niced up their hair. Lipstick of all colours sexed up their mouths. I swear I saw Jonah's tongue escape from his jaws. (And I didn't know where to ogle first, myself.) They were serving drinks, patties

and sausages in buttered rolls. A mountain of chocolate muffins sat on the kitchen table. My taste buds demanded some
action. And then I remembered our special assembly. Sweet
sauces!

'Welcome to the party!' a brother hollered in my ear. He
looked at Boy from the Hills in his school uniform. 'Love it!
Love it!'

I ignored him and tweeted into Bit's ear. 'Are you thinking
what I'm thinking?'

'Yep,' Bit replied. 'They're serving the food jacked from our
school kitchen.'

'What do we do?' asked Venetia. 'The feds are on the case,
you know. I ain't getting my backside slandered cos of this.'

'Me either,' added Jonah.

'You think you're the only ones?' said Bit.

Saira shrugged. 'Why are you fretting? We're not involved.
We didn't swipe any food. What have we got to fret about?
Let's sample a pattie each, ask someone if we can use their
phone and bounce out.'

Whatever worries I had, I wasn't gonna say no to a chicken
pattie. Saira caught the attention of one of the chicks in the
kitchen. 'Can we have drinks and a pattie each?' she asked.

'Sure. What would you like?' the chick asked.

It was weird. No one had asked us who we were yet they
were serving us no questions, like we'd been invited. Jonah,
Bit and me had a Coke, Boy from the Hills had an orange
juice while Saira asked for an apple juice. Venetia's eyes grew
large as she was served her sparkling wine. We each had a
chicken pattie.

The main noise was coming from the front room. The castle was jam-packed but we just about managed to squeeze our way to where all the drama was taking place. Rolling in with two pretty girls was a definite advantage – brothers gave us space. When we got there, two fit chicks, dressed in black leggings, name-brand trainers, half-cut vests and black head-bands were preparing to have a dance-off. Sweat glistened from their abs. Glow bangles with LED lights glammed up their ankles and gold jewellery sparkled in their belly buttons. A brother was in a corner playing music from a laptop linked up to speakers. There was no other furniture. The windows were opened wide. Ravers surrounded the dancers with their fists pumping the air, chanting on their favourite. Others were clapping and banging the walls.

'Go, North Leg! Go, North Leg! Go, North Leg!' chanted one set of fans.

'Go, Belly Blender! Go, Belly Blender! Go, Belly Blender!' yelled the other supporters.

I sampled my snack while my eyes feasted on the scene. (The chicken pattie was a dose overcooked but my belly wasn't grumping.)

The music paused. The two chicks sized each other up from scalp to liccle toe like Rocky and Apollo Creed. The sound system kicked in again. The bassline nearly knocked my ass over. The rave queens then performed some mad body-popping, belly-churning, waist-crunching, leg-twist-ing, high-kicking, shoulder-juggling moves – they were kick-ass incredible. Boy from the Hills looked like he had stepped into another world – I didn't think they had raves like this in

Ripcorn Wood. They didn't even have them like this in South Crong – not that I knew of anyway. Bless a fit butt! If this was what I would be able to sample on the regular when I reached sixteen, then that birthday couldn't come rapid enough.

'Go, North Leg! Go, North Leg! Go, North Leg!'

'Go, Belly Blender! Go, Belly Blender! Go, Belly Blender!'

The rhythm of the bass forced me to nod my head. My left foot started to bounce. Dance-heads pounded the walls. Saira and Venetia tapped their feet. Bit looked on mesmerised as Jonah's tongue dangled out another inch.

The dance-off finished to a mad roar from the crowd. The DJ picked up his microphone and hollered, 'Who's chanting for Queen Belly Blenderrrrrr?!'

Belly Blender did a stomach-churning move, a spin and performed the splits as her fans went nuts.

'Who's chanting for Madame North Leggggg?!'

Madame North Leg gripped her straight left leg against her ear and held the pose. She almost kissed the light bulb with her toes. Her crew stomped the floor as they chanted her name. I saw a French flag being waved in a corner. *'Allez, Madame Magnafique! Belle!'*

'I wanna marry them both,' tweeted Jonah into my ear. 'And I won't be taking their sexy selves to any cinema or bowling alley! I'll just carry them around in my rucksack and when I'm bored, take them out and watch those chicks dance. All day! You don't see their vibes on *Strictly Come Dancing*. And everybody on *Britain's Got Talent* is lame to these chicks.'

'You're not wrong,' I agreed. 'But stop perving.'

'I'm *not* perving!' protested Jonah. 'Can't a bruv enjoy two chicks dancing?'

'Yeah, but keep your tongue on lock and wipe up your drool.'

As North Leg and Belly Blender mopped up their sweat, the DJ announced his decision.

'Madame North Leg booted up a storm in this month of June as her toes kissed the moon! She can spin like a ball on a roulette wheel, her French peeps say she's the real deal from Lille! Nuff talent in her heels! Queen Belly Blender can stir up her abs like a roundabout full of hot-wheeling cabs! If you look too close at her belly flow, your eyes get hypnotised, your brain's on go-slow. Double the dip, redder than raw, squeeze my pip, goddam it's a drawwwwww!'

Every fan booed a mad boo. North Leg and Belly Blender hugged each other. Boy from the Hills tried to say something as the music started again. 'That ... those were the most mind-messing, belly-button-popping, sickest moves I have ever seen. *Wow!*'

'Calm down, Boy,' I laughed. 'Don't stroke out on me.'

'Should we ask somebody if we can use their phone?' Boy from the Hills asked.

'In a minute,' replied Saira. 'I'm getting my groove on.'

Saira and Venetia started to dance. I couldn't believe it! We bruvs swapped glances. All we could do was sink our patties, drain our drinks and watch the show. I was thinking about doing my little Mars-walk-bounce thing that I did in my dungeon when no one was around but thought better of it. Venetia was nearly as good as Belly Blender and North Leg.

Loving the girls' moves, Bit's grin was wider than the Crong circular while Jonah was still gazing at the dancers – Cupid had blazed an arrow in his ass.

'Who wants another drink?' I asked after a while.

The girls didn't hear me but Jonah and Bit wanted another Coke.

'I'll be back soon,' I said. 'And Jonah, I'm begging you . . . please, please don't dance. Don't do it, bruv.'

'Screw you!'

'And *stop perving*!' I joked.

'Screw you with a wire brush dipped in smoking acid!'

# 23

# The Black Garages

Boy from the Hills decided to roll with me.

We made our way back to the kitchen. The crowd in the hallway was huge and brothers didn't step back and allow us to squeeze through like they had done for Saira and Venetia. Boy from the Hills crunched someone's toe and got a Crongton glare. Finally, we made it through. There were about four or five others who were ahead of us in the drinks queue.

The DJ was spanking up the bass when Boy from the Hills said, 'I'm gonna go for a wine this time. Maybe a rosé if they've got it.'

'I'm on that too.' I nodded. 'A wine and a rosé! Not sure what a rosé is but why the freak not? I'm already in a pot of trouble anyway. In fact, it might be a neat idea to be liquor-bombed by the time my bro knows about our situation – he's gonna flip.'

'I wonder whose rave this is,' said Boy from the Hills.

Just then, I saw a brother standing near the drawbridge with a white patch on his head. *Oh no!* Is that Festus Livingstone?

'My mum will be good about it,' Boy from the Hills went on. 'She's cool like that. All she will say is that I should have dinged her if I was going out with bredrens or cruising to a party. She gets tired of me always blocking in my yard at weekends. She's always telling me to get my butt out more. *Why don't you play rugby or cricket or something?* She's always on my case about that. So . . . '

I had stopped listening. I looked again at the guy with the patch-head. It was definitely Festus damn Livingstone. I couldn't freaking believe it! He looked a planet bigger than he did on the bus but maybe that was my messed-up memory, or fear, or whatever. Hard-road bruvs were bouncing through the flat with crates of beer. They were all wearing black T-shirts, name-brand tracksuit tops and black jeans. Festus's crew! *Battering rams!* Cold skinny worms slithered through my veins. My forehead bubbled in sweat. *Oh God!*

'McKay, what's a matter?' Boy from the Hills asked.

I didn't answer. He followed my gaze.

'Shit on a stick!' he exclaimed.

'We have to disappear, quick-time!' I said. 'We have to tell the others.'

We turned and barged our way through the crowd. Behind us we heard cries of, 'Mind your backs! Liquor crew coming through! Mind your backs!' as Livingstone's posse headed towards the kitchen.

I almost tripped over a chick's leg as I entered the front

room. Boy from the Hills steadied me. We scanned the floor frantically. *Where are they?* In the middle of the room was my answer. Bit and Jonah were busting moves alongside Venetia and Saira. They were laughing and smiling, loving up the vibes. Panic invaded my hard drive so I just bounced people out of my way to get to my bredrens.

'Mind yourself, Fat Boy!' said a brother.

'Hey, King Tubby!' called out a chick. 'Take your freaking time!'

I ignored the insults and finally managed to grab Venetia's arm. 'We have to step!' I shouted.

She pulled her arm away and carried on grooving. 'I'm not ready to step yet,' she yelled, skilfully avoiding any spillage of wine while she danced. 'A couple more tunes and then we'll bounce. Did you get me another wine?'

'Er, no. But I have to . . .'

'McKay,' Venetia cut my flow, 'it's been a cradazy night, this is the bomb, chillax yourself and starrrrrt bubbling!'

I could hardly hear what she was saying over the banging noise. Boy from the Hills managed to get Jonah's attention. He pushed his mouth close to Jonah's ear and shouted down it. 'Festus is in the yard!'

Jonah stopped dancing. The only things moving were his eyeballs. Dread slobbered his face. 'Festus?' he repeated. 'Festus Livingstone?'

'*Festus Livingstone!*' I said again.

Jonah turned his head to the hallway. Saira and Venetia stopped grooving. Festus's crew were still carrying crates into the kitchen. Bit watched with his mouth open.

'Is there another way out?' Jonah wondered.

'This is a flat,' replied Boy from the Hills. 'One way in, one way out. Unless you wanna think about the window.'

'*I don't freaking believe it,*' raged Jonah. '*Don't believe it!*'

'Calm yourself down,' said Bit. 'They only know what McKay looks like, remember.'

'Thanks,' I said.

'What are we gonna do? Maybe if we just park in a corner they won't notice us?' said Venetia.

'And say while we're in that damn corner they *do* notice us?' said Jonah.

It was hard to think with the pounding music. I glanced at Bit and he was shaking his head. Doom filled his eyes. Jonah was looking at the open window like it was a proper option. We were two storeys up. Boy from the Hills was checking the hallway.

'That's a no-no!' I said.

'You could make it!' urged Jonah. 'Maybe you can cushion the impact if you land like one of those commandoes? You sort of bend your knees and roll at the same time as you land.'

'Do I look like a freaking commando?' I protested. 'You go first!'

Jonah didn't take up my invitation.

'They're in the kitchen,' watched Saira. 'Nobody's jumping out of the damn window. Let's try and roll out now. McKay, just turn the other way when we pass. We'll be good.'

Venetia sank the rest of her wine and dropped her paper cup. She sucked in a long breath. I didn't feel good. Not good at all. Something nasty was chomping the inside of my stomach. I felt like I was gonna be sick.

Saira led the way. Bit was next, followed by Venetia. I was in the middle with Jonah behind me. Boy from the Hills was last. Ravers twerked, grooved and bubbled all around us. The castle was rocking. They were all chanting to the music.

*'WHOA HOH! WHOA HOH! WHOA HOH!'*

The DJ hyped up the crowd.

*'I am the tongue-smacker! The dictionary specialist, thesaurus master, lyrics on flow like a news-printer! Quicker than a computer! More words per second than the steps of a caterpillar! My delivery more precise than the world's greatest wicket-taker, commentator par-excellence for any dance-off hour, Crongton's very own master-rapper! Too damn bad for Simon Cowell and his X-Factor! Unlike Cheryl I don't need no freaking auto-tuner. I'm hotter than a blazing thermometer! I'm so fresh I make other MCs look like a Jurassic chapter. If they try to test me I rap them up like an apple turnover with my lyrical blender. To conquer me you're gonna need a vocabulary defibrillator. My peeps love me so much they want me to be their Parliament member. Chicks are so desperate for me to stay a night over, they tranquilise their mothers and overdose their fathers. God made me and his creations will never get better. They call me MC Jack Riddler, the twerk-a-dub grime doctor. Not even a Jedi master could find me a worthy competitor! Chant WHOA if you love my lyrical stamina!'*

*'WHOA HOH! WHOA HOH! WHOA HOH!'*

We managed to make it out of the front room but the hallway was still corked. Our steps turned into little shuffles. Rave-heads were still chatting about the dance-off between Belly Blender and North Leg. Headway was slow. I wanted to grab one of the balloons and use it to hide my face.

*Maybe if I hold a whole bunch I could float out of the window?*
*Why did that chick call me King Tubby?*
*Focus, McKay! The crap is swimming neck-high.*

Saira neared the kitchen. We could hear the clink of bottles being placed on a table and into the fridge. Someone was using a bottle opener. A blast of heat roasted everybody nearby as somebody opened the oven. I turned my body away. My undergarms stuck to me like chewing gum to a tramp's heel. Six new ravers had just entered the castle. We couldn't move a centimetre. I dared not look around. Our bodies kissed the wall to let the dance-heads through. It was a relief to see Venetia start rolling again.

The drawbridge was open! Safety was in sight. The bouncer who had hit on Saira was singing to another chick who was about to step inside.

*'I'll, do, anything, for you, Miss Ripeness, anything, cos you, mean, everything to me . . . '*

Then I heard a voice behind me.

'Check out this clown who comes to a dance-off rave in his freaking school uniform!'

I turned around. I couldn't help myself. Festus had bounced out of the kitchen. He was pointing at Boy from the Hills. He had a mad grin on his face. 'Haven't you got any garms?' he mocked. 'Go back to your yard, Sweep Head, and come back with some decent brands!'

Everyone stared at Boy from the Hills. A few people laughed. Suddenly Jonah barged past me in a frantic panic, trying to make a bolt for the drawbridge. Festus scanned in the hallway. His eyes locked on mine. For a short second I imagined I had a big neon light above my head that spelled **NESTA'S BRO**. I didn't know why but I glanced at the white plaster on Festus's head – *My bruv did that!* – *then* looked away. But it was too damn late.

Somehow I got my legs moving and stomped towards freedom, arms flailing around, trying to push away anybody in my way. Someone's drink spilled across my back. I think I knocked a bomb-head over once I got outside. I bounced down the concrete steps like a giant American football – ricocheting in all directions. I smacked into walls and crashed my knees again. I heard my bredrens shouting but I couldn't quite make out what they were saying. I tripped over when I reached ground level. The back of my head kissed the concrete. Someone, a girl, was screaming but I couldn't tell if it was Saira or Venetia.

'Jonah! Get your ass back here! *We can't leave him! We can't leave him! Jonah! Jonah! Come back! Come back!'*

I was lying on my back. I tried to focus. Three fat moons danced above me. My knees were killing me and my head was ding-donging. Name-brand trainers were gathering all around me. Black. There must've been about five pairs. I looked up and saw a face. I already knew who it would belong to: Festus Livingstone. He was grinning – the kinda evil grin that promised some *Twelve Years a Slave*, messed-up torture. His teeth were so damn white. All I could think in that moment – crazy as it sounds – was, *He must attack his plaque twice a day.*

'Nesta's fat-ass bro,' Festus said to his bredrens. 'Spitting image.'

He booted me in my side. Agony blazed along my back. I heard laughter. I looked around for my bredrens.

'Leave him alone!'

My eyes followed the voice. It was Venetia. She was behind me with Saira, Bit and Boy from the Hills. Jonah was a couple of metres behind them. *Why haven't they hot-toed away? They had the chance.*

I felt another kick in my right thigh. The pain spread to the rest of my body. All I could do was cover my seed-bags, close my eyes and grit my molars. *Daaaaad! Nestaaaaa!* I screamed in my head.

'You see what your crazy-ass bro done to me!' raged Festus. He pointed to the white plaster on his head. 'You see what he freaking done? He had the nerve to wheel up to our ends and then red up my head! I swear on North Crong blood that he's gonna *pay* for that disrespect!'

'Leave him alone!' screamed Venetia once again. 'It wasn't him who mauled your head. What's he done to you? Freak all!'

Festus ignored her. He knelt down and stared right at me. I could sniff the beer on his breath. His goatee wasn't trimmed. He had a red spot that uglied up the corner of his left nostril.

'I swear to God I'm gonna shank your bro's ribs before the night is done! Believe me on that score! And before he blows his last he's gonna tell me where Manjaro's chicken self is hiding out!'

Hearing Festus's nasty messed-up voice made me shiver like a scalped polar bear stepping through a blizzard. Dizziness and pain made my sight blurry but something glinted against the moonlight above me. I tried to get up but my legs wouldn't respond. I couldn't hear the music any more.

'You're from South Crong!' said Festus. 'Maybe *you* know where that pussy is.'

'He's got a blade!'

Someone screamed. I heard a buzz of voices above me.

'Not here, Festus!' warned a voice. 'Nuff people are watching. Not here!'

'He hasn't done you anything!' shrieked Saira. 'None of us know where Manjaro is. Your beef is with his bro. What's a matter with you? *Gitsin!* Let him *go!*'

'Shut that bitch up!'

I heard a scuffle, some punching and slapping. A body hit the ground.

'Get your freaking hands off me! You ugly piece of pig shit! Get your freaking hands off me!'

Another smack and a punch. Then I heard muffled screams. 'You pig scab! You ugly freaking trog! Get . . . freaking . . . off me!'

'So you think you're bad too? You wanna rescue your bitch and be a graveyard hero? There's nuff of them in the cemetery. Keep your fists on pause, Dwarfie, and breathe another day.'

I tried to turn around to see what was going down but some throbbing pain from the back of my head stopped me from doing so. My knees buckled. I willed myself not to cry in front of the hood-rats.

'Let's take these South Crong pussies to the garages,' Festus said. 'We'll make them spill there. It's not too much of a trod from here.'

'Let them go,' another voice urged. 'They're just school kids, Fest. They can't do us shit. Let's slide back to the rave – I wanna see the next dance-off.'

'I'm on that too,' another agreed.

'Haven't you seen what this fat-ass's bro done to my freaking head? I'm *not* gonna let that pass, bruv. No freaking way! Besides, they might snitch to the feds. South Crong pussies are always spilling to the feds. And they might know where Manjaro is.'

'Major Worries told us not to waste our time with South Crong cadets,' a different voice said. 'He said to go after Pinchers' soldiers. And the feds are kinda well busy tonight – trying to stop the madness in Crong central.'

'And I hear this Nesta bruv is always on his lonesome. He doesn't step with Pinchers or any other crew.'

'And he marked me for life!' Festus raged. 'You forget that? Weren't you freaking there? Eleven stitches that pussy gave me! *Eleven!* How would you feel if everyone's chatting about how a South Crong pussy red up your head and sparked you out? I *know* soldiers are laughing behind my back. Do you know how I feel when the Major looks at my head? He thinks I'm a weak-heart.'

'He doesn't think that! Trust me.'

'*Yes, he does!*' Festus roared. 'What do you know? When Nesta hears what's going down with his fat-ass bro, he'll have to step it up to the garages . . . then I'll deal with him neatly – shank him up good and proper. They won't bend up laughing behind my back then! And the Major will give me props and let me step up – especially if I give him info about Manjaro.'

I glanced at Bit. *His mind must be drenched in fear.* The dread churning up inside of me messed up my breathing. I felt myself being dragged to my feet. The cold chill of a blade was held against my neck. One side of it was jagged. Someone shrieked. I didn't know why but I had this vision of Mum teaching me how to slice onions.

*'Hold it firmly with your fingertips. Always cut away from the body.'*

'Step with me, Fat Boy,' Festus ordered. 'You're my bait. And if any of your bredrens try to slide, I swear, your neck's spurting untold red.'

My mouth went dry. I could now feel my pulse behind my ears. I managed to glance behind. My bredrens were with me. Saira and Venetia were crying. Bit was trying to comfort them. Tears were in Jonah's eyes too. Boy from the Hills looked in proper shock. Festus's crew rolled behind them.

Every step hurt. The back of my head felt damp and my tongue was pounding again.

'Do we have to do this now?' one of Festus's crew asked. 'Did you see how many chicks were there at the rave?'

Festus let go of me and hot-stepped to his bredren. He still had the blade in his hand. Everyone stopped. Cold necks and guillotines! This G could switch quicker than a remote control with new batteries. I had this mad urge to sit down but I decided not to. Meanwhile, Festus put an arm around his bredren's neck like he was the Godfather. He smiled like the Joker in *Batman*.

'Is that why you follow me?' Festus challenged, pushing up his face real close. 'Just to jack liquor from stores and hunt chicks? We're *soldiers*! Are you tuning into that? Are you on this or not? *Tell me now!'*

I didn't know about the brother but I nearly let something drop from my backside. The stress and pain were getting too much. I sat my ass down in the middle of the road.

'I'm on it,' said the brother.

'Nice to know you're on my wavelength,' said Festus. His attention switched to me. 'Get your fat ass up!'

I did what I was told. Festus hot-toed up to me and punched me in the back. The pain vibrated up to my head.

*'Leave him alone!'*

'Do what I say and you might piss again tomorrow,' Festus warned. 'It's your bro who won't see daylight again.'

We rolled away from the Crongton circular to Notre Dame Road. We would've been better off if we'd stayed the night on Fireclaw Heath.

We made a right turn into a street of low-level slabs. I started to count the Volkswagen Golfs parked in the road. I got up to three. Maybe it distracted me from what might happen next. I guessed it was something like one or two o'clock in the morning. Dad would be on his mid-shift break. I wondered if he'd tried to call me. Nesta would've been dinging me. He was probably looking for my ass right now.

We passed the slabs. They were three storeys high. I thought about screaming for help but I booted that idea out of my head. That blade was too long. Too shiny. Too jagged. And too close to my skin. If he etched and sketched that into my chest I wouldn't see another morning. I would never become a chef owning untold restaurants. Never get married to a cute chick with dimples and live in a castle with two kitchens. Never chillax in my basement cinema watching my *Hobbit* trilogy.

Saira had stopped crying. Venetia stepped with her arms folded. She was the only one who looked calm.

On my eighth birthday Mum took me to Warwick Castle. That was our best ever day. I couldn't believe I was inside a *real* castle. I imagined all the people in history who had been mauled, savaged and uber-tortured there. I hot-toed it along the castle's long stone corridors like I'd OD'd on sherbet and fizzy drinks.

Mum bought me a T-shirt, a plastic sword and a wooden shield. We had a picnic in the grounds – she'd made carrot cake. I loved it to the max. She told me how she baked it, measuring and mixing, blending and folding, lushing it up with a lick of butter icing.

Dad had stayed behind to watch Nesta play football for his Sunday team, so I had Mum to myself, which I secretly loved. We sang songs on the train on the way back to South Crong.

'Festival and dumplings all in a row!
Make sure your windows are shut, be careful of the
   greedy crows!
Don't tell your sis, don't tell your bro,
Sweet up your plate with ackee and saltfish and
   your stomach will glow!'

I thought I might have blacked out or lost myself somehow, because next thing I knew we had reached the Crong circular. On the other side of the road was North Crong ends. The tall slabs searched for the moon. Some windows were lit, some weren't. A fox was checking out the food that spilled out from an overturned bin. I heard fed sirens in the distance and watched the passing cars, praying that one of them would belong to the feds.

Luck kissed our asses goodbye.

I thought again of those knights who were killed at Warwick Castle.

Saira started sobbing again. Venetia was still strangely calm.

'You lot can go as soon as Nesta shows his chicken butt,' Festus said to my bredrens as we crossed the road. 'So stop your wailing. Your fat-ass friend here is gonna invite him to join our liccle private rave ...'

Festus led the way down side roads and alleyways. There was something in the air. I couldn't quite guess what it was. I found it difficult to breathe. My knees were about to flop on me. North Crong soldier graffiti, a small 'n' sprayed in black within a big 'C', marked every slab. On one block wall was a painted image of a giant Major Worries stepping through North Crong ends. His feet were the size of dustbin trucks and his fists could've Godzillared council slabs.

I turned around to glance at Jonah and he was staring at the ground as he trod. He could easily have blazed away. But he didn't. At that moment I felt a mad love for him and all of my crew. They could have left my ass to face my fate alone. But they chose not to.

We eventually came to a narrow street behind a tall slab. A row of garages ran parallel to the road. Fear twisted my stomach so hard I almost puked. I couldn't fake bravery any more. Tears spilled from my eyes. I looked up and started to count the satellite dishes that were fixed on to the slab. Another distraction. Clothes were hanging off balconies. Some kid was bawling on the fifth or sixth floor. Someone on the second was playing a loud computer game. It was all so . . . normal.

Festus stopped. He dug into his pocket to grab his mobile.

'Hold them there,' he ordered his foot soldiers and bounced away a few metres.

I swapped glances with my bredrens. They looked so exhausted but they all had crazy concern and love in their eyes, even Boy from the Hills although I hardly knew him. I could feel it. This was a doomed situation but their courage gave me a dose of hope.

Festus talked into his phone, walking here and there and waving his spare arm about like he was proper vex at something. Whoever he was talking to had pissed him off big time. He killed the call and rolled back to us. He searched his bredrens' faces.

'The Major's not coming. He's busy on a mission. Open up the garage.'

'Are you sure about this?' a brother said. 'We're not in any beef with these young cadets. Haven't we freaked them out enough?'

'Open up the freaking garage!'

A brother dug out a bunch of keys from his pocket, pushed

one in the lock and flipped open a garage door. It was proper dark inside.

'*I'm not going in!*' Saira screamed. '*Siktir git! I'm not going in!*'

'Kill that bitch's noise,' ordered Festus.

The same brother who opened the garage door back-handed Saira across her face.

'*Think you're a man beating down a girl! Your mum must be well proud, you piece of shit! Siktir git!*'

She reeled backwards from the punch that followed.

# 24

## Chocolate Bars in the Dark

They pushed Saira inside first. Festus raised his right foot and booted me in next. I stumbled but didn't want to fall over – I didn't want to give him the pleasure. The others didn't have to be told. They shuffled in quietly. Someone slapped on a light. A naked bulb flickered into life and out again. Festus pulled the garage drawbridge closed. My heart sunk with it. Darkness fell. Saira screamed a mad scream. The bulb rebooted itself and shone a sickly yellow. Spiderwebs clung to every corner. North Crong graffiti scrawled up the ceiling. I could smell piss and alcohol.

There was an eaten-out sofa in the middle of the floor with a scarred, stabbed-up table beside it. Resting on the table was a big glass ashtray spilling rocket butts and a world of cigarette ash. A pack of cards was next to that. Posters of sexy chicks gazed down from the red-brick walls. Bottles of beer, cans of fizzy drinks, Rizla packets, untold cigarette packs and a variety of chocolate bars filled three shelves fixed to the end wall. The floor was dusty. A toolbox, surrounded by different sized spanners and Allen keys, rested in a corner. Beside it was a small boom box and a selection of blank CDs.

'Give them a bar each,' ordered Festus. 'It might shut up the loud one. I dunno what she's bawling about – I'm not gonna trouble her. What kinda rep would I get if soldiers know me for banging down chicks? The Major wouldn't love that.'

'What kinda rep would you get for jacking chicks?' Saira spat.

Festus ignored her.

A brother wearing black leather gloves collected six Mars bars. He handed them out. None of us accepted.

'Suit yourselves!'

Four brothers parked on the sofa. One of them started to wrap a rocket. My bredrens stood by a wall. Festus couldn't keep still. He stepped this way and that. My eyes followed him. He only stopped to grab a beer. He opened it with a bottle opener that he carried in his pocket. He sank a dose before wiping his lips with the back of his hand. He looked at me.

'*Call* him!' he demanded.

I didn't respond. Festus tipped more liquor down his throat. He mopped his mouth again.

'*Call him!*'

'He hasn't got a phone! None of us do!' screamed Saira.

'What do you mean?' asked Festus.

'We got jacked up Notre Dame,' revealed Bit.

Festus started to laugh. A horrible sounding cackle. Two of

his bredrens joined in. I wondered if they'd ever bucked into G-Gore from the Hunchbackers.

'Glad you find it funny,' said Saira.

I glanced at Venetia to see how she was. She was very still. She was staring at Festus with a mad intensity.

'Not your day, is it?' Festus chuckled. 'But no worries. Fat Boy can use my phone. My calls are free after seven at night. You wouldn't believe the load of apps I've got.'

One of Festus's bredrens giggled again.

Festus took out his phone. He bounced up to me. *'Call him!'* I knew Nesta's number off by heart. I wished I didn't. Festus slammed his phone into my left hand. My body jolted at his touch. The dread in my stomach churned over once more and I could feel the munched remains of the chicken pattie rising in my chest. I had never hated someone like I hated Festus. For a short second I wondered what he'd do if I puked up over him. He might delete me but it would be worth it to the max.

Saira had her hand over her mouth. Jonah was shutting and opening his eyes like he wanted to wake up somewhere else. Bit's mouth was wide open. Boy from the Hills looked like he needed resuscitating. And Venetia still had her gaze locked on Festus's every move – if her eyeballs could have fired lasers, Festus would've been a pile of ashes in a short second.

Festus owned one of them phones where the keypad was too small for the fingers. I dialled Nesta's number very slowly. I didn't want to make a mistake. I felt all eyes were on me. The light bulb faded before flicking into life again. I wondered where Nesta could be. Out looking for me perhaps. Or chillaxing with Yvonne?

If Festus knew anything about my bro he wouldn't pick a war with him. Nesta had so much rage in him since Mum died. He wouldn't mouse out with anybody. Not even Manjaro.

Nesta would give Festus a fight he wouldn't believe.

'*Who's this?*' Nesta answered.

'It's McKay.'

'Where the frigging blazes are you? I've been dinging your mobile for hours! I swear, if you're looting and getting yourself involved in the madness in Crong central I'm gonna kuff you so hard you're gonna think the town hall memorial stone is headbutting you! And I'm gonna double-kuff you on top of that for not picking up your damn phone!'

Festus snatched the phone off me. A Mr Burns-like grin spread over his face. 'Recognise my voice, pussy?!'

Festus switched the phone to speaker. He smiled at his bredrens – one of them laughed. Nesta didn't respond.

'I said, do you recognise my voice, pussy?'

'Who's this? Jonah? Bit? I'm not in the frigging mood to play games so put McKay back on.'

Festus glanced at his crew again. They nodded at him. Festus raised a thumb. I thought I was gonna be sick.

'I've got your bike ... I've got your fat-ass bro.'

Silence.

'Did you freaking hear me?!' Festus suddenly raged. 'I've got your fat-ass bro!'

Festus turned to me and pushed his hand into my face. 'Tell him!' he screamed. He backhanded me. 'Tell him!'

One of the girls shrieked. Festus passed me the phone. I felt the heat on my left cheek. I didn't know what to say. 'Sorry,' I managed. 'Sorry . . . '

I couldn't think of anything else. Tears spilled from my eyes once more. Festus snatched the phone. 'So what are you gonna do, pussy? You have half an hour. If I don't see your ass in that time, your fat-ass bro's head's gonna spill red. Up to you, pussy!'

There was a long pause. It was unbearable. I felt like my head was gonna explode like a fat firework in a microwave. I glanced at everyone's faces and they were tuning their ears intently. *What's Nesta thinking?* Finally, he spoke.

'Where are you?' he asked.

'The black garages,' Festus replied. 'Indica Lane. Garage number seven. You're always wheeling to ends where you don't belong so you should find it quick-time. Come if you think you're militant enough. Don't expect to make it back to your barracks.'

Another pause. A heavy worm with a snowflake jacket skated down my spine. Bit and Jonah wiped their faces. Saira mopped her tears with a tissue. Boy from the Hills kept very still, his eyes vacant. He looked a world paler since we rolled into the garage but that could've been the yellow light. Venetia stood with her arms folded. She followed Festus's every move with intense eyes. I didn't think Nesta would call the feds. I wondered if he'd ding Dad.

'You still there, pussy?' Festus asked. 'Or are you mousing out?'

'I'm here,' replied Nesta. His voice was calm – like he was the cool kid replying to a teacher's registration call. 'Now, hear this good, loud and clear . . . I swear on my mum's grave that if you even scratch McKay's liccle toe I'm gonna slice you up like a Friday night kebab, stomp on you like I'm making French wine and pulp you like a Wrigley's chewing gum. You might think you can terrorise me but if you mess with my fam I'm gonna go all-out Godfather on you. I *swear* to God *that's* what's gonna go down . . . Ring the alarm – I'm coming.'

Nesta deleted the call.

I had to swallow the sick that was building up in my throat. I felt dizzy. Festus turned to his bredrens. He grinned at them once more. One of them fidgeted. Another took in a mad gulp of air. Their eyes didn't seem so confident. I guessed the garage was just as much a prison to them as it was for me.

Festus switched his attention to me again. 'When he comes you can step. Maybe you can escort his organs in the ambulance.'

Someone giggled a nervous giggle. Saira wailed once more, covering her mouth with her hands. Jonah and Bit sat down. Their backs were against the red brick wall. Boy from the Hills hardly moved – he was still gazing into space. Venetia still had her arms folded, her gaze forever following Festus.

Festus parked on the armrest of the sofa. He picked up the cards and began to shuffle them. He was very good at it. His bredren had finished wrapping his rocket. He sparked it with a lighter. Another brother got up and grabbed a beer. He borrowed Festus's bottle opener, sank a good dose and sat down again. The breath of weed filled the garage. Smoke king-cobra'd up towards the light bulb. I wanted to vomit. Or sink a chocolate bar. I was too scared to do either.

Dropping the cards on the floor, Festus began to step up and down the garage. He stroked his blade with his thumb like it was a comfort toy. I wondered how many people he had shanked with it. Sweat dripped off me like water from a squeezed sponge.

One of the brothers sitting on the sofa began to tap his feet. *Plat, plat, plat!* The sound of it mauled my nerves. *Plat, plat, plat!* I had never wanted to break someone's leg as much as his. *Plat, plat, plat!* Then we heard a car pull up. *Nesta?* But Nesta didn't have a car. Maybe he had brought a crew with him. *Plat, plat, plat!*

'*Shut up!*' Festus ordered.

Festus couldn't take the foot-slapping any more than I could. For the first time that night, I actually felt grateful to him.

Jonah and Bit slowly stood up. I was on hyper-drive. I could feel my pulse in places I'd never felt it before. Festus took off his jacket. He flexed his shoulders, tightened the grip on his blade. I could see the veins and tissues in his wrist and forearm stand out. His shoulders were so wide they seemed to be in different postcodes. His biceps had intricate detail in them. He took up his position close to the garage door. He was intent on revenge.

I wanted to do something. I couldn't stand there and watch my brother's body being ripped open. But I was no hero. *What can I do?*

We heard a car door slam. I didn't have to be a Jedi to sense Nesta was outside.

Seconds later, there was this insane clanging on the garage door.

*Blangggg! Blangggg! Blangggg!*

That was Nesta, but he wasn't using his fists. He *had* brought something. Mad relief pinballed through me.

*'McKay! You in there? McKay!'*

My lips moved but I couldn't say a word. The four brothers sitting on the sofa got up to their feet in a rush. Three of them looked proper scared. One of them took out a penknife from an inside pocket. Another picked up a long screwdriver from the toolbox. The guy with the penknife swapped it for a hammer. Festus passed his blade from one hand to another.

*'McKay! Say something! Are you in there?'*

Saira, Boy from the Hills, Bit and Jonah backed away to the end wall. Venetia stood her ground. She looked trance-like calm. She was taking something out of her rucksack. Sweat blurred my vision.

'Open it,' ordered Festus, looking at his bredrens.

Festus's crew swapped frenzied glances.

*Blangggg! Blangggg! Blangggg!*

*'McKay! McKay! Open this freaking door!'*

*Blangggg! Blangggg! Blangggg!*

'Open it now!' Festus demanded.

The brother wearing the black gloves stepped forward. He glanced behind before placing his right hand on the lever of the garage door. Fear seized his eyes. He started to lift. He paused. A shaft of street-light lit up his name-brand trainers.

*'McKay!'*

Festus shifted his weight from right foot to left foot. Sweat cooked his forehead. He held his blade in his right hand. His muscles tensed. The stream of light had now reached knee-high. My inner voice screamed at me. *Do something, McKay!* Maybe I could just crash on him.

I took a stride. Then I heard an *'Uuuurrrrhhhh!'*

*'Aman Allahim!'* Saira screamed.

Festus was reeling like someone had blazed his kneecaps. Something shiny was in his neck. He was trying to take it out. Venetia slowly stepped back from him. Her eyes looked like they couldn't believe what she had just done. Blood dripped over her right hand. Her fingers were stretched. Her mouth was open but no sound came out. Her back hit the wall but her eyes never left Festus.

*'Uuuurrrrgggghhhh!'*

Festus dropped to the ground. He fought for breath. One of his bredrens dropped his screwdriver and went to help him. The rest of his crew hot-toed it out of there – one of them dropped a hammer on his frenetic dash out. Nesta rushed in, carrying an axe – the handle was almost as long as Liccle Bit's legs.

*Mother-freaking beanstalks! Where in Crongton did he get that from?*

Collie Vulture was with him. He was swinging a cricket bat. He didn't need it.

I looked again at Festus. The file part of a toenail clipper stuck out of his neck. Shock slapped my whole body. Vomit shot up from my throat. I puked up over the playing cards. The guy with the black leather gloves was madly trying to stop the bleeding. He looked around, I guessed for something to absorb the blood. He ended up using an oily rag from the toolbox. Festus was sort of wriggling and squirming on the floor. His face was twisting and creasing in agony. He was making this ugly gargling noise – like an alien taking cough medicine. His tongue looked like it was trying to escape from his mouth.

I turned my head. Venetia buried her head into Bit's chest. Her eyes were shut tight. Saira hugged them both.

Nesta dropped his axe. He took out his phone and made a call. Jonah hot-stepped out. Boy from the Hills followed him.

'Need an ambulance,' Nesta spoke into his phone. He was calm, like he had made similar calls before. 'Someone's been stabbed. Indica Lane, North Crongton – by the garages. You don't need to know who's calling. Just send an ambulance quick-time. Indica Lane. I don't know the postcode.'

Nesta killed the call. 'McKay!' he called. 'Get your ass in the car. All of you get in the car.'

Bit and Saira helped Venetia step out of the garage. Collie Vulture led them to a Mini parked at the end of the street.

*A Mini? Are you freaking kidding me?*

I followed them. My body was still shaking.

'McKay!' Nesta yelled again. 'Move it! The feds and the medics will be here in a hurry.'

I glanced behind. The brother with the red-stained gloves was cradling Festus's head with one hand while pressing the rag to his neck with the other. His lips were wobbling. Festus's eyes were closing and opening. Blood drowned the dust. I couldn't help thinking that Festus was gonna need another big white plaster to match the one slapped on his head.

## 25

## Ghost Town

I don't know how we managed it but six of us squeezed on to the back seat. Boy from the Hills sat on one of my legs and Jonah sat on the other. Saira and Venetia parked themselves on Bit – their heads kissed the roof. Pain rushed from my knees. Nesta put the axe in the boot and crouched in the passenger seat. Collie Vulture was behind the wheel, the cricket bat tucked in beside him. He turned the key in the ignition. Nothing. He switched again and this time the engine rocked into life. It wasn't exactly *The Fast and the Furious*! The car's headlights lit up the street. The radio came on. I wound down my window. The cool air chilled my forehead. I didn't want to think about the nail file or remember the look of shock on Festus's face as he saw his own blood spilling on to the garage floor.

I wanted to hear Nesta's voice. Just so I could really believe we were escaping this madness.

*It could've been my big bro lying in the dust with a blade sticking out of his neck.*

'Where you get the wheels?' I asked.

'Man—'

'Don't ask,' interrupted Nesta.

'Is he,' Venetia started, 'is he gonna be all right?'

No one answered.

'Is he gonna be all right?!' Venetia repeated. *'IS HE GONNA BE ALL RIGHT?!'*

'I don't know,' Nesta replied. 'You skewered him good. If they can stop his blood spilling he'll have a chance.'

It was unreal.

Venetia crossed herself and closed her eyes. Tears rolled down her face. Saira found a tissue and started to wipe the blood off Venetia's right hand. Festus's blood. It was no PS4 game. It was no DVD.

What could have driven her to such violence? When I thought about it, she'd been so calm – so collected – but the attack was impulsive. I thought about Collette, and about everything that had gone down this evening. Maybe the emotional baggage just got too heavy for her; she just couldn't take any more and flipped out.

Opera music was playing on the radio. Nobody asked to change the station. Again I wondered whose wheels we were rammed into.

Collie Vulture made his way to the Crong circular. He kept his speed well below the limit but it was still a bumpy ride with six of us in the back. As we got closer to Crong central I could hear burglar alarms holler into the night. Smoke was rising from at least three places. Petrol fumes polluted the air. The odd fed car sped past and a helicopter was circling somewhere above us. Streets leading to Crong central were blocked by barriers and fed vans. I kept my face close to the open window in case I puked up again.

'The feds have choked-up all roads to Crong central,' said Collie Vulture. 'About an hour ago, hood-rats set fire to that posh restaurant.'

'Posha Nostra,' said Nesta. 'That Italian place. When that went up the feds got mad and started to charge in for real. Nuff rodents got arrested hot-toeing up Crong Broadway – they wanted to blitz the two jeweller's shops up there. Keep on the Crong circular till we get to Crong Heath.'

'That's where I live,' said Boy from the Hills. 'Can you drop me off there?'

The opera singing continued on the radio. Venetia cried silently. I glanced at her and wondered if she'd ever get over this mad night. I didn't think I would.

'What . . . what am I gonna say?' she asked.

'That you defended yourself,' replied Saira. 'That cradazy prick had a blade in his hand, V. He could've carved any one of us in there.'

'Saira's not wrong,' said Bit. 'It was a stressful situation. No one can blame you for what happened. Give thanks and praises that we're alive. That Festus is the living psycho. Even his bredrens didn't wanna follow his madness.'

'You're braver than a world of hard-core brothers that I know,' said Nesta.

'What hard-core bruvs do you know?' I asked.

Nesta gave me a hard look that I saw in the rear mirror. 'You think fear wasn't stroking my head when we hot-wheeled up there?' he admitted. 'That could've been me lying on that garage floor, laced in the neck with his blade. As I see it, you saved my behind, and your crew. Don't try to stress out yourself. Nuff respect due.'

Bit nodded. 'Nesta's not wrong.'

'But,' Venetia started. 'But what if he dies? What if the feds come around? What am I gonna say to my fam? What will they say at my church? My pops is gonna go cradazy – he switches on me if I'm late back from school or even if I pinch my liccle sister.'

'He should feel blessed that you're OK,' said Bit. 'I am.'

'Look at how many peeps saw Festus beat down McKay outside the rave,' recalled Jonah. 'And they all saw him hold-ing a blade to McKay's throat like he was gonna etch and sketch him. And then he jacked us! He took the living liberty!'

'But Festus might die,' she managed before trauma slob-bered her again.

'We'll go up with you to your yard,' offered Saira. 'And I don't care if we have to block there for the rest of the night, week or month. We'll back you to the max to your fam, the feds and anyone else.'

'I'm on that,' said Bit.

'And me too,' I agreed.

Venetia was calm for a few seconds before she collapsed into tears again. None of us could think of any lyric to make her feel better. Instead, we just kinda hugged her the best way we could in the cramped back seat.

It took us fifteen minutes to drive to Crongton Heath. Boy from the Hills directed Collie Vulture to Ripcorn Wood. Collie Vulture had to swerve as a fox rolled casually across the road. We passed big castles with long drive-ins and front gardens spacious enough to ride a pony. Everything was so quiet. It didn't seem real.

'Are you sure you live up here?' Nesta asked Boy from the Hills.

'Yeah,' Boy from the Hills replied. 'Lived up here all my days. It's proper quiet in these ends until our neighbour gets some man to trim his branches with a chainsaw.'

When we pulled up, we all bounced out apart from Venetia. It felt good to stretch my legs but I had to spit out the rest of the vomit that was sitting at the top of my chest.

'You sure you don't want me to step with you so I can back you up to your fam?' Boy from the Hills offered to Venetia.

Venetia shook her head. She tried to smile. Her hands were trembling. 'That's all right,' she said. 'Thanks and praises for having my back but Bit and Saira can come with me. I hope to see you at school . . . sometime.'

'You will,' Boy from the Hills said. 'You saved our skins, toes and everything else!'

'Thanks,' Venetia replied. 'Colin's your name, isn't it?'

Boy from the Hills nodded. 'You remembered!'

'I don't know a damn what's gonna happen to me but thanks for helping me out, Colin. Take care.'

'Nothing's gonna happen to you!' said Bit.

'Can we delete the long goodbyes?' said Collie Vulture. 'This car's not exactly mine.'

'Then whose car is it?' I wanted to know. 'Anybody I know?'

'*Don't* ask,' shouted Nesta. 'Just be glad you're getting a ride home from North Crong.'

Nesta looked proper angry. I decided to drop the issue but it was downloaded into my hard drive.

Suddenly, Saira wrapped her arms around Boy from the Hills's neck and kissed him on a cheek. Jealousy slapped hard.

'When the crap has died down we'll roll up to your yard,' she suggested to Boy from the Hills. 'And smack some balls around on your pool table!'

'I'm on that,' Boy from the Hills replied with the biggest smile of the night. 'I'm gonna hold you to that.'

Saira smiled. 'I might get a cradazy urge to drag your bushy self to a barber but you're all right!'

Envy hoofed my chest again.

Boy from the Hills waved goodbye and rolled through his gates. We all climbed back into the Mini. Three turns of the ignition later, it bounced into life. Collie Vulture did a U-turn and we were hot-wheeling towards South Crong.

South Crong wasn't the neatest place on earth but when we reached the outskirts it looked like the prettiest housing estate in the world.

*Bless the tall bins! It's good to be back on home ends.*

'If he does survive,' said Nesta, 'I don't think Festus will spill to the feds. Rep means everything to brothers like that. He's not gonna want it known that he got burst by a chick. In fact he'd do anything to stop that living fact from spilling out.'

'But if he lives he's gonna want some effed-up revenge,' replied Collie Vulture. 'He's not gonna go all *Frozen* and chant "Let It Go", either.'

Nesta thought about it. 'No, he won't,' he said.

Saira was stroking Venetia's hair, trying to comfort her. Bit held her hand. The tears kept rolling.

'Who's next?' asked Collie Vulture.

'We better take V home,' answered Saira. 'We'll go up with her.'

'Where does she live?' Collie Vulture wanted to know.

'Somerleyton House,' Bit replied.

'The tall, long slab,' Collie Vulture recognised.

I looked out of the window. Hood-rats were still on the streets as well as a few others. Some were pushing supermarket trolleys and baby buggies filled with trainers, clothes, chocolate bars, cigarette boxes, liquor, fizzy-drink bottles, mobile phones, laptops, game consoles and a world of other stuff. We passed two slabs where South Crongtonians were partying like it was 2099. I wondered if these ravers would bless their eyes on a dance-off between two flexible chicks like we had. There wasn't a fed in sight.

'Oh my freaking days!' remarked Jonah. 'I can't believe I missed it. I could've got myself a new phone!'

'Be careful what you wish for,' said Nesta. 'The feds have arrested a world of riot rodents and they're not done yet. When they scan all the CCTV they're gonna arrest a trailer-load more. Trust me, most of them are gonna be sinking oats for the longest time.'

We pulled up outside Somerleyton House. Bit climbed

out first and helped Venetia to her feet. The rest of us followed. My knees were still killing me but I didn't want to show it.

'My pops is probably out looking for me,' said Venetia. She looked up to her floor and tears dripped down her cheeks again. 'He's gonna erupt on so many levels.'

'I don't wanna downplay it but however your pops reacts is the least of your worries,' said Nesta. 'Tell him the dirty truth – Festus and his crew jacked you and he was threatening allsorts. Be glad you're safe back in your yard. Hug everybody in your fam – even your cat if you've got one. And if I were you I'd block there for the time being. *No* more missions!'

Nesta gave me a hard look.

Venetia and Saira embraced us like we were long lost fam – that felt better. We were now all so close.

'You can all get emotional later,' said Collie Vulture. 'I've gotta get these wheels back otherwise someone might wanna burst me.'

'Who?' I wanted to know.

Nesta's face told me I wasn't getting an answer.

Jonah and me stepped back into the Mini. Bit rolled away, linking arms with Venetia and Saira.

'Say Festus does live,' I said out loud. 'Do you think he'll hunt us down?'

'So for all our days we'll have to look over our shoulders?' said Jonah.

'Take every day as it comes,' said Nesta. 'The madness of this night hasn't even booted in yet. I'm not gonna lie – brothers like him know how to hold on to beef – that's the

Crongton way. This all started with me ... sorry for getting you bruvs caught up in this macho drama.'

'You were only defending yourself,' I said.

'Yeah.' Nesta nodded. 'But look what it led to. Sorry.'

The journey continued in silence. I couldn't remember the last time Nesta said sorry to me – or anyone really.

We pulled up outside Jonah's slab and I jumped out with him. A few parents were out on the balconies looking around the estate for their kids. Smoke was still rising in Crong central. A burglar alarm screamed over Wareika Way. Supermarket trolleys were dumped near the big slab dustbins.

'You want me to bounce up with you?' I offered to Jonah. 'Offer you some kinda backup as your parents maul your ears? I know your mum's gonna switch big time.'

'That's all right,' replied Jonah. 'I'll deal with it. And if they launch a cuss attack I'll tell them to deal with their issues too! I'm gonna tell them I don't love them raging at each other day after freaking day. It's got to the point where I can't sample sleep in my yard cos of them two.'

'You sure?' I asked.

'No, I'm not sure,' Jonah replied, 'but I'll live. I better go and see Bit's fam as well – tell them he's OK. In fact I'll do that first.'

Then Jonah did something he'd never done before. He hugged me. It took me a few seconds to find my voice.

'Thanks ... thanks for staying with my ass,' I said. 'With your rapid toes you could've got away.'

'How could I do that?' Jonah replied. 'I've known you all my days. You're ... you're like a brother.'

'Thanks again,' I said. 'I owe you big time.'

'By the way,' Jonah said. 'I think Saira likes me. There was a world of love in her hug goodbye to me.'

'She hugged me tighter and kissed me on the cheek,' I argued. 'Saira and me are gonna be linking soon. Sometime in the sweet future she's gonna bring me breakfast in bed!'

'She kissed me too!' Jonah grinned. 'If we were on our lonesome our tongues would've locked.'

'And then a rhino twerked on Mars!' I laughed.

'*McKay!*' Nesta hollered.

Jonah turned, hot-toed away and bounced up the steps of his slab. I stood there watching him spring up to his floor. *Broken lifts! When she claps her eyes on Jonah's ass, Mrs Hani might be tempted to fling her son over the balcony with all the fam's debt tied to his ankles.*

'*McKay!*' Nesta roared again. 'I haven't got all night!'

I stepped back into the Mini. I had the back seat to myself. Collie Vulture switched off the radio. I wanted it back on – I didn't love the opera singing but it kinda calmed me down.

'Are you coming back to my yard?' Collie Vulture asked Nesta.

'No,' Nesta replied. 'I have to spill a dose of reality to my liccle bro. Tell Yvonne I'll ding her later.'

'What reality?' I wanted to know.

'You'll find out soon enough.'

'I know you're gonna cuss me about tonight,' I said. 'So can't it wait till the morning? My legs are killing me, my mouth is proper sore and my bed's wondering where my ass has been.'

Nesta stared through the windscreen as Collie Vulture managed to start the Mini first time. 'I'm not gonna cuss you,' he said. 'It's about Mum. It can't wait any more – should've told you a long time ago.'

'What about Mum?' I pressed.

Nesta didn't respond. He continued to gaze through the windscreen. He slapped on the radio again. He fiddled with the tuning knob.

'What about Mum?' I repeated, this time louder.

'When we get back to our yard!'

# 26

## Nesta's Revelation

Collie Vulture dropped us off outside our slab. 'I better get the wheels back to you-know-who,' he said.

I didn't say anything. I just stared at Nesta. Nesta looked away.

I had never felt better entering our castle. Dickins House! Nesta made for the kitchen and grabbed one of Dad's vodka-lemonade bottles. I crashed on the sofa in the front room and closed my eyes. I wanted to treat my knees with disinfectant and wash out my mouth with something but I was too damn tired.

'Don't go to sleep yet,' Nesta told me, taking a seat at the dinner table.

'Nesta, I know I done a serious wrong,' I said. 'But my eyes are dropping, bruv. Thanks big time for coming to get me. It's been a mental night – I thought that was it, over, thought I was gonna be graveyarded.'

'I'll make you a coffee,' Nesta offered. 'It'll keep your eyes open. I want you to hear what I've gotta say.' He bounced back into the kitchen and I heard him filling the kettle.

*Kiss my knights.* Nesta had never made me a hot drink in all my days.

'How much sugar you take?' he shouted.

'Two!' I replied.

Three minutes later he returned with a mug of coffee that looked all wrong – too much damn milk. I didn't complain but I didn't drink it, either. He parked beside me on the sofa. He locked his fingers together. My nerves started to kick like Madame North Leg was dancing inside my belly.

'Why didn't you answer your phone?' Nesta asked.

I didn't know how to answer.

'Tell me! Why didn't you answer your phone?'

I swallowed a big dose of spit. 'We got jacked up in Notre Dame.'

'Notre Dame!' Nesta repeated. 'What were you doing up there?'

'We were getting back Venetia's phone. Her boyfriend – some long bruv called Sergio – her ex-boyfriend. He napped it. So we rolled up there to get it back.'

Nesta shook his head. I tried the coffee. It wasn't good.

'So who jacked your phone?' Nesta wanted to know. 'The Hunchbackers?'

I nodded.

'G-Gore?' Nesta guessed. 'He's a pussy.'

'Yep – G-Gore. He beat down Venetia though.'

'He beat down Venetia? A chick-croker! He's even more of a pussy!'

'He scared the living kidneys out of me.'

'That's what he does to cadets,' Nesta said. 'He wouldn't try that crap on me. When this is all done I'm gonna have a word with him.'

'We just wanted to get Venetia's phone back.'

Nesta leaned towards me. '*Why* didn't you tell me you were rolling up to Notre Dame?'

'Er . . .' I didn't want to remind him about the fact he'd been storm-trooped away by the feds, about how angry he'd been, how nobody could talk to him when he was like that.

'I would've helped you out! Don't I look after you? Don't I have your back?'

'Yeah, you do.'

Nesta shook his head again. He stood up and grabbed his bottle from the dinner table. He sank half of it in one gulp, keeping his eyes on me.

'The important thing is that you're safe.'

'Are you gonna tell Dad?' I asked.

'No. But you will,' Nesta replied. 'He might've tried to ding you. In fact I was trying to ding him but couldn't get through.'

Ugh. *I'll be on a mad curfew till I'm a grandpa.*

'Now hear me good, McKay.' Nesta sank the rest of his drink. 'Mum . . .'

'What about Mum?' I wanted to know.

'On . . . on the day she . . .'

Nesta couldn't finish his sentence. I knew what he meant though.

'I didn't go school that day,' Nesta continued.

'So?' I replied.

Nesta gave me a rapid glance before he switched his attention to his fingers once more. 'I skipped school nuff days that term – Collie Vulture, Sergeant Rizzla and me would chill up by the skate park burning rockets. Anyway, on *that* day the school decided to ding Mum – they couldn't get hold of Dad cos he was at work.'

I shrugged – I couldn't quite get what Nesta was trying to say. 'Why you dragging this up?' I asked him. 'I don't like to think of *that* day.'

'You don't get it, do you?' Nesta suddenly raised his voice.

'Get what?'

'It's cos of *me*!'

'What's cos of you?'

'McKay, just listen,' he said in a whisper.

I gave him my full attention.

'Mum had just stepped out to go shopping when she got the call. She decided to roll towards the school instead of Crong central. She wasn't meant to be on Larch Road.'

Larch Road. I still couldn't return to that street. I couldn't even speak its name. The street it happened. That car. Her body.

'If it wasn't for me she wouldn't have been there! *It was my fault. Me!*'

I'd never seen Nesta cry before. He was leaking lakes, shaking his head. He covered his face with his hands and his chest heaved up and down. I stood up and went to him. I placed an arm around his shoulder. He brushed me off.

'Aren't you mad? Say something! Do something! Cuss me! Take someting and lick me with it! Why aren't you mad?'

I didn't know what to say. Tears flooded my eyes too.

'You're my big bro,' I managed. 'It wasn't you driving the car. Nesta – it's not your fault. You can't do this to yourself, bro. Mum wouldn't blame you and neither will I.'

Nesta covered his eyes again. I placed my arm around his shoulders once more and this time he didn't swipe it off.

Sometime that morning, Nesta cleaned and treated my knees with cotton wool and a dose of disinfectant – it stung like crazy. He did it all very carefully and silently. Lovingly, really. He fetched my pillow and duvet from my bedroom and I fell asleep on the sofa. He knew that since Mum passed I preferred to sleep on the couch rather than in my own dungeon. Dad was against it but Nesta didn't care. I'm not sure if I was dreaming but I think he kissed me on the forehead, like Mum used to.

I woke up to bright sunlight licking through the lounge window. I sat up and heard Nesta and Dad talking. They were sitting opposite each other at the dinner table. They were speaking calmly, mugs of coffee in front of them. (As well as a few empty vodka-lemonade bottles.)

'Dad . . . Nesta.'

They turned their heads. Dad smiled at me. He got up and came over. He was still wearing his work boots. He placed his hand on my cheek like he usually did but this time his touch felt warmer, more comforting. He looked tired.

'Are you OK, McKay?'

I nodded. 'I think so.'

'Your brother has told me all about what happened last night.'

'He has?'

I swapped looks with Nesta. He shrugged and showed me his palms. 'You were asleep.'

'It wasn't my fault, Dad,' I defended myself. 'We only went up to Notre Dame to get Venetia's phone back, but we got jacked by this crew and then this racist cabbie wouldn't take us back to South Crong cos we didn't have the full fare and then . . . '

'It's all right, McKay,' Dad said. 'You're safe now. Back with us. We'll talk about it later. If you want to. But for now, what would you like for breakfast? Or should I say lunch? It's after twelve.'

'Breakfast?' I repeated. 'Er . . . I dunno.'

'Your brother went out early this morning and bought some sausages and eggs. You want some?'

I looked at Nesta. I couldn't remember the last time he had done any shopping. He might've bought a pint of milk six months ago, but no more than that.

'Er. Yes. I'm on that.'

'Stay here and rest,' Dad ordered. 'I'll get it for you. Would you like an orange juice?'

Suddenly, I remembered Festus, the nail file, the blood. 'Festus! Is he—?'

'*Later*,' interrupted dad. 'Nesta and me will look after you, get you up to spec.'

Nesta nodded.

It was unreal that the two of them were on point. Suddenly the reality slapped me. They'd wrapped this all up while I was asleep, figuring out what was best and what wasn't – still keeping me out, treating me like a kid.

Dad kept on patting my head as I was sinking breakfast. The sausages were a dose undercooked – I couldn't be arsed to point it out to him. Still couldn't believe they swapped their thoughts on my drama behind my back. My temper started to brew.

'We phoned the hospital. This Festus guy is critical but stable. That's all we know,' said Dad. 'We don't know if the police have been involved but they haven't called. Even if they are it was self-defence.'

'We don't want you to stress out yourself,' said Nesta. 'You haven't done any wrong.'

'Nesta's gonna stay with you for the next few days,' said Dad. 'Just to keep an eye on you while I'm at work, maybe walk with you to school and pick you up.'

'And if you get any ideas about leaving South Crong I'm gonna kuff you all over!' Nesta warned. 'So *don't* even test me on that!'

*There he goes, kicking off again! Always threatening me!*

'You don't have to go school on Monday,' said Dad. 'You can stay here for as long as it takes – from what Nesta tells me what you all witnessed is gonna take its toll.'

The glinting, silver nail clipper flashed into my mind, larger in memory than it was in real life. The inside of my head started to cook on gas mark nine.

'That's all the both of you do!' I raged. 'Telling me to do this and that! Threatening me with a kuff! Leaving me here on my lonesome and thinking it's all right! Keeping things between yourselves and not telling me a damn nish! Ain't I worth telling, too dumb to understand, like a kid, like the freaking family dog who has to shut up and go sit in its corner? But wait – it's OK you telling me to ignore crusty men banging down our gates. Do you know what it's like when I bounce down the steps and I'm thinking what the freak am I gonna do if I crash into one of them debt brothers? I'm old enough to cope with *that* shit apparently! I cook for you, clean the freaking castle for you, step in to calm it down when you two are warring but you STILL treat me like a freaking kid? Don't you *ever* think about how I feel? What *I* think? No, you freaking don't! I've had enough of it!'

Dad and Nesta didn't reply.

Dad looked at Nesta – I guessed he was hoping he'd help him out.

'The both of us are sorry.'

'We were saying earlier that the three of us need to sit down and talk,' Nesta said. 'Everyone has a say. Everything on the table. Everyone *has* to listen.'

'Everything?' I repeated. 'Everyone?'

Dad nodded.

'I'm on that,' I agreed. 'As long as you two don't shut me up, ignore what I've got to say or threaten to kuff me. It's not playing like that again!'

'I hear you,' Nesta said.

'You're grown,' Dad said. 'I have to respect that now.'

There was a long, awkward silence where we all kinda looked at the walls. No one moved. I think they were trying to get their heads around my rage. I was too. I had never spilled a dose of anger like that before. *While they're still shocked I might as well ride with it.*

'And I *want* to go school,' I insisted. 'I wanna see my bredrens!'

Nesta and Dad glanced at each other once more.

'I understand that,' Nesta said. 'But I'm not having you bouncing around the ends on your own!'

'I have to agree,' Dad said. 'You're grown, McKay. But you're still only fourteen.'

'But—' I argued.

'No buts!' Dad gave me an old-school Crongton stare.

'It's not negotiable,' Nesta cut in.

Silence. I realised I didn't have a case. I could have been carved with the rest of my friends by Festus Livingstone or the Hunchbackers. I had to expect some kinda fallout.

'You say you don't want me to hide things from you,' Dad said. 'So I'm gonna share this straight. I called the loan company this morning. We've agreed a repayment plan. It's gonna be tough and I have to work a lot of overtime but I've got to start somewhere.'

I looked at Nesta. He was nodding.

'I just hope that gets the bailiffs off my back,' Dad said. 'It's not right how they hunt down people for money they haven't got.'

'So no more bailiffs banging down our drawbridge?' I asked.

'I should have never put you into that position,' Dad apologised. 'I'm really sorry for that. It won't happen again.'

'And I'm sorry for ...' Nesta paused. He peered into my eyes. 'Well, you know what I'm sorry for. I won't drop you into any of my dramas ever again.'

Was I hearing right? *Lick my cupcakes!*

Last night scared the living ribs out of me but Dad's and Nesta's words gave my insides a glow – like things were gonna get better. Maybe just a liccle better but it was a start.

# 27

# Lamb Kofta and Pool

I spent the entire weekend fretting about my bredrens – I couldn't even swap lyrics with them on the phone – but taking up a world of space in my hard drive and overriding everything was the fate of Festus. Was he dead or alive?

Dad and Nesta had my ass on lockdown. To fill my time I cooked. Nesta and Dad were seriously impressed with the jerk chicken Sunday dinner that I served up with boiled rice, steamed broccoli, roasted carrots and parsnips. I sexed it all up with spicy gravy. I was amazed that Nesta actually bounced to the supermarket and bought the ingredients. We chased that down with jam roly-poly and custard. Dad licked his plate clean and smiled at me.

'*This* is what you're good at!' he said. 'You're a natural cook. That's the way to go – make use of your talents.'

'Dad's not wrong,' Nesta agreed. 'I still don't know zero nish what I'm good at.'

'You'll find it if you keep on looking in the right places,' cut in Dad.

'But you're blessed in the cooking game,' Nesta resumed. 'That chicken was the living thumb-licker!'

'So can I go and see Bit and Jonah?' I asked hopefully.

'*No!*'

I had to wait until Monday morning to see my bredrens. Nesta ignored my complaining and rolled with me to school. He even stood outside the gates and watched me step in.

'I'll be back at three-thirty on the damn dot! I've got people to see.'

'Who?' I asked.

Nesta gave me fierce eyes again. 'I know we promised to be more open with you but there are some tings I can't spill.'

'But—'

'But nothing!' Nesta cut me off.

There was a frenzied buzz in registration. Everyone was talking about the riot and what they had jacked from the stores – Kiran Cassidy had a stash of mobile phones and chocolate bars to sell.

Meanwhile, Jonah, Bit and me were chatting about something else entirely.

'Anyone hear about Festus – is he dead?' Jonah wanted to know.

'My dad called the hospital and they told him Festus was critical but stable.'

'What does that mean?' asked Bit.

'That he's OK for now but the Grim Reaper has got a dose of hope,' I said.

'What about the feds?' Jonah wanted to know. 'My mum will blow another boiler if the feds in the white shell suits slap on our gates and ask if they can take a DNA sample from my ass.'

I stared at Jonah. 'Did you tell your fam about Festus?'

Jonah took his time in answering. 'No,' he finally replied. 'Mum was blistering my ears so much I could hardly get a lyric in – in the end I just wanted to get to my room and catch some sleep.'

'I hear that.' Bit nodded. 'When I got in my sis went nuts. She thought the feds had arrested me. I think she might've smacked me down for good if I'd carried in any jacked goods. When I told them what happened with Festus they were shocked, but kinda relieved. They hugged and kissed me all over like I survived a plane crash or something. My sis even made my breakfast this morning ... Sisters are funny.'

'Anyone seen Venetia or Saira?' I asked.

Bit and Jonah shook their heads.

'What about Boy from the Hills?' I wanted to know.

'He's here,' said Jonah. 'He was late. He's gonna link with us at break.'

At break time we were reunited with Saira, Venetia and Boy from the Hills. We rolled to a quiet corner in the playground. Saira did most of the talking as Venetia kept very quiet.

'I didn't even know I had so much fam,' Saira explained.

'Uncles, aunts, cousins I've never met, all there in our liccle front room wanting to know where my skin had been all night! I just ignored them and bounced up to my room.'

'There was only Mum waiting for me,' Boy from the Hills said. 'She was mad with the feds cos they wouldn't send someone around when she called them to report me missing.'

We all looked at Venetia. Nobody asked her what her weekend had been like. I couldn't even guess.

'Why don't you guys come around my yard this Wednesday?' said Boy from the Hills. 'My mum wants to meet my new friends. What do you say? Are you on it?'

'I'm on that,' I said. 'But I'm on lockdown till my birthday. My pops won't even let me pick up the post.'

'I'm on a serious curfew too,' said Jonah. 'My mum won't even let me take out the rubbish.'

'And me three,' added Bit. 'My sis says that if I go on another mission she'll bury me under our toilet.'

'Me too,' said Venetia. She looked up and half-smiled. 'My dad ... wasn't happy.'

'I'm on it.' Saira nodded. 'But I'll have to sneak by a world of family to get to your yard. Are you doing anything for your birthday, McKay?'

'Dad's taking me bowling – Nesta promised to come too. I was gonna ask you guys.'

'We're all on that,' said Bit.

I felt warm inside when I saw everyone nod.

'Maybe coming to my yard can be an early part of the celebration,' said Boy from the Hills.

'But that won't change my lockdown status,' said Saira.

'We kinda guessed that you'd all be grounded,' said Boy from the Hills. 'So my mum is willing to pick you up from school and drop you all off to your yards when we're done for the night – she's got a people carrier.'

We glanced at each other. 'For real?' I asked. 'Your mum would do that?'

Boy from the Hills nodded.

'My fam can't say no to that!' said Saira. 'I'm definitely on it! Can I bring something to cook? I wanna give you guys a taste of lamb kofta.'

'Yeah,' Boy from the Hills smiled. 'Bring what you like.'

'I'm on it too!' Jonah said.

'And me three!' said Bit.

'And can we use the pool table?' I asked.

'As long as you don't break the cue when I beat you,' laughed Boy from the Hills.

'Can you come, Venetia?' I asked.

Venetia stared at the ground once more.

'It won't be the same without you, V,' said Saira. 'Chat to your dad. Tell him it's McKay's early birthday treat. *Please!* If it makes him happy we'll ask Boy from the ... I mean Colin's mum to hear our confessions and traumas. She's some sort of therapist, ain't she?'

'Yep, she is.' Boy from the Hills nodded.

'Saira's not wrong,' added Bit.

'I'll chat to him,' agreed Venetia. 'But I can't promise any-thing ... If he agrees maybe I can make a cake or something?'

'He can't say no,' I said. 'Venetia, you're the VIP, you have to come.'

Then I heard a loud voice. 'McKay! McKay!'

It was coming from outside the school gates. 'McKay! McKay!'

It was Nesta. He sounded like a fireman shouting to check if anybody was left in a burning building. I glanced at my bredrens and their smiles had dropped. He was an instant reminder of what happened on *that* Friday night. In my head the nail clipper grew large.

I rolled through the school gates towards Nesta. His eyes were intense, unblinking. He glanced over his left shoulder twice. 'He's out!' he said. 'Festus went back to his yard this morning – they sewed him up.'

'Venetia will be proper relieved,' I said. 'And that goes for the rest of us.'

'McKay, listen to me carefully. I'm sorry, bruv, but Dad will pick you up from school this afternoon. I have to take a low profile for the time being.'

'Why?' I asked.

'Cos the word on road is that *I* shanked Festus. He's lied big time to protect his rep – can't be known he got burst by a girl. The whole of North Crong are gonna be targeting my ribs.'

It took me a few seconds to download Nesta's revelation. I glanced behind to check on my bredrens. They were all looking at me.

'But it was . . . '

'Yes, I know,' said Nesta. 'It's the living lie. As I said, Festus will say and do anything to save his rep.'

'What you gonna do?'

'As I said I'll keep a low profile for the next few days,' he answered. 'I'll relax my toes at Yvonne's yard for a day or so. Then I'll leave South Crong.'

'Leave?'

'Got no choice,' Nesta said. 'It'll be better for you if I go missing. For now. Anyway, I'm getting tired of Crong. I need to work out what I wanna do with my life, try to figure out what I'm good at – Yvonne says she don't want no waste-man. And once I get settled I'm gonna see a counsellor or something. You know, about Mum. Dad's looking it up for me.'

'But you've always been strong for me, Nesta.'

'But not strong for myself,' Nesta admitted.

He breathed in deep, trying to control his emotions.

'I need *help*, McKay. Real help. And you know what, it don't mean you're a pussy if you look for it. There ain't no shame on that. But I have to leave this place to get it. Living in the ends is just . . . just too much. You hearing me?'

'You can't leave!'

I could feel the tears forming in my eyes. I sniffed to try to get rid of them.

'I've talked to Dad, bruv – it's for the best. I'm marked, McKay. Major Worries is gonna be on my case. I don't wanna stay here and have to look around every corner for a waiting blade. That's no life. That's not living. That's hiding.'

I didn't know what to say.

'In a mad way, I prefer it this way – better for Major Worries to hunt me than hunt you and your crew. What's the point of flinging a javelin if there's no stadium to fling it in? But you'll still have to be proper careful. *Don't* go on any stupid missions!'

282

I couldn't stop the tears any longer.

'Promise me something, McKay,' Nesta said.

'What?' I asked.

'Make something of yourself at this place,' he insisted. 'You've been blessed with a talent. I didn't do anything while I was here – do something with your cooking.'

'I am – this morning I bucked into Ms Penn. I'm gonna join her cooking club.'

'Good – that'll keep you in the right lane.'

He looked over his shoulder again and started to roll away.

'When will you be back?' I called.

Nesta stopped in his tracks and turned around.

'I'll be back to kuff you if you mess up. And I might send a liccle someting for your birthday. Make sure you give Dad a good game of bowling – he hates to lose.'

I watched Nesta, hands in pockets, disappear up the street.

I ignored the blast of the bell telling us to get back to lessons.

Tears were dripping off my chin.

'Oh, by the way,' Nesta shouted. 'They found my bike! Can you believe that shit! Dad's picking it up later.'

I turned around and managed a smile. 'You're joking with me?'

'No, I'm not. On the level! Dad and Yvonne didn't believe it either. Walk good!'

I returned to my bredrens. They saw the tears in my eyes. They didn't bomb me with questions. Instead, they group-hugged me. I felt good. I wasn't on my lonesome. Nor was anyone else in my crew.

**If any of the issues in this book have affected you, you might find some of the following organisations helpful.**

### ChildLine

ChildLine is the free helpline for young people in the UK. You can call, email or chat online to them confidentially about any problem you might have.

Confidential helpline: 0800 1111

Website: www.childline.org.uk

### Gangsline

Gangsline is a non-profit organisation established in 2007 to provide help and support to young men and women involved in gang culture.

Confidential helpline: 0800 032 9538

Website: www.gangsline.com

### NSPCC

Whether you're thinking about joining a gang, are already involved or want to leave, you can call the NSPCC's 24-hour helpline anonymously or find out more information on their website.

Confidential helpline: 0808 800 5000

Website: www.nspcc.org.uk/preventing-abuse/keeping-

children-safe/staying-safe-away-from-home/
gangs-young-people

## Safe

Run by the Metropolitan Police, Safe is a website that provides information and advice on many different aspects of life, specifically for young people, including gangs and group violence and knife and gun crime.

Website: www.safe.met.police.uk

## Winston's Wish

Winston's Wish is a charity that supports bereaved young people in the UK. They have information on their website, an area to ask questions, and you can use their message boards to talk to other people like you.

Website: foryoungpeople.winstonswish.org.uk

# COOK LIKE THE SOUTH CRONG CREW

## Mckay's Jerk Chicken Stir-Fry

**INGREDIENTS**

4 chicken fillets
1 tablespoon Jamaican jerk seasoning
2 teaspoons paprika
2 teaspoons garlic powder
2 teaspoons of parsley
1 teaspoon ground black pepper
Olive oil
3 chopped spring onions
Quarter chopped green pepper
Stir-fry vegetable mix

**METHOD**

Chop and dice chicken fillets. Place in a large bowl and mix and season with jerk seasoning, paprika, garlic powder, parsley and black pepper.

Line a wok or a large frying pan with olive oil. Heat pan. Add chopped spring onions and green pepper. Stir in the chicken. When chicken seals and changes colour, add stir-fry vegetable mix. Cook over a medium heat for about 25–30 minutes, stirring as you go.

**SERVE**

Serve with boiled white rice or boiled pasta.

Enjoy!

# Mrs Hani's Chocolate Cupcakes

## INGREDIENTS

40g cocoa powder

4 tbsp boiled water

3 eggs

175g unsalted butter (softened)

165g unrefined golden caster sugar

115g self-raising white flour

## INGREDIENTS FOR CHOCOLATE ICING

60g unsalted butter

30g cocoa powder

250g unrefined golden icing sugar

3 tbsp milk

## METHOD

Line two 12-hole muffin tins with paper cases. Sift the cocoa powder into a bowl, pour in the boiling water and stir into a thick paste. Add the remaining cake ingredients and mix with an electric hand whisk or beat with a wooden spoon until creamy.

Divide the mixture equally between the 24 paper cases. Bake in a preheated oven at 200 degrees C/gas mark 6 for about ten minutes until well risen and springy to the touch. Take out and cool in the cases on a wire rack.

To make the chocolate icing, melt the butter and pour it into a bowl. Sift in the cocoa powder and stir in the icing sugar a little at a time until it is spreadable. If the icing is too thick, gradually add the milk until you reach the required consistency. Use a palette knife to spread the icing and leave to set before serving.

# Saira's Lamb Koftas

**INGREDIENTS**

900g lean lamb mince
2 mint leaves, finely chopped
2 teaspoons paprika
2 teaspoons ground coriander
1 teaspoon ground black pepper
1 teaspoon garlic powder
Olive oil
2 onions, finely chopped
Quarter chopped green pepper

**METHOD**

Using a large bowl, mix and season the mince with mint, paprika, coriander, black pepper and garlic powder. Roll and press into meatballs to prepare for frying.

Line a large frying pan or wok with olive oil. Fry the onions and green pepper before adding the meatballs. Cook on a medium heat for 20–25 minutes occasionally stirring so the meatballs do not stick.

**SERVE**

Serve with boiled white rice, pitta or nan bread and salad or vegetables of your choice.

# ACKNOWLEDGEMENTS

May I thank my editor and apprentice map-maker, Sarah Castleton, for her keen eye and gently encouraging me to produce the best work I can. Also, a loud Crongton shout-out to the rest of the brilliant team behind me at Atom/ Little, Brown (I promise I'll pop into the office more often!)

Take a bow Ms Laura Susijn, my ever patient and support-ive agent. Crongton salutes to Courttia Newland, Sandra Agard, Irenosen Okojie, Yvvette Edwards, Esther Poyer, Yvonne Archer, Nadifa Mohamed, Dreda Say Mitchell, Lemn Sissay, Lara Bellini, Vanessa Walters, Sunny Singh, Rosie Canning, Joy Francis & Words of Colour, the fabulous team behind Black Bookswap, school, college, university and prison librarians who have welcomed me so warmly and supplied me with mint teas, chocolate cakes and custard creams, Simon O'Hagan of the Independent, who regularly unleashes the voice of this lost boy from Brixton, Tom Murray, one of our greatest singer-songwriters (still can't believe you penned a song about one of my fictional characters!), the members of CWISL, Beverley Birch, talent spotter supreme, who many years ago suggested, 'Alex, you should think about writing a Young Adult novel!' Last of all, a Brixtonian tip of the head to all you readers out there – I couldn't do what I do without you. Simple as. You may be unaware, but you guys and gals have kept me going through difficult times. Thank you all xxx